TRAILIN

TRAILIN'

By
MAX BRAND

Introduction to the Bison Book Edition
by Richard W. Etulain

University of Nebraska Press
Lincoln and London

First Bison Book printing: 1994
Most recent printing indicated by the last digit below:
10   9   8   7   6   5   4   3   2   1

Library of Congress Cataloging-in-Publication Data
Brand, Max, 1892–1944.
Trailin' / by Max Brand; introduction to the Bison book edition by
Richard W. Etulain.
p. cm.
"Bison."
ISBN 0-8032-1247-X
ISBN 0-8032-6116-0 (pbk.)
I. Title.
PS3511.A87T737   1994
813'.52—dc20
94-13998
CIP

∞

To

ROBERT HOBART DAVIS
Maker of Books and Men

INTRODUCTION

by Richard W. Etulain

Those acquainted with the life story of Frederick Schiller Faust will not be surprised that his larger-than-life heroes often begin as underdogs or outsiders, but through a series of courageous and nearly unbelievable acts of hard work, consistency, and doggedness prove their mettle and gain considerable self-understanding in the process. Such actions summarized Faust's own life, a story line he used hundreds of times in his western tales.

Indeed, Faust's life was a continual sequence of unusual events. Born in Seattle in 1892 and orphaned in his early teens, he spent most of his first years on the West Coast. Working on farms in California's interior valleys as a teenager, Faust graduated from high school in Modesto and then entered the University of California in 1911. Spending four years at Berkeley, he left without a degree because his independent attitudes and actions roused the wrath of the president. While at California, Faust gained a reputation as a rebellious student, with obvious writing talent and a romantic disposition. After abandoning the Bay Area in 1915, he hopscotched around the country before landing in New York City two years later. Suffering a few months of near starvation while trying to place his first stories, Faust then met editor and agent Robert H. (Bob) Davis of the Munsey publications syndicate who encouraged him to persevere and helped place his first stories. (It was to Davis, "Maker of Books and Men," that Faust dedicated *Trailin'*.) Once the trickle of publication began in 1917, it quickly became a stream and then a deluge.

Exhibiting the indefatigable energies of his superheroes and displaying similar drives to succeed, Faust became a veritable fiction factory throughout the rest of his life. From 1917 until his death in 1944, he poured out thirty million words, more than 500 novels, from his red-hot typewriter. Of these, nearly 350 were Western serials or novels. Earning sometimes more than $100,000 a year, he moved his wife (they had married in 1917) and family to Italy in 1925, where they remained, living like royalty in a giant Florentine villa before moving to Hollywood in 1938. Churning out Westerns, mysteries, historical adventure novels, and several other kinds of popular fiction under nearly twenty pen names (the best known of which was Max Brand) he earned millions of dollars but spent lavishly to maintain his entourage and expensive style of living.

Later, when a tightening Depression undercut some of Faust's better-paying pulp fiction markets, particularly *Western Story Magazine,* he moved in other directions. By the middle 1930s slick magazines such as *Collier's* and *Saturday Evening Post* began publishing his serials and stories. Equally lucrative was his work in Hollywood, where he was paid $1,500 per week—and that figure soon doubled—for writing scripts. Although Faust's enormous income solved his material needs, it failed to satisfy his aesthetic desires. Sometimes denouncing his boilerplate fiction as western "junk," he dreamed instead of producing memorable poetry. Some of his verse was published, but it never drew the attention for which Faust hungered. Nor was he able to solve the family problems and personal dissatisfactions that ate at him. Driven to succeed but dissatisfied with his achievements, Faust constantly sought new quests to satisfy his longings. Hoping that participation in active service during World War II might satiate some of his desire for adventure, he applied for and received permission to report front-line action in Europe. Tragically, soon after he arrived an exploding enemy shell mortally wounded him, and he died the next day, May 12, 1944.

Even though *Trailin'* first appeared as a serial in the pulp magazine *All-Story Weekly* and was published as a novel in 1920, within the first three years of Max Brand's career, he already displayed an adept hand at writing popular fiction. Obviously he had learned early important tricks in producing pulp fiction. For example, as the plot of *Trailin'* develops and new threads of the story are braided into the narrative, Brand is able, through cut-away chapters ("meanwhile back at the ranch"), to keep three or four subplots marching along in unison. While the hero and his girl try to escape, the villain is in close pursuit, but trouble is brewing back on the home range, and other decisions hog-tie residents of a nearby town. Equally impressive is Brand's ability to supply the right mix of necessary ingredients for the Western. Those addicted to this popular genre expected lively narratives with a plethora of conflict, speedy jaunts crisscrossing open landscapes, and heart-warming romance. Brand abundantly supplied these needed elements—and more.

Although not as well-known as *The Untamed* (1919) or *Destry Rides Again* (1930), *Trailin'* nonetheless reveals much about Brand's place in the historical development of the Western. Launching his career nearly a generation after Owen Wister's novel *The Virginian* (1902) helped to define the Western, and beginning publication about a decade after the appearance of Zane Grey's *Heritage of the Desert* (1910) and *Riders of the Purple Sage* (1912), Brand built on their traditions and popularity even as he turned out Westerns of his own kind. Although he too capitalized on the familiar triplex of action, romance, and the conflict between heroes and villains in a frontier setting that defined the Western, Brand added new ingredients as well as unusual emphases. For one, unlike most other writers, he rarely gave his stories specific settings; rather, the action took place, as it does in *Trailin'*, in a magical, generic West. Nor was Brand much interested in incorporating historical events or persons into his Westerns. Instead, he invests his stories with epic-like overtones. Allusions to Homer, to other ancients, and to a mysterious, hazy past enlarge the meaning here of the hero's Oedipal search for his father—his trailin' becomes The Quest of all young men on such journeys.

The plot of *Trailin'* revolves around familiar themes, then, a young man's search for his father, and himself. Beginning *in medias res,* Brand uses a dramatic scene in which Anthony Woodbury, who seems to be a greenhorn easterner, tops a rough bronc that riders in the touring Wild West show at Madison Square Garden tout as unconquerable. Who is this polo-playing New Yorker who exhibits extraordinary strength, courage, and skill? That question drives the opening chapters and becomes the central idea of the developing plot. We soon learn that Anthony doesn't know his own origins, although he thinks Long Islander John Woodbury is his real father. After a series of enigmatic events, Anthony sets out in pursuit of William Drew, a gigantic westerner who witnessed Anthony's sensational ride in the arena and who duels and kills his father, whose real name is John Bard.

The novel then takes up the "trailin'" theme. Anthony goes west to apprehend his father's murderer. There, he encounters some of the usual cast of characters in a Western: a hardcase, Steve Nash, who becomes the villain; Sally Fortune, whom Anthony comes to love; townsmen, cowboys, and outlaws, who play thickening bit parts; and Drew, whose looming grey presence shadows Anthony's search and his own mysterious story. Showcasing his talents as a storyteller, Brand keeps control of several thematic strands of his narrative: villain versus hero, a developing romance, and the hero's search for his father—all against an appealing background of high mountains, limpid lakes, and rushing streams.

These familiar components deserve further discussion. Readers of Westerns, who early in the twentieth century were primarily city dwellers, expected clearcut distinctions between the East and the West, easterners and westerners. Anthony Bard, on the surface, seems a greenhorn because of his dress and his speech, but also a man of immense strength and drive because, as it turns out, he is a pure-bred Westerner. In Brand's formula, the hero's drive, tenacity, and bravery are clear examples of a western character and code at odds with those peculiarities considered eastern—polished speech, limited physical capabilities, and little or no knowledge of the out-of-doors. Moreover, in the closing sections of the novel, Anthony plays out the struggle between masculinity and love that Wister introduced and Grey used repeatedly. The hero has to battle the villain and throttle evil forces—a man's gotta do what a man's gotta do—before he is worthy of thinking of a future with Sally. Finally, the action takes place at the end of, or near the close of, the frontier. And Drew, who turns out to be Anthony's real father, is a holdover from the ancient Old West when titanic forces vied for control. Although the West has rapidly changed, with ranches and towns dotting the landscape, ties between the past and the present are symbolized in Anthony's inheritance of his father's strength and resilience. The Old West may have disappeared over the horizon, but its spirit and achievements will be passed on, as they are here from Drew to his son.

Not every reader, in the 1920s or now, will be entirely satisfied with all of *Trailin'*. Sometimes the identities of the hero, heroine, and villain are asserted more often than dramatized. Nor is the plot line, frequently unbelievable, likely to please everyone. Quite simply, Brand is not always adept at creating complex personalities, even when he obviously labors to do so. During several paragraphs of interior monologue, for example, Anthony must reflect on why he will not climb into bed with Sally even though she seems willing and may even tempt him. The author likewise falters in all the space given to why Drew cannot, in a brief, straightforward conversation, explain to his son their tangled heritage.

One can easily make too much of these shortcomings, however, if the desires of readers of Westerns are not kept in mind. These aficionados are not likely to look for excessively complex, ambivalent characters. How can one identify, for instance, with Anthony or dislike Nash if they persistently waver between good and evil. And in the 1920s a Western hero, not even the villain, could seduce the heroine. Readers are likely also to forgive Brand for his rambling plot because he keeps his characters in high gear, stuffing his plot with numerous action and adventure scenes, the *sin qua non* of all Westerns.

In short, *Trailin'* remains a winning novel because it illustrates the typical qualities of hundreds of Max Brand's alluring Westerns. Smoothly written, carrying a cast of magnetic characters, and portraying a magic, archetypal West, *Trailin'* clearly incorporates those qualities that make its creator one of the all-time, popular writers of Westerns.

CONTENTS

Contents

TRAILIN'

CHAPTER I

"LA-A-A-DIES AN' GEN'L'MUN"

ALL through the exhibition the two sat unmoved; yet on the whole it was the best Wild West
show that ever stirred sawdust in Madison Square
Garden and it brought thunders of applause from
the crowded house. Even if the performance could
not stir these two, at least the throng of spectators
should have drawn them, for all New York was
there, from the richest to the poorest; neither the
combined audiences of a seven-day race, a prize-
fight, or a community singing festival would make
such a cosmopolitan assembly.

All Manhattan came to look at the men who
had lived and fought and conquered under the
limitless skies of the Far West, free men, wild men
—one of their shrill whoops banished distance and
brought the mountain desert into the very heart

1

of the unromantic East. Nevertheless from all these thrills these two men remained immune.

To be sure the smaller tilted his head back when the horses first swept in, and the larger leaned to watch when Diaz, the wizard with the lariat, commenced to whirl his rope; but in both cases their interest held no longer than if they had been old vaudevillians watching a series of familiar acts dressed up with new names.

The smaller, brown as if a thousand fierce suns and winds had tanned and withered him, looked up at last to his burly companion with a faint smile.

"They're bringing on the cream now, Drew, but I'm going to spoil the dessert."

The other was a great, grey man whom age apparently had not weakened but rather settled and hardened into an ironlike durability; the winds of time or misfortune would have to break that stanch oak before it would bend.

He said: "We've half an hour before our train leaves. Can you play your hand in that time?"

"Easy. Look at 'em now—the greatest gang of liars that never threw a diamond hitch! Ride? I've got a ten-year kid home that would laugh at 'em all. But I'll show 'em up. Want to know my little stunt?"

"I'll wait and enjoy the surprise."

The wild riders who provoked the scorn of the smaller man were now gathering in the central space; a formidable crew, long of hair and brilliant as to bandannas, while the announcer thundered through his megaphone:

"La-a-a-dies and gen'l'mun! You see before you the greatest band of subduers and breakers of wild horses that ever rode the cattle ranges. Death defying, reckless, and laughing at peril, they have never failed; they have never pulled leather. I present 'Happy' Morgan!"

Happy Morgan, yelling like one possessed of ten shrill-tongued demons, burst on the gallop away from the others, and spurring his horse cruelly, forced the animal to race, bucking and plunging, half way around the arena and back to the group. This, then, was a type of the dare-devil horse breaker of the Wild West? The cheers travelled in waves around and around the house and rocked back and forth like water pitched from side to side in a monstrous bowl.

When the noise abated somewhat, "And this, la-a-a-dies and gen'l'mun, is the peerless cow-puncher, 'Bud Reeves.'"

Bud at once imitated the example of Happy Morgan, and one after another the five remaining riders followed suit. In the meantime a number

of prancing, kicking, savage-eyed horses were
brought into the arena and to these the master of
ceremonies now turned his attention.

"From the wildest regions of the range we have
brought mustangs that never have borne the
weight of man. They fight for pleasure; they buck
by instinct. If you doubt it, step down and try
'em. One hundred dollars to the man who sticks
on the back of one of 'em—but we won't pay the
hospital bill!"

He lowered his megaphone to enjoy the laughter,
and the small man took this opportunity to say:
"Never borne the weight of a man! That chap in
the dress-suit, he tells one lie for pleasure and ten
more from instinct. Yep, he has his hosses beat.
Never borne the weight of man! Why, Drew, I
can see the saddle-marks clear from here; I got a
mind to slip down there and pick up the easiest
hundred bones that ever rolled my way."

He rose to make good his threat, but Drew cut
in with: "Don't be a damn fool, Werther. You
aren't part of this show."

"Well, I will be soon. Watch me! There goes
Ananias on his second wind."

The announcer was bellowing: "These man-
killing mustangs will be ridden, broken, beaten
into submission in fair fight by the greatest set of

horse-breakers that ever wore spurs. They can ride anything that walks on four feet and wears a skin; they can——"

Werther sprang to his feet, made a funnel of his hand, and shouted: "Yi-i-i-ip!"

If he had set off a great quantity of red fire he could not more effectively have drawn all eyes upon him. The weird, shrill yell cut the ringmaster short, and a pleased murmur ran through the crowd. Of course, this must be part of the show, but it was a pleasing variation.

"Partner," continued Werther, brushing away the big hand of Drew which would have pulled him down into his seat; "I've seen you bluff for two nights hand running. There ain't no man can bluff all the world three times straight."

The ringmaster retorted in his great voice: "That sounds like good poker. What's your game?"

"Five hundred dollars on one card!" cried Werther, and he waved a fluttering handful of greenbacks. "Five hundred dollars to any man of your lot—or to any man in this house that can ride a *real* wild horse."

"Where's your horse?"

"Around the corner in a Twenty-sixth Street stable. I'll have him here in five minutes."

"Lead him on," cried the ringmaster, but his voice was not quite so loud.

Werther muttered to Drew:

"Here's where I hand him the lemon that'll curdle his cream," and ran out of the box and straight around the edge of the arena. New York, murmuring and chuckling through the vast galleries of the Garden, applauded the little man's flying coat-tails.

He had not underestimated the time; in a little less than his five minutes the doors at the end of the arena were thrown wide and Werther reappeared. Behind him came two stalwarts leading between them a rangy monster. Before the blast of lights and the murmurs of the throng the big stallion reared and flung himself back, and the two who lead him bore down with all their weight on the halter ropes. He literally walked down the planks into the arena, a strange, half-comical, half-terrible spectacle. New York burst into applause. It was a trained horse, of course, but a horse capable of such training was worth applause.

At that roar of sound, vague as the beat of waves along the shore, the stallion lurched down on all fours and leaped ahead, but the two on the halter ropes drove all their weight backward and checked the first plunge. A bright-coloured scarf waved from a nearby box, and the monster swerved away. So, twisting, plunging, rearing, he was worked down the arena. As he came opposite a box in which sat a tall young man in evening clothes the latter rose and shouted: "Bravo!"

The fury of the stallion, searching on all sides for a vent but distracted from one torment to another, centred suddenly on this slender figure. He swerved and rushed for the barrier with ears flat back and bloodshot eyes. There he reared and struck at the wood with his great front hoofs; the boards splintered and shivered under the blows.

As for the youth in the box, he remained quietly erect before this brute rage. A fleck of red foam fell on the white front of his shirt. He drew his handkerchief and wiped it calmly away, but a red stain remained. At the same time the two who led the stallion pulled him back from the barrier and he stood with head high, searching for a more convenient victim.

Deep silence spread over the arena; more hushed and more hushed it grew, as if invisible blankets of soundlessness were dropping down over the stirring masses; men glanced at each other with a vague surmise, knowing that this was no part of the performance. The whole audience drew forward to the edge of the seats and stared, first at the monstrous horse, and next at the group of men who could "ride anything that walks on four feet and wears a skin."

Some of the women were already turning away their heads, for this was to be a battle, not a game; but the vast majority of New York merely watched and waited and smiled a slow, stiff-lipped smile. All the surroundings were changed, the flaring electric lights, the vast roof, the clothes of the multitude, but the throng of white faces was the same as that pale host which looked down from the sides of the Coliseum when the lions were loosed upon their victims.

As for the wild riders from the cattle ranges, they drew into a close group with the ringmaster between them and the gaunt stallion, almost as if the fearless ones were seeking for protection. But the announcer himself lost his almost invincible *sang-froid;* in all his matchless vocabulary there were no sounding phrases ready for this occasion, and little Werther strutted in the centre of the great arena, rising to his opportunity.

He imitated the ringmaster's phraseology: "La-a-a-dies and gen'l'mun, the price has gone up. The 'death-defyin', dare-devils that laugh at danger' ain't none too ready to ride my hoss. Maybe the price is too low for 'em. It's raised.

One thousand dollars—cash—for any man in hearin' of me that'll ride my pet."

There was a stir among the cattlemen, but still none of them moved forward toward the great horse; and as if he sensed his victory he raised and shook his ugly head and neighed. A mighty laugh answered that challenge; this was a sort of "horse-humour" that great New York could not overlook, and in that mirth even the big grey man, Drew, joined. The laughter stopped with an amazing suddenness making the following silence impressive as when a storm that has roared and howled about a house falls mute, then all the dwellers in the house look to one another and wait for the voice of the thunder. So all of New York that sat in the long galleries of the Garden hushed its laughter and looked askance at one another and waited. The big grey man rose and cursed softly.

For the slender young fellow in evening dress at whom the stallion had rushed a moment before was stripping off his coat, his vest, and rolling up the stiff cuffs of his sleeves. Then he dropped a hand on the edge of the box, vaulted lightly into the arena, and walked straight toward the horse.

CHAPTER II

SPORTING CHANCE

IT might easily have been made melodramatic by any hesitation as he approached, but, with a businesslike directness, he went right up to the men who held the fighting horse.

He said: "Put a saddle on him, boys, and I'll try my hand."

They could not answer at once, for Werther's "pet," as if he recognized the newcomer, made a sudden lunge and was brought to a stop only after he had dragged his sweating handlers around and around in a small circle. Here Werther himself came running up, puffing with surprise.

"Son," he said eagerly, "I'm not aiming to do you no harm. I was only calling the bluff of those four-flushers."

The slender youth finished rolling up his left sleeve and smiled down at the other

"Put on the saddle," he said.

Werther looked at him anxiously; then his eyes

brightened with a solution. He stepped closer and laid a hand on the other's arm.

"Son, if you're broke and want to get the price of a few squares just say the word and I'll fix you. I been busted myself in my own day, but don't try your hand with my hoss. He ain't just a buckin' hoss; he's a man-killer, lad. I'm tellin' you straight. And this floor ain't so soft as the sawdust makes it look," he ended with a grin.

The younger man considered the animal seriously.

"I'm not broke; I've simply taken a fancy to your horse. If you don't mind, I'd like to try him out. Seems too bad, in a way, for a brute like that to put it over on ten thousand people without getting a run for his money—a sporting chance, eh?"

And he laughed with great good nature.

"What's your name?" asked Werther, his small eyes growing round and wide.

"Anthony Woodbury."

"Mine's Werther."

They shook hands.

"City raised?"

"Yes."

"Didn't know they came in this style east of the Rockies, Woodbury. I hope I lose my thousand, but if there was any betting I'd stake ten to one against you."

In the meantime, some of the range-riders had thrown a coat over the head of the stallion, and while he stood quivering with helpless rage they flung a saddle on and drew the cinches taut.

Anthony Woodbury was saying with a smile: "Just for the sake of the game, I'll take you on for a few hundred, Mr. Werther, if you wish, but I can't accept odds."

Werther ran a finger under his collar apparently to facilitate breathing. His eyes, roving wildly, wandered over the white, silent mass of faces, and his glance picked out and lingered for a moment on the big-shouldered figure of Drew, erect in his box. At last his glance came back with an intent frown to Woodbury. Something in the keen eyes of the laid raised a responsive flicker in his own.

"Well, I'll be damned! Just a game, eh? Lad, no matter on what side of the Rockies you were born, I know your breed and I won't lay a penny against your money. There's the hoss saddled and there's the floor you'll land on. Go to it— and God help you!"

The other shook his shoulders back and stepped toward the horse with a peculiarly unpleasant smile, like a pugilist coming out of his corner toward an opponent of unknown prowess.

He said: "Take off the halter."

One of the men snapped viciously over his shoulder: "Climb on while the climbing's good. Cut out the bluff, partner."

The smile went out on the lips of Woodbury. He repeated: "Take off the halter."

They stared at him, but quickly began to fumble under the coat, unfastening the buckle. It required a moment to work off the heavy halter without giving the blinded animal a glimpse of the light; then Woodbury caught the bridle reins firmly just beneath the chin of the horse. With the other hand he took the stirrup strap and raised his foot, but he seemed to change his mind about this matter.

"Take off the blinder," he ordered.

It was Werther who interposed this time with: "Look here, lad, I know this hoss. The minute the blinder's off he'll up on his hind legs and bash you into the floor with his forefeet."

"Let him go," growled one of the cowboys. "He's goin' to hell making a gallery play."

But taking the matter into his own hands Woodbury snatched the coat from the head of the stallion, which snorted and reared up, mouth agape,

ears flattened back. There was a shout from
the man, not a cry of dismay, but a ringing battle
yell like some ancient berserker seeing the first
flash of swords in the mêlée. He leaped forward,
jerking down on the bridle reins with all the force
of his weight and his spring. The horse, caught
in mid-air, as it were, came floundering down on
all fours again. Before he could make another
move, Woodbury caught the high horn of the saddle and vaulted up to his seat. It was gallantly
done and in response came a great rustling from
the multitude; there was not a spoken word, but
every man was on his feet.

Perhaps what followed took their breaths and
kept them speechless. The first touch of his rider's
weight sent the stallion mad, not blind with fear
as most horses go, but raging with a devilish cunning like that of an insane man, a thing that made
the blood run cold to watch. He stood a moment
shuddering, as if the strange truth were slowly
dawning on his brute mind; then he bolted straight
for the barriers. Woodbury braced himself and
lunged back on the reins, but he might as well have
tugged at the mooring cable of a great ship; the
bit was in the monster's teeth.

Then a whisper reached the rider, a universal
hushing of drawn breath, for the thousands were

tasting the first thrill and terror of the combat. They saw a picture of horse and man crushed against the barrier. But there was no such stupid rage in the mind of the stallion.

At the last moment he swerved and raced close beside the fence; some projecting edge caught the trousers of Woodbury and ripped away the stout cloth from hip to heel. He swung far to the other side and wrenched back the reins. With stiff-braced legs the stallion slid to a halt that flung his unbalanced rider forward along his neck. Before he could straighten himself in the saddle, the horse roared and came down on rigid forelegs, yet by a miracle Woodbury clung, sprawled down the side of the monster, to be sure, but was not quite dismounted.

Another pitch of the same nature would have freed the stallion from his rider beyond doubt, but he elected to gallop full speed ahead the length of the arena, and during that time, Woodbury, stunned though he was, managed to drag himself back into the saddle. The end of the race was a leap into the air that would have cleared a five-bar fence, and down pitched the fighting horse on braced legs again. Woodbury's chin snapped down against his breast as though he had been struck behind the head with a heavy bar, but though his

brain was stunned, the fighting instinct remained
strong in him and when the stallion reared and
toppled back the rider slipped from the saddle in
the nick of time.

Fourteen hundred pounds of raging horseflesh
crashed into the sawdust; he rolled like a cat to his
feet, but at the same instant a flying weight leaped
through the air and landed in the saddle. The
audience awoke to sound—to a dull roar of noise;
a thin trickle of blood ran from Woodbury's mouth
and it seemed that the mob knew it and was yelling
for a death.

There followed a bewildering exhibition of such
bucking that the disgruntled cowboys forgot their
shame and shouted with joy. Upon his hind legs
and then down on his forefeet with a sickening
heartbreaking jar the stallion rocked; now he
bucked from side to side; now rose and whirled
about like a dancer; now toppled to the ground
and twisted again to his feet.

Still the rider clung. His head rocked with the
ceaseless jars; the red-stained lips writhed back
and showed the locked teeth. Yet, as if he scorned
the struggles of the stallion, he brought into play
the heavy quirt which had been handed him as he
mounted. Over neck and shoulders and tender
flanks he whirled the lash; it was not intelligence

fighting brute strength, but one animal conquering another and rejoicing in the battle.

The horse responded, furiously he responded, but still the lash fell, and the bucking grew more cunning, perhaps, but less violent. Yet to the wildly cheering audience the fight seemed more dubious than ever. Then, in the very centre of the arena, the stallion stopped in the midst of a twisting course of bucking and stood with widely braced legs and fallen head. Strength was left in him, but the cunning, savage mind knew defeat.

Once more the quirt whirled in the air and fell with a resounding crack, but the stallion merely switched his tail and started forward at a clumsy stumbling trot. The thunder of the host was too hoarse for applause; they saw a victory and a defeat but what they had wanted was blood, and a death. They had had a promise and a taste; now they hungered for the reality.

Woodbury slipped from the saddle and gave the reins to Werther. Already a crowd was growing about them of the curious who had sprung over the barriers and swarmed across the arena to see the conqueror, for had he not vindicated unanswerably the strength of the East as compared with that of the West? Boys shouted shrilly; men shouldered each other to slap him on the back;

2

but Werther merely held forth the handful of greenbacks. The conqueror braced himself against the saddle with a trembling hand and shook his head.

"Not for me," he said, "I ought to pay you—ten times that much for the sport—compared to this polo is nothing."

"Ah," muttered those who overheard, "polo! That explains it!"

"Then take the horse," said Werther, "because no one else could ride him."

"And now any one can ride him, so I don't want him," answered Woodbury.

And Werther grinned. "You're right, boy. I'll give him to the iceman."

The big grey man, William Drew, loomed over the heads of the little crowd, and they gave way before him as water divides under the prow of a ship; it was as if he cast a shadow which they feared before him.

"Help me through this mob," said Woodbury to Werther, "and back to my box. Devil take it, my overcoat won't cover that leg."

Then on him also fell, as it seemed, the approaching shadow of the grey man and he looked up with something of a start into the keen eyes of Drew.

"Son," said the big man, "you look sort of

familiar to me.   I'm asking your pardon, but who
was your mother?"

The eyes of young Woodbury narrowed and the
two stood considering each other gravely for a
long moment.

"I never saw her," he said at last, and then
turned with a frown to work his way through the
crowd and back to his box.

The tall man hesitated a moment and then
started in pursuit, but the mob intervened.   He
turned back to Werther.

"Did you get his name?" he asked.

"Fine bit of riding he showed, eh?" cried the
little man, "and turned down my thousand as
cool as you please.   I tell you, Drew, there's some
flint in the Easterners after all!"

"Damn the Easterners.   What's his name?"

"Woodbury.   Anthony Woodbury."

"Woodbury?"

"What's wrong with that name?"

"Nothing.   Only I'm a bit surprised."

And he frowned with a puzzled, wistful expression, staring straight ahead like a man striving to
solve a great riddle.

CHAPTER III

SOCIAL SUICIDE

At his box, Woodbury stopped only to huddle into his coat and overcoat and pull his hat down over his eyes. Then he hurried on toward an exit, but even this slight delay brought the reporters up with him. They had scented news as the eagle sights prey far below, and then swooped down on him. He continued his flight shaking off their harrying questions, but they kept up the running fight and at the door one of them reached his side with: "It's Mr. Woodbury of the Westfall Polo Club, son of Mr. John Woodbury of Anson Place?"

Anthony Woodbury groaned with dismay and clutched the grinning reporter by the arm.

"Come with me!"

Prospects of a scoop of a sizable nature brightened the eyes of the reporter. He followed in all haste, and the other news-gatherers, in obedience to the exacting, unspoken laws of their craft, stood back and followed the flight with grumbling envy.

On Twenty-Sixth Street, a little from the corner of Madison Avenue, stood a big touring car with the chauffeur waiting in the front seat. There were still some followers from the Garden.

Woodbury jumped into the back seat, drew the reporter after him, and called: "Start ahead, Maclaren—drive anywhere, but get moving."

"Now, sir," turning to the reporter as the engine commenced to hum, "what's your name?"

"Bantry."

"Bantry? Glad to know you."

He shook hands.

"You know me?"

"Certainly. I cover sports all the way from polo to golf. Anthony Woodbury—Westfall Polo Club—then golf, tennis, trap shooting——"

"Enough!" groaned the victim. "Now look here, Bantry, you have me dead to rights—got me with the goods, so to speak, haven't you?"

"It was a great bit of work; ought to make a first-page story."

And the other groaned again. "I know—son of millionaire rides unbroken horse in Wild West show—and all that sort of thing. But, good Lord, man, think what it will mean to me?"

"Nothing to be ashamed of, is it? Your father'll be proud of you."

Woodbury looked at him sharply.

"How do you know that?"

"Any man would be."

"But the notoriety, man! It would kill me with a lot of people as thoroughly as if I'd put the muzzle of a gun in my mouth and pulled the trigger."

"H-m!" muttered the reporter, "sort of social suicide, all right. But it's news, Mr. Woodbury, and the editor——"

"Expects you to write as much as the rest of the papers print—and none of the other reporters know me."

"One or two of them might have."

"But my dear fellow—won't you take a chance?"

Bantry made a wry face.

"Madison Square Garden," went on Woodbury bitterly. "Ten thousand people looking on—gad, man, it's awful."

"Why'd you do it, then?"

"Couldn't help it, Bantry. By Jove, when that wicked devil of a horse came at my box and I caught a glimpse of the red demon in his eyes— why, man, I simply had to get down and try my luck. Ever play football?"

"Yes, quite a while ago."

"Then you know how it is when you're in the

bleachers and the whistle blows for the game to begin. That's the way it was with me. I wanted to climb down into the field—and I did. Once started, I couldn't stop until I'd made a complete ass of myself in the most spectacular style. Now, Bantry, I appeal to you for the sake of your old football days, don't show me up—keep my name quiet."

"I'd like to—damned if I wouldn't—but—a scoop——"

Anthony Woodbury considered his companion with a strange yearning. It might have been to take him by the throat; it might have been some gentler motive, but his hand stole at last toward an inner coat pocket.

He said: "I know times are a bit lean now and then in your game, Bantry. I wonder if you could use a bit of the long green? Just now I'm very flush, and——"

He produced a thickly stuffed bill-fold, but Bantry smiled and touched Woodbury's arm.

"Couldn't possibly, you know."

He considered a moment and then, with a smile: "It's a bit awkward for both of us, isn't it? Suppose I keep your name under my hat and you give me a few little inside tips now and then on polo news, and that sort of thing?"

"Here's my hand on it. You've no idea what a load you take off my mind."

"We've circled about and are pretty close to the Garden again. Could you let me out here?"

The car rolled to an easy stop and the reporter stepped out.

"I'll forget everything you wish, Mr. Woodbury."

"It's an honour to have met you, sir. Use me whenever you can. Good night."

To the chauffeur he said: "Home, and make it fast."

They passed up Lexington with Maclaren "making it fast," so that the big car was continually nosing its way around the machines in front with much honking of the horn. At Fifty-Ninth Street they turned across to the bridge and hummed softly across the black, shimmering waters of the East River; by the time they reached Brooklyn a fine mist was beginning to fall, blurring the wind-shield, and Maclaren slowed up perceptibly, so that before they passed the heart of the city, Woodbury leaned forward and said: "What's the matter, Maclaren?"

"Wet streets—no chains—this wind-shield is pretty hard to see through."

"Stop her, then. I'll take the wheel the rest of the way. Want to travel a bit to-night."

The chauffeur, as if this exchange were something he had been expecting, made no demur, and a moment later, with Woodbury at the wheel, the motor began to hum again in a gradually increasing crescendo. Two or three motor-police glanced after the car as it snapped about corners with an ominous skid and straightened out, whining, on the new street; but in each case, having made a comfortable number of arrests that day, they had little heart for the pursuit of the grey monster through that chill mist.

Past Brooklyn, with a country road before them, Woodbury cut out the muffler and the car sprang forward with a roar. A gust of increasing wind whipped back to Maclaren, for the wind-shield had been opened so that the driver need not look through the dripping glass and mingling with the wet gale were snatches of singing.

The chauffeur, partly in understanding and partly from anxiety, apparently, caught the side of the seat in a firm grip and leaned forward to break the jar when they struck rough places. Around an elbow turn they went with one warning scream of the Klaxon, skidded horribly at the sharp angle of the curve, and missed by inches a car from the opposite direction.

They swept on with the startled yell of the other

party ringing after them, drowned at once by the crackling of the exhaust. Maclaren raised a furtive hand to wipe from his forehead a moisture which was not altogether rain, but immediately grasped the side of the seat again. Straight ahead the road swung up to meet a bridge and dropped sharply away from it on the further side. Maclaren groaned but the sound was lost in the increasing roar of the exhaust.

They barely touched that bridge and shot off into space on the other side like a hurdler clearing an obstacle. With a creak and a thud the big car landed, reeled drunkenly, and straightened out in earnest, Maclaren craned his head to see the speedometer, but had not the heart to look; he began to curse softly, steadily.

When the muffler went on again and the motor was reduced to a loud, angry humming, Woodbury caught a few phrases of those solemn imprecations. He grinned into the black heart of the night, streaked with lines of grey where therein entered the halo of the headlights, and then swung the car through an open, iron gate. The motor fell to a drowsily contented murmur that blended with the cool swishing of the tires on wet gravel.

"Maclaren," said the other, as he stopped in front of the garage, "if everyone was as good a passenger as you I'd enjoy motoring; but after all, a car can't act up like a horse." He concluded gloomily: "There's no fight in it."

And he started toward the house, but Maclaren, staring after the departing figure, muttered: "There's only one sort that's worse than a damn fool, and that's a young one."

It was through a door opening off the veranda that Anthony entered the house, stealthily as a burglar, and with the same nervous apprehension. Before him stretched a wide hall, dimly illumined by a single light which splashed on the Italian table and went glimmering across the floor. Across the hall was his destination—the broad balustraded staircase, which swept grandly up to the second floor. Toward this he tiptoed steadying himself with one hand against the wall. Almost to his goal, he heard a muffled footfall and shrank against the wall with a catlike agility, but, though the shadow fell steep and gloomy there, luck was against him.

A middle-aged servant of solemn port, serene with the twofold dignity of double chin and bald head, paused at the table in his progress across the room, and swept the apartment with the judicial eye of one who knows that everything is as it should be but will not trust even the silence of

night. So that bland blue eye struck first on the
faintly shining top hat of Anthony, ran down his
overcoat, and lingered in gloomy dismay on the
telltale streak of white where the trouser leg
should have been.

What he thought not even another Œdipus
could have conjectured. The young master very
obviously did not wish to be observed, and in such
times Peters at could be blinder than the bat noon-
day and more secret than the River Styx. He
turned away, unhurried, the fold of that double
chin a little more pronounced over the severe
correctness of his collar.

A very sibilant whisper pursued him. He
stopped again, still without haste, and turned not
directly toward Anthony, but at a discreet angle,
with his eyes fixed firmly upon the ceiling.

CHAPTER IV

A SESSION OF CHAT

THE whisper grew distinct in words.

"Peters, you old numskull, come here!"

The approach of Peters was something like the sidewise waddle of a very aged crab. He looked to the north, but his feet carried him to the east. That he was much moved was attested by the colour which had mounted even to the gleaming expanse of that nobly bald head.

"Yes, Master Anthony—I mean Mr. Anthony?"

He set his teeth at the *faux pas*.

"Peters, look at me. Confound it, I haven't murdered any one. Are you busy?"

It required whole seconds for the eyes to wheel round upon Anthony, and they were immediately debased from the telltale white of that leg to the floor.

"No, sir."

"Then come up with me and help me change. Quick!"

He turned and fled noiselessly up the great stairs, with Peters panting behind. Anthony's overcoat was off before he had fairly entered his room and his coat and vest flopped through the air as Peters shut the door. Whatever the old servant lacked in agility he made up in certain knowledge; as he laid out a fresh tuxedo, Anthony changed with the speed of one pursued. The conversation was spasmodic to a degree.

"Where's father? Waiting in the library?"

"Yes. Reading, sir."

"Had a mix-up—bully time, though—damn this collar! Peters, I wish you'd been there— where's those trousers? Rub some of the crease out of 'em—they must look a *litile* worn."

He stood at last completely dressed while Peters looked on with a shining eye and a smile which in a younger man would have suggested many things.

"How is it? Will I pass father this way?"

"I hope so, sir."

"But you don't think so?"

"It's hard to deceive him."

"Confound it! Don't I know? Well, here's for a try. Soft-foot it down stairs. I'll go after you and bang the door. Then you say good-evening in a loud voice and I'll go into the library. How's that?"

"Very good—your coat over your arm—so! Just ruffle your hair a bit, sir—now you should do very nicely."

At the door: "Go first, Peters—first, man, and hurry, but watch those big feet of yours. If you make a noise on the stairs I'm done with you."

The noiselessness of the descending feet was safe enough, but not so safe was the chuckling of Peters for, though he fought against the threatening explosion, it rumbled like the roll of approaching thunder. In the hall below, Anthony opened and slammed the door.

"Good-evening, Mr. Anthony," said Peters loudly, too loudly.

"Evening, Peters. Where's father?"

"In the library, sir. Shall I take your coat?"

"I'll carry it up to my room when I go. That's all."

He opened the door to the library and entered with a hope that his father would not be facing him, but he found that John Woodbury was not even reading. He sat by the big fire-place smoking a pipe which he now removed slowly from his teeth.

"Hello, Anthony."

"Good-evening, sir."

He rose to shake hands with his son; they might

have been friends meeting after a separation so long that they were compelled to be formal, and as Anthony turned to lay down his hat and coat he knew that the keen grey eyes studied him carefully from head to foot.

"Take this chair."

"Why, sir, wouldn't dream of disturbing you."

"Not a bit. I want you to try it; just a trifle too narrow for me."

John Woodbury rose and gestured his son to the chair he had been occupying. Anthony hesitated, but then, like one who obeys first and thinks afterward, seated himself as directed.

"Mighty comfortable, sir."

The big man stood with his hands clasped behind him, peering down under shaggy, iron-grey brows.

"I thought it would be. I designed it myself for you and I had a pretty bad time getting it made."

He stepped to one side.

"Hits you pretty well under the knees, doesn't it? Yes, it's deeper than most."

"A perfect fit, father, and mighty thoughtful of you."

"H-m," rumbled John Woodbury, and looked about like one who has forgotten something. "What about a glass of Scotch?"

"Nothing, thank you—I—in fact I'm not very strong for the stuff."

The rough brows rose a trifle and fell.

"No? But isn't it usual? Better have a go."

Once more there was that slight touch of hesitancy, as if the son were not quite sure of the father and wished to make every concession.

"Certainly, if it'll make you easier."

There was an instant softening of the hard lines of the elder Woodbury's face, as though some favour of import had been done him. He touched a bell-cord and lowered himself with a little grunt of relaxation into a chair. The chair was stoutly built, but it groaned a little under the weight of the mighty frame it received. He leaned back and in his face was a light which came not altogether from the comfortable glow of the fire.

And when the servant appeared the big man ordered: "Scotch and seltzer and one glass with a pitcher of ice."

"Aren't you taking anything, sir?" asked Anthony.

"Who, me? Yes, yes, of course. Why, let me see—bring me a pitcher of beer." He added as the servant disappeared: "Never could get a taste for Scotch, and rye doesn't seem to be—er—good form. Eh, Anthony?"

3

"Nonsense," frowned the son, "haven't you a right to be comfortable in your own house?"

"Come, come!" rumbled John Woodbury. "A young fellow in your position can't have a boor for a father, eh?"

It was apparently an old argument between them, for Anthony stared gloomily at the fire, making no attempt to reply; and he glanced up in relief when the servant entered with the liquor. John Woodbury, however, returned to the charge as soon as they were left alone again, saying: "As a matter of fact, I'm about to set you up in an establishment of your own in New York." He made a vastly inclusive gesture. "Everything done up brown—old house—high-class interior decorator, to get you started with a splash."

"Are you tired of Long Island?"

"*I'm* not going to the city, but you will."

"And my work?"

"A gentleman of the class you'll be in can't callous his hands with work. I spent my life making money; you can use your life throwing it away—like a gentleman. But"—he reached out at this point and smashed a burly fist into a palm hardly less hard—"but I'll be damned, Anthony, if I'll let you stay here in Long Island wasting your time riding the wildest horses you can get and practising with an infernal revolver. What the devil do you mean by it?"

"I don't know," said the other, musing. "Of course the days of revolvers are past, but I love the feel of the butt against my palm—I love the kick of the barrel tossing up—I love the balance; and when I have a six-shooter in my hand, sir, I feel as if I had six lives. Odd, isn't it?" He grew excited as he talked, his eyes gleaming with dancing points of fire. "And I'll tell you this, sir: I'd rather be out in the country where men still wear guns, where the sky isn't stained with filthy coal smoke, where there's an horizon wide enough to breathe in, where there's man-talk instead of this damned chatter over tea-cups———"

"Stop!" cried John Woodbury, and leaned forward, "no matter what fool ideas you get into your head—you're *going* to be a *gentleman!*"

The swaying forward of that mighty body, the outward thrust of the jaws, the ring of the voice, was like the crashing of an ax when armoured men meet in battle. The flicker in the eyes of Anthony was the rapier which swerves from the ax and then leaps at the heart. For a critical second their glances crossed and then the habit of obedience conquered.

"I suppose you know, sir."

The father stared gloomily at the floor.

"You're sort of mad, Anthony?"

Perhaps there was nothing more typical of Anthony than that he never frowned, no matter how angered he might be. Now the cold light passed from his eyes. He rose and passed behind the chair of the elder man, dropping a hand upon those massive shoulders.

"Angry with myself, sir, that I should so nearly fall out with the finest father that walks the earth."

The eyes of the grey man half closed and a semblance of a smile touched those stiff, stern lips; one of the great work-broken hands went up and rested on the fingers of his son.

"And there'll be no more of this infernal Western nonsense that you're always reverting to? No more of this horse-and-gun-and-hell-bent-away stuff?"

"I suppose not," said Anthony heavily.

"Well, Anthony, sit down and tell me about to-night."

The son obeyed, and finally said, with difficulty: "I didn't go to the Morrison supper."

A sudden cloud of white rose from the bowl of Woodbury's pipe.

"But I thought——"

"That it was a big event? It was—a fine thing

for me to get a bid to; but I went to the Wild West show instead. Sir, I know it was childish, but—I couldn't help it! I saw the posters; I thought of the horse-breaking, the guns, the swing and snap and dash of galloping men, the taint of sweating horses—and by God, sir, I *couldn't* stay away! Are you angry?"

It was more than anger; it was almost fear that widened the eye of Woodbury as he stared at his son. He said at last, controlling himself: "But I have your word; you've given up the thought of this Western life?"

"Yes," answered Anthony, with a touch of despair, "I have given it up, I suppose. But, oh, sir—" He stopped, hopeless.

"And what else happened?"

"Nothing to speak of."

"After you come home you don't usually change your clothes merely for the pleasure of sitting with me here."

"Nothing escapes you, does it?" muttered Anthony.

"In your set, Anthony, that's what they'd call an improper question."

"I could ask you any number of questions, sir, for that matter."

"Well?"

"That room over there, for instance, which you always keep locked. Am I never to have a look at it?"

He indicated a door which opened from the library.

"I hope not."

"You say that with a good deal of feeling. But there's one thing more that I have a right to hear about. My mother! Why do you never tell me of her?"

The big man stirred and the chair groaned beneath him.

"Because it tortures me to speak of her, Anthony," said the husky voice. "Tortures me, lad!"

"I let the locked room go," said Anthony firmly, "but my mother—she is different. Why, sir, I don't even know how she looked! Dad, it's my right!"

"Is it? By God, you have a right to know exactly what I choose to tell you—no more!"

He rose, strode across the room with ponderous steps, drew aside the curtains which covered the view of the garden below, and stared for a time into the night. When he turned he found that Anthony had risen—a slender, erect figure. His voice was as quiet as his anger, but an inward

quality made it as thrilling as the hoarse boom of
his father.

"On that point I stick. I must know something
about her."

"Must?"

"In spite of your anger. That locked room is
yours; this house and everything in it is yours;
but my mother—she was as much mine as yours,
and I'll hear more about her—who she was, what
she looked like, where she lived——"

The sharply indrawn breath of John Woodbury
cut him short.

"She died in giving birth to you, Anthony."

"Dear God! She died for me?"

And in the silence which came over the two men
it seemed as if another presence were in the room.
John Woodbury stood at the fire-place with bowed
head, and Anthony shaded his eyes and stared at
the floor until he caught a glimpse of the other and
went gently to him.

He said: "I'm sorrier than a lot of words could
tell you. Will you sit down, sir, and let me tell
you how I came to press home the question?"

"If you want to have it that way."

They resumed their chairs.

CHAPTER V

"IT will explain why I changed my clothes after I came home. You see, toward the end of the show a lot of the cowboys rode in. The ringmaster was announcing that they could ride anything that walked on four feet and wore a skin, when up jumped an oldish fellow in a box opposite mine and shouted that he had a horse which none of them could mount. He offered five hundred dollars to the man who could back him; and made it good by going out of the building and coming back inside of five minutes with two men leading a great stallion, the ugliest piece of horseflesh I've ever seen.

"As they worked the brute down the arena, it caught sight of my white shirt, I suppose, for it made a dive at me, reared up, and smashed its fore-hoofs against the barrier. By Jove, a regular man-eater! Brought my heart into my mouth to see the big devil raging, and I began to yearn to get astride him and to—well, just fight to see which of us would come out on top. You know?"

The big man moistened his lips; he was strangely excited.

"So you climbed into the arena and rode the horse?"

"Exactly! I knew you'd understand! After I'd ridden the horse to a standstill and climbed off, a good many people gathered around me. One of them was a big man, about your size. In fact, now that I look back at it, he was a good deal like you in more ways than one; looked as if time had hardened him without making him brittle. He came to me and said: 'Excuse me, son, but you look sort of familiar to me. Mind telling me who your mother was?' What could I answer to a——"

A shadow fell across Anthony from the rising height of his father. As he looked up he saw John Woodbury glance sharply, first toward the French windows and then at the door of the secret room.

"Was that all, Anthony?"

"Yes, about all."

"I want to be alone."

The habit of automatic obedience made Anthony rise in spite of the questions which were storming at his lips.

"Good-night, sir."

"Good-night, my boy."

At the door the harsh voice of his father overtook him.

"Before you leave the house again, see me, Anthony."

"Yes, sir."

He closed the door softly, as one deep in thought, and stood for a time without moving. Because a man had asked him who his mother was, he was under orders not to leave the house. While he stood, he heard a faint click of a snapping lock within the library and knew that John Woodbury had entered the secret room.

In his own bedroom he undressed slowly and afterward stood for a long time under the shower, rubbing himself down with the care of an athlete, thumbing the soreness of the wild ride out of the lean, sinewy muscles, for his was a made strength built up in the gymnasium and used on the wrestling mat, the cinder path, and the football field. Drying himself with a rough towel that whipped the pink into his skin, he looked down over his corded, slender limbs, remembered the thick arms and Herculean torso of John Woodbury, and wondered.

He sat on the edge of his bed, wrapped in a bathrobe, and pondered. Stroke by stroke he built the

picture of that dead mother, like a painter who
jots down the first sketch of a large composition.
John Woodbury, vast, blond, grey-eyed, had given
him few of his physical traits. But then he had
often heard that the son usually resembled the
mother. She must have been dark, slender, a frail
wife for such a giant; but perhaps she had a
strength of spirit which made her his mate.

As the picture drew out more clearly in the mind
of Anthony, he turned from the lighted room,
threw open a window, and leaned out to breathe
the calm, damp air of night.

It was infinitely cool, infinitely fresh. To his
left a row of young trees darted their slender tops
at the sky like shadowy spearheads. The smell of
wet leaves and the wet grass beneath rose up to
him. To the right, for his own room stood in a
wing of the mansion, the house shouldered its way
into the gloom, a solemn, grey shadow, netted in a
black tracery of climbing vine. In all the stretch
of wall only two windows were lighted, and those
yellow squares, he knew, belonged to his father.
He had left the secret room, therefore.

As he watched, a shadow brushed slowly across
one of the drawn shades, swept the second, and
returned at once in the opposite direction. Back
and forth, back and forth, that shadow moved, and

as his eye grew accustomed to watching, he caught quite clearly the curve of the shoulders and the forward droop of the head.

It was not until then that the first alarm came to Anthony, for he knew that the footsteps of the big grey man were dogged by fear. He could no more conceive it than he could imagine noon and midnight in conjunction, and feeling as guilty as if he had played the part of an eavesdropper he turned away, snapped off the lights, and slipped into bed.

The pleasant warmth of sleep would not come. In its place the images of the day filed past him like the dance of figures on a motion picture screen, and always, like the repeated entrance of the hero, the other images grew small and dim. He saw again the burly stranger wading through the crowd in the arena, shaking off the packed mob as the prow of a stately ship shakes off the water, to either side.

At length he started out of bed and glanced through the window. The moving shadow still swept across the lighted shades of his father's room; so he donned bathrobe and slippers and went down the long hall. At the door he did not stop to knock, for he was too deeply concerned by this time to pay any heed to convention. He

grasped the knob and threw the door wide open.
What happened then was so sudden that he could
not be sure afterward what he had seen. He was
certain that the door opened on a lighted room, yet
before he could step in the lights were snapped
out.

He was staring into a deep void of night; and a
silence came about him like a whisper. Out of that
silence he thought after a second that he caught
the sound of a hurried breathing, louder and louder,
as though someone were creeping upon him. He
glanced over his shoulder in a slight panic, but
down the grey hall on either side there was nothing
to be seen. Once more he looked back into the
solemn room, opened his lips to speak, changed his
mind, and closed the door again.

Yet when he looked down again from his own
room the lights shone once more on the shades of
his father's windows. Past them brushed the
shadow of the pacing man, up and down, up and
down. He turned his eyes away to the jagged tops
of the young trees, to the glimpses of dark fields
beyond them, and inhaled the scent of the wet,
green things. It seemed to Anthony as if it all were
hostile—as though the whole outdoors were besieging this house.

He caught the sway of the pacing figure whose

shadow moved in regular rhythm across the yellow shades. It entered his mind, clung there, and finally he began to pace in the same cadence, up and down the room. With every step he felt that he was entering deeper into the danger which threatened John Woodbury. What danger? For answer to himself he stepped to the windows and pulled down the shades. At least he could be alone.

CHAPTER VI

JOHN BARD

THERE is no cleanser of the mind like a morning bath. The same cold, whipping spray which calls up the pink blood, glowing through the marble of the skin, drives the ache of sleep from the brain, and washes away at once all the recorded thoughts of yesterday. So in place of a crowded slate of wonders and doubts, Anthony bore down to the breakfast table a willingness to take what the morning might bring and forget the night before.

John Woodbury was already there, helping himself from the covered dishes, for the meal was served in the English style. There was the usual "Good-morning, sir," "Good-morning, Anthony," and then they took their places at the table. A cautious survey of the craglike face of his father showed no traces of a sleepless night; but then, what could a single night of unrest mean to that body of iron?

He ventured, remembering the implied com-

47

mand to remain within the house until further
orders: "You asked me to speak to you, sir, before
I left the house. I'd rather like to take a ride this
morning."

And the imperturbable voice replied: "You've
worn your horses out lately. Better give them a
day of rest."

That was all, but it brought back to Anthony
the thought of the shadow which had swept cease-
lessly across the yellow shades of his father's room;
and he settled down to a day of reading. The
misty rain of the night before had cleared the sky
of its vapours, so he chose a nook in the library
where the bright spring sun shone full and the
open fire supplied the warmth. At lunch his father
did not appear, and Peters announced that the
master was busy in his room with papers. The
afternoon repeated the morning, but with less unrest on the part of Anthony. He was busy with
L'Assommoir, and lost himself in the story of down-
fall, surrounding himself with each unbeautiful
detail.

Lunch was repeated at dinner, for still John
Woodbury seemed to be "busy with papers in his
room." A fear came to Anthony that he was to
be dodged indefinitely in this manner, deceived
like a child, and kept in the house until the silent

drama was played out. But when he sat in the
library that evening his father came in and quietly
drew up a chair by the fire. The stage was ideally
set for a confidence, but none was forthcoming.
The fire shook long, sleepy shadows through the
room, the glow of the two floor-lamps picked out
two circles of light, and still the elder man sat
over his paper and would not speak.

L'Assommoir ended, and to rid himself of the
grey tragedy, Anthony looked up and through
the windows toward the bright night which lay
over the gardens and terraces outside, for a full
moon silvered all with a flood of light. It was a
waiting time, and into it the old-fashioned Dutch
clock in the corner sent its voice with a monotonous, softly clanging toll of seconds, until Anthony
forgot the moonlight over the outside terraces to
watch the gradual sway of the pendulum. A
minute, spent in this manner, was equal to an hour
of ordinary time. Fascinated by the sway of the
pendulum he became conscious of the passage of
existence like a river broad and wide and shining
which flowed on into an eternity of chance and
left him stationary on the banks.

The voice which sounded at length was as dim
and visionary as a part of his waking dream. It
was like one of those imagined calls from the world

4

of action to him who stood there, watching reality
run past and never stirring himself to take advantage of the thousand opportunities for action.
He would have discarded it for a part of his dream,
had not he seen John Woodbury raise his head
sharply, heard the paper fall with a dry crackling
to the floor, and watched the square jaw of his
father jut out in that familiar way which meant
danger.

Once more, and this time it was unmistakably
clear: "John Bard,—John Bard, come out to
me!"

The big, grey man rose with widely staring eyes
as if the name belonged to him, and strode with a
thumping step into the secret room. Hardly had
the clang of the closing door died out when he reappeared, fumbling at his throat. Straight to Anthony he came and extended a key from which
dangled a piece of thin silver chain. It was the
key to the secret room.

He took it in both hands, like a young knight
receiving the pommel of his sword from him who
has just given the accolade, and stared down at it
until the creaking of the opened French windows
startled him to his feet.

"Wait!" he called, "I will go also!"

The big man at the open window turned.

"You will sit where you are now," said his harsh voice, "but if I don't return you have the key to the room."

His burly shoulders disappeared down the steps toward the garden, and Anthony slipped back into his chair; yet for the first time in his life he was dreaming of disobeying the command of John Woodbury. Woodbury—yet the big man had risen automatically in answer to the name of Bard. John Bard! It struck on his consciousness like two hammer blows wrecking some fragile fabric; it jarred home like the timed blow of a pugilist. Woodbury? There might be a thousand men capable of that name, but there could only be one John Bard, and that was he who had disappeared down the steps leading to the garden. Anthony swerved in his chair and fastened his eyes on the Dutch clock. He gave himself five minutes before he should move.

The watched pot will never boil, and the minute hand of the big clock dragged forward with deadly pauses from one black mark to the next. Whispers rose in the room. Something fluttered the fallen newspaper as if a ghost-hand grasped it but had not the strength to raise; and the window rattled, with a sharp gust of wind. The last minute Anthony spent at the open French window with a backward eye on the clock; then he raced down the steps as though in his turn he answered a call out of the night.

The placid coolness of the open and the touch of moist, fresh air against his forehead mocked him as he reached the garden, and there were reassuring whispers from the trees he passed; yet he went on with a long, easy stride like a runner starting a distance race. First he skirted the row of poplars on the drive; then doubled back across the meadow to his right and ran in a sharp-angling course across an orchard of apple trees. Diverging from this direction, he circled at a quicker pace toward the rear of the grounds and coursed like a wild deer over a stretch of terraced lawns. On one of these low crests he stopped short under the black shadow of an elm.

In the smooth-shaven centre of the hollow before him, the same ground over which he had run and played a thousand times in his childhood, he saw two tall men standing back to back, like fighters come to a last stand and facing a crowd of foes. They separated at once, striding out with a measured step, and it was not until they moved that he caught the glint of metal at the side of one of them and knew that one was the man who had answered to the name of John Bard and the other was the grey man who had spoken to him at the Garden the night before. He knew it not so much by the testimony of his eyes at that dim distance as by a queer, inner feeling that this must be so. There was also a sense of familiarity about the whole thing, as if he were looking on something which he had seen rehearsed a thousand times.

As if they reached the end of an agreed course, the two whirled at the same instant, the metal in their hands glinted in an upward semicircle, and two guns barked hoarsely across the lawns.

One of them stood with his gun still poised; the other leaned gradually forward and toppled at full length on the grass. The victor strode out toward the fallen, but hearing the wild yell of Anthony he stopped, turned his head, and then fled into the grove of trees which topped the next rise of ground. After him, running as he had never before raced, went Anthony; his hand, as he sprinted, already tensed for the coming battle; two hundred yards at the most and he would reach the lumbering figure which had plunged into the night of the trees; but a call reached him as sharp as the crack of the guns a moment before: "Anthony!"

His head twitched to one side and he saw John Bard rising to his elbow. His racing stride shortened choppily.

"Anthony!"

He could not choose but halt, groaning to give up the chase, and then sped back to the fallen man. At his coming John Bard collapsed on the grass, and when Anthony knelt beside him a voice in rough dialect began, as if an enforced culture were brushed away and forgotten in the crisis: "Anthony, there ain't no use in followin' him!"

"Where did the bullet strike you? Quick!"

"A place where it ain't no use to look. I know!"

"Let me follow him; it's not too late——"

The dying man struggled to one elbow.

"Don't follow, lad, if you love me."

"Who is he? Give me his name and——"

"He's acted in the name of God. You have no right to hunt him down."

"Then the law will do that."

"Not the law. For God's sake swear——"

"I'll swear anything. But now lie quiet; let me——"

"Don't try. This couldn't end no other way for John Bard."

"Is that your real name?"

"Yes. Now listen, Anthony, for my time's short."

He closed his eyes as if fighting silently for strength.

Then: "When I was a lad like you, Anthony—"
That was all. The massive body relaxed; the head
fell back into the dewy grass. Anthony pressed
his head against the breast of John Bard and it
seemed to him that there was still a faint pulse.
With his pocket knife he ripped away the coat
from the great chest and then tore open the shirt.
On the expanse of the hairy chest there was one
spot from which the purple blood welled; a deadly
place for a wound, and yet the bleeding showed
that there must still be life.

He had no chance to bind the wound, for John
Bard opened his eyes again and said, as if in his
dream he had still continued his tale to Anthony.

"So that's all the story, lad. Do you forgive
me?"

"For what, sir? In God's name, for what?"

"Damnation! Tell me; do you forgive John
Bard?"

He did not hear the answer, for he murmured:
"Even Joan would forgive," and died.

CHAPTER VII

BLUEBEARD'S ROOM

As Anthony Woodbury, he knelt beside the dying. As Anthony Bard he rose with the dead man in his arms a mighty burden even for his supple strength; yet he went staggering up the slope, across a level terrace, and back to the house. There it was Peters who answered his call, Peters with a flabby face grown grey, but still the perfect servant who asked no questions; together they bore the weight up the stairs and placed it on John Bard's bed. While Anthony kept his steady vigil by the dead man, it was Peters again who summoned the police and the useless doctor.

To the old, uniformed sergeant, Anthony told a simple lie. His father had gone for a walk through the grounds because the night was fine, and Anthony was to join him there later, but when he arrived he found a dying man who could not even explain the manner of his death.

"Nothin' surprises me about a rich man's

56

death," said the sergeant, "not in these here days of anarchy. Got a place to write? I want to make out my report."

So Anthony led the grizzled fellow to the library and supplied him with what he wished. The sergeant, saying good-bye, shook hands with a lingering grip.

"I knew John Woodbury," he said, "just by sight, but I'm here to tell the world that you've lost a father who was just about all man. Solong; I'll be seein' you again."

Left alone, Anthony Bard went to the secret room. The key fitted smoothly into the lock. What the door opened upon was a little grey apartment with an arched ceiling, a place devoid of a single article of furniture save a straight-backed chair in the centre. Otherwise Anthony saw three things—two pictures on the wall and a little box in the corner. He went about his work very calmly, for here, he knew, was the only light upon the past of John Bard, that past which had lain passive so long and overwhelmed him on this night.

First he took up the box, as being by far the most promising of the three to give him what he wished to know; the name of the slayer, the place where he could be found, and the cause of the slaying. It held only two things; a piece of dirty silk and a small oil can; but the oil can and the black smears on the silk made him look closer, closer until the meaning struck him in a flare, as the glow of a lighted match suddenly illumines, even if faintly, an entire room.

In that box the revolver had lain, and here every day through all the year, John Bard retired to clean and oil his gun, oil and reclean it, keeping it ready for the crisis. That was why he went to the secret room as soon as he heard the call from the garden, and carrying that gun with him he had walked out, prepared. The time had come for which he had waited a quarter of a century, knowing all that time that the day must arrive. It was easy to understand now many an act of the big grim man; but still there was no light upon the slayer.

As he sat pondering he began to feel as if eyes were fastened upon him, watching, waiting, mocking him, eyes from behind which stared until a chill ran up his back. He jerked his head up, at last, and flashed a glance over his shoulder.

Indeed there was mockery in the smile with which she stared down to him from her frame, down to him and past him as if she scorned in him all men forever. It was not that which made Anthony close his eyes. He was trying with all his might to conjure up his own image vividly. He looked again, comparing his picture with this portrait on the wall, and then he knew why the grey man at the Garden had said: "Son, who's your mother?" For this was she into whose eyes he now stared.

She had the same deep, dark eyes, the same black hair, the same rather aquiline, thin face which her woman's eyes and lovely mouth made beautiful, but otherwise the same. He was simply a copy of that head hewn with a rough chisel—a sculptor's clay model rather than a smoothly finished reproduction.

Ah, and the fine spirit of her, the buoyant, proud, scornful spirit! He stretched out his arms to her, drew closer, smiling as if she could meet and welcome his caress, and then remembered that this was a thing of canvas and paint—a bright shadow; no more.

To the second picture he turned with a deeper hope, but his heart fell at once, for all he saw was an enlarged photograph, two mountains, snow-topped in the distance, and in the foreground, first a mighty pine with the branches lopped smoothly from the side as though some tremendous ax had trimmed it, behind this a ranch-house, and farther back the smooth waters of a lake.

He turned away sadly and had reached the door when something made him turn back and stand once more before the photograph. It was quite the same, but it took on a different significance as he linked it with the two other objects in the room, the picture of his mother and the revolver box. He found himself searching among the forest for the figures of two great grey men, equal in bulk, such Titans as that wild country needed.

West it must be, but where? North or South? West, and from the West surely that grey man at the Garden had come, and from the West John Bard himself. Those two mountains, spearing the sky with their sharp horns—they would be the pole by which he steered his course.

A strong purpose is to a man what an engine is to a ship. Suppose a hull lies in the water, stanchly built, graceful in lines of strength and speed, nosing at the wharf or tugging back on the mooring line, it may be a fine piece of building but it cannot be much admired. But place an engine in the hull and add to those fine lines the purr of a motor— there is a sight which brings a smile to the lips and a light in the eyes. Anthony had been like the unengined hulk, moored in gentle waters with never the hope of a voyage to rough seas. Now that his purpose came to him he was calmly eager, almost gay in the prospect of the battle.

On the highest hill of Anson Place in a tomb overlooking the waters of the sound, they lowered the body of John Bard.

Afterward Anthony Bard went back to the secret room of his father. The old name of Anthony Woodbury he had abandoned; in fact, he felt almost like dating a new existence from the moment when he heard the voice calling out of the garden: "John Bard, come out to me!" If life was a thread, that voice was the shears which snapped the trend of his life and gave him a new beginning. As Anthony Bard he opened once more the door of the chamber.

He had replaced the revolver of John Bard in the box with the oiled silk. Now he took it out again and shoved it into his back trouser pocket, and then stood a long moment under the picture of the woman he knew was his mother. As he stared he felt himself receding to youth, to boyhood, to child days, finally to a helpless infant which that woman, perhaps, had held and loved. In those dark, brooding eyes he strove to read the mystery of his existence, but they remained as unriddled as the free stars of heaven.

He repeated to himself his new name, his real

name: "Anthony Bard." It seemed to make him a stranger in his own eyes. "Woodbury" had been a name of culture; it suggested the air of a long descent. "Bard" was terse, short, brutally abrupt, alive with possibilities of action. Those possibilities he would never learn from the dead lips of his father. He sought them from his mother, but only the painted mouth and the painted smile answered him.

He turned again to the picture of the house with the snow-topped mountains in the distance. There surely, was the solution; somewhere in the infinite reaches of the West.

Finally he cut the picture from its frame and rolled it up. He felt that in so doing he would carry with him an identification tag—a clue to himself. With that clue in his travelling bag, he started for the city, bought his ticket, and boarded a train for the West.

CHAPTER VIII

MARTY WILKES

THE motion of the train, during those first two days gave Anthony Bard a strange feeling that he was travelling from the present into the past. He felt as if it was not miles that he placed behind him, but days, weeks, months, years, that unrolled and carried him nearer and nearer to the beginning of himself. He heard nothing about him; he saw nothing of the territory which whirled past the window. They were already far West before a man boarded the train and carried to Bard the whole atmosphere of the mountain desert.

He got on the train at a Nebraska station and Anthony sat up to watch, for a man of importance does not need size in order to have a mien. Napoleon struck awe through the most gallant of his hero marshals, and even the porter treated this little brown man with a respect that was ludicrous at first glimpse.

He was so ugly that one smiled on glancing at

him. His face, built on the plan of a wedge, was extremely narrow in front, with a long, high-bridged nose, slanting forehead, thin-lipped mouth, and a chin that jutted out to a point, but going back all the lines flared out like a reversed vista. A ridge of muscle crested each side of the broad jaws and the ears flaunted out behind so that he seemed to have been built for travelling through the wind.

The same wind, perhaps, had blown the hair away from the upper part of his forehead, leaving him quite bald half way back on his head, where a veritable forest of hair began, and continued, growing thicker and longer, until it brushed the collar of his coat behind.

When he entered the car he stood eying his seat for a long moment like a dog choosing the softest place on the floor before it lies down. Then he took his place and sat with his hands folded in his lap, moveless, speechless, with the little keen eyes straight before him—three hours that state continued. Then he got up and Anthony followed him to the diner. They sat at the same table.

"The journey," said Anthony, " is pretty tiresome through monotonous scenery like this."

The little keen eyes surveyed him a moment before the man spoke.

"There was buffalo on them plains once."

If someone had said to an ignorant questioner, "This little knoll is called Bunker Hill," he could not have been more abashed than was Anthony, who glanced through the window at the dreary prospect, looked back again, and found that the sharp eyes once more looked straight ahead without the slightest light of triumph in his coup. Silence, apparently, did not in the least abash this man.

"Know a good deal about buffaloes?"

"Yes."

It was not the insulting curtness of one who wishes to be left in peace, but simply a statement of bald fact.

"Really?" queried Anthony. "I didn't think you were as old as that!"

It appeared that this remark was worthy of no answer whatever. The little man turned his attention to his order of ham and eggs, cut off the first egg, manœuvred it carefully into position on his knife, and raised it toward a mouth that stretched to astonishing proportions; but at the critical moment the egg slipped and flopped back on the plate.

"Missed!" said Anthony.

He couldn't help it; the ejaculation popped out

of its own accord. The other regarded him with grave displeasure.

"If you had your bead drawed an' somebody jogged your arm jest as you pulled the trigger, would you call it a miss?"

"Excuse me. I've no doubt you're extremely accurate."

"I ne'er miss," said the other, and proved it by disposing of the egg at the next imposing mouthful.

"I should like to know you. My name is Anthony Bard."

"I'm Marty Wilkes. H'ware ye?"

They shook hands.

"Westerner, Mr. Wilkes?"

"This is my furthest East."

"Have a pleasant time?"

A gesture indicated the barren, brown waste of prairie.

"Too much civilization."

"Really?"

"Even the cattle got no fight in 'em." He added, "That sounds like I'm a fighter. I ain't."

"Till you're stirred up, Mr. Wilkes?"

"Heat me up an' I'll burn. So'll wood."

"You're pretty familiar with the Western country?"

"I get around."

"Perhaps you'd recognize this."

He took a scroll from his breast pocket and unrolled the photograph of the forest and the ranchhouse with the two mountains in the distance. Wilkes considered it unperturbed.

"Them are the Little Brothers."

"Ah! Then all I have to do is to travel to the foot of the Little Brothers?"

"No, about sixty miles from 'em."

"Impossible! Why, the mountains almost overhang that house."

Wilkes handed back the picture and resumed his eating without reply. It was not a sullen resentment; it was hunger and a lack of curiosity. He was not "heated up."

"Any one," said Anthony, to lure the other on, "could see that."

"Sure; any one with bad eyes."

"But how can you tell it's sixty miles?"

"I've been there."

"Well, at least the big tree there and the ranchhouse will not be *very* hard to find. But I suppose I'll have to travel in a circle around the Little Brothers, keeping a sixty-mile radius?"

"If you want to waste a pile of time. Yes."

"I suppose you could lead me right to the spot?"

"I could."

"How?"

"That's about fifty-five miles straight north-east of the Little Brothers."

"How the devil can you tell that, man?"

"That ain't hard. They's a pretty steady north wind that blows in them parts. It's cold and it's strong. Now when you been out there long enough and get the idea that the only things that live is because God loves 'em. Mostly it's jest plain sand and rock. The trees live because they got protection from that north wind. Nature puts moss on 'em on the north side to shelter 'em from that same wind. Look at that picture close. You see that rough place on the side of that tree—jest a shadow like the whiskers of a man that ain't shaved for a week? That's the moss. Now if that's north, the rest is easy. That place is north-east of the Little Brothers."

"By Jove! how did you get such eyes?"

"Used 'em."

"The reason I'd like to find the house is be-cause——"

"Reasons ain't none too popular with me."

"Well, you're pretty sure that your suggestion will take me to the spot?"

"I'm sure of nothing except my gun when the weather's hot."

"Reasonably sure, however? The pine trees and the house—if I don't find one I'll find the other."

"The house'll be in ruins, probably."

"Why?"

"That picture was taken a long time ago."

"Do you read the mind of a picture, Mr. Wilkes?"

"No."

"The tree, however, will be there."

"No, that's chopped down."

"That's going a bit too far. Do you mean to say you know that this particular tree is down?"

"That's first growth. All that country's been cut over. D' you think they'd pass up a tree the size of that?"

"It's going to be hard," said Anthony with a frown, "for me to get used to the West."

"Maybe not."

"I can ride and shoot pretty well, but I don't know the people, I haven't worn their clothes, and I can't talk their lingo."

"The country's mostly rocks when it ain't ground; the people is pretty generally men and women; the clothes they wear is cotton and wool, the lingo they talk is English."

It was like a paragraph out of some book of ultimate knowledge. He was not entirely contented with his statement, however, for now he qualified it as follows: "Maybe some of 'em don't talk good book English. Quite a pile ain't had much eddication; in fact there ain't awful many like me. But they can tell you how much you owe 'em an' they'll understand you when you say you're hungry. What's your business? Excuse me; I don't generally ask questions."

"That's all right. You've probably caught the habit from me. I'm simply going out to look about for excitement."

"A feller gener'ly finds what he's lookin' for. Maybe you won't be disappointed. I've knowed places on the range where excitement growed like fruit on a tree. It was like that there manna in the Bible. You didn't have to work none for it. You jest laid still an' it sort of dropped in your mouth."

He added with a sigh: "But them times ain't no more."

"That's hard on me, eh?"

"Don't start complainin' till you miss your feed. Things are gettin' pretty crowded, but there's ways of gettin' elbow room—even at a bar."

"And you really think there's nothing which distinguishes the Westerner from the Easterner?"

"Just the Western feeling, partner.   Get that an' you'll be at home."

"If you were a little further East and said that, people might be inclined to smile a bit."

"Partner, if they did, they wouldn't finish their smile.   But I heard a feller say once that the funny thing about men east and west of the Rockies was that they was all——"

He paused as if trying to remember.

"Well?"

"Americans, Mr. Bard."

CHAPTER IX

"THIS PLACE FOR REST"

As the white heat of midday passed and the shadows lengthened more and more rapidly to the east, the sheep moved out from the shade and from the tangle of the brush to feed in the open, and the dogs, which had laid one on either side of the man, rose and trotted out to recommence their vigil; but the shepherd did not change his position where he sat cross-legged under the tree.

Alternately he stroked the drooping moustache to the right and then to the left, with a little twist each time, which turned the hair to a sharp point in its furthest downward reach near his chin. To the right, to the left, to the right, to the left, while his eyes, sad with a perpetual mist, looked over the lake and far away to the white tops of the Little Brothers, now growing blue with shadow.

Finally with a brown forefinger he lifted the brush of moustache on his upper lip, leaned a little, and spat. After that he leaned back with a sigh of content; the brown juice had struck fairly and squarely on the centre of the little stone which for the past two hours he had been endeavouring vainly to hit. The wind had been against him.

All was well. The spindling tops of the second-growth forest pointed against the pale blue of a stainless sky, and through that clear air the blatting of the most distant sheep sounded close, mingled with the light clangour of the bells. But the perfect peace was broken rudely now by the form of a horseman looming black and large against the eastern sky. He trotted his horse down the slope, scattered a group of noisy sheep from side to side before him, and drew rein before the shepherd.

"Evening."

"Evening, stranger."

"Own this land?"

"No; rent it."

"Could I camp here?"

The shepherd lifted his moustache again and spat; when he spoke his eyes held steadily and sadly on the little stone, which he had missed again.

"Can't think of nobody who'd stop you."

"That your house over there? You rent that?"

He pointed to a broken-backed ruin which stood on the point of land that jutted out onto the waters of the lake, a crumbling structure slowly blackening with time.

"Nope."

A shadow of a frown crossed the face of the stranger and was gone again more quickly than a cloud shadow brushed over the window on a windy city in March.

"Well," he said, "this place looks pretty good to me. Ever fish those streams?"

"Don't eat fish."

"I'll wager you're missing some first-class trout, though. By Jove, I'd like to cast a couple of times over some of the pools I've passed in the last hour! By the way, who owns that house over there?"

"Same feller that owns this land."

"That so? What's his name?"

The other lifted his shaggy eyebrows and stared at the stranger.

"Ain't been long around here, eh?"

"No."

"William Drew, he owns that house."

"William Drew?" repeated the rider, as though imprinting the word on his memory. "Is he home?"

"Maybe."

"I'll ride over and ask him if he can put me up."

"Wait a minute. He may be home, but he lives on the other side of the range."

"Very far from here?"

"A piece."

"How'll I know him when I see him?"

"Big feller—grey—broad shoulders."

"Ah!" murmured the other, and smiled as though the picture pleased him. "I'll hunt him up and ask him if I can camp out in this house of his for a while."

"Well, that's your party."

"Don't you think he'd let me?"

"Maybe; but the house ain't lucky."

"That so?"

"Sure. There's a grave in front of it."

"A grave? Whose?"

"Dunno."

"Well, it doesn't worry me. I'll drop over the hill and see Drew."

"Maybe you'd better wait. You'll be passin' him on the road, like as not."

"How's that?"

"He comes over here on Tuesdays once a month; to-morrow he's about due."

"Good. In the meantime I can camp over there by that stream, eh?"

"Don't know of nobody who'd stop you."

"By the way, what brings Drew over here every month?"

"Never asked him. I was brung up not to ask questions."

The stranger accepted this subtle rebuke with such an open, infectious laugh that the shepherd smiled in the very act of spitting at the stone, with the result that he missed it by whole inches.

"I'll answer some of the questions you haven't asked, then. My name is Anthony Bard and I'm out here seeing the mountains and having a bully time in general with my rod and gun."

The sad eyes regarded him without interest, but Bard swung from his horse and advanced with outstretched hand.

"I may be about here for a few days and we might as well get acquainted, eh? I'll promise to lay off the questions."

"I'm Logan."

"Glad to know you, Mr. Logan."

"Same t' you. Don't happen to have no fine-cut about you?"

"No. Sorry."

"So'm I. Ran out an' now all I've got is plug. Kind of hard on the teeth an' full of molasses."

"I've some pipe tobacco, though, which might do."

He produced a pouch which Logan opened, taking from it a generous pinch.

"Looks kind of like fine-cut—smells kind of like the real thing"—here he removed the quid from his mouth and introduced the great pinch of tobacco— "an' I'll be damned if it don't taste a pile the same!"

The misty eyes centred upon Bard and a light grew up in them.

"Maybe you'd put a price on this tobacco, stranger?"

"It's yours," said Bard, "to help you forget all the questions I've asked."

The shepherd acted at once lest the other might change his mind, dumping the contents of the pouch into the breast pocket of his shirt. Afterward his gaze sought the dim summits of the Little Brothers, and a sad, great resolution grew up and hardened the lines of his sallow face.

"You can camp with me if you want—partner."

A cough, hastily summoned, covered Bard's smile.

"Thanks awfully, but I'm used to camping alone—and rather like it that way."

"Which I'd say, the same goes here," responded the shepherd with infinite relief, "I ain't got much use for company—away from a bar. But I could

show you a pretty neat spot for a camp, over there
by the river."

"Thanks, but I'll explore for myself."

He swung again into the saddle and trotted
whistling down the slope toward the creek which
Logan had pointed out. But once fairly out of
sight in the second-growth forest, he veered
sharply to the right, touched his tough cattle-pony
with the spurs, and headed at a racing pace straight
for the old ruined house.

Even from a distance the house appeared unmistakably done for, but not until he came close
at hand could Bard appreciate the full extent of
the ruin. Every individual board appeared to be
rotting and crumbling toward the ground, awaiting
the shake of one fierce gust of wind to disappear
in a cloud of mouldy dust. He left his horse with
the reins hanging over its head behind the house
and entered by the back door. One step past the
threshold brought him misadventure, for his foot
drove straight through the rotten flooring and his
leg disappeared up to the knee.

After that he proceeded more cautiously, following the lines of the beams on which the boards were
nailed, but even these shook and groaned under his
weight. A whimsical fancy made him think of the
fabled boat of Charon which will float a thousand

bodiless spirits over the Styx but which sinks to the water-line with the weight of a single human being.

So he passed forward like one in a fabric of spider-webs almost fearing to breathe lest the whole house should puff away to shreds before him. Half the boards, fallen from the ceiling, revealed the bare rafters above; below there were ragged holes in the flooring. In one place a limb, torn by lightning or wind from its overhanging tree, had crashed through the corner of the roof and dropped straight through to the ground.

At last he reached a habitable room in the front of the house. It was a new shell built inside the old wreck, with four stout corner-posts supporting cross-beams, which in turn held up the mouldering roof. In the centre was a rude table and on either side a bunk built against the wall. Perhaps this was where Drew lived on the occasions of his visits to the old ranchhouse.

Out of the gloom of the place, Bard stepped with a shrug of the shoulders, like one who shakes off the spell of a nightmare. He strode through the doorway and took the slant, warm sun of the afternoon full in his face.

He found himself in front of the only spot on the entire premises which showed the slightest care, the mound of a grave under the shelter of two trees whose branches were interwoven overhead in a sort of impromptu roof. From the surface of the mound all the weeds and grasses had been carefully cleared away, and around its edge ran a path covered with gravel and sand. It was a well-beaten path with the mark of heels still comparatively fresh upon it.

The headstone itself bore not a vestige of moss, but time had cracked it diagonally and the chiselled letters were weathered away. He studied it with painful care, poring intently over each faint impression. He who cared for the grave had apparently been troubled only to keep the stone free from dirt—the lettering he must have known by heart. At length Bard made out this inscription:

HERE SLEEPS

JOAN

WIFE OF WILLIAM DREW

———

SHE CHOSE THIS PLACE FOR REST

———

CHAPTER X

A BIT OF STALKING

It seemed as if the peaceful afternoons of Logan were ended forever, for the next day the scene of interruption was repeated under almost identical circumstances, save that the tree under which the shepherd sat was a little larger. Larger also was the man who rode over the brow of the hill to the east. The most durable cattle-pony would have staggered under the bulk of that rider, and therefore he rode a great, patient-eyed bay, with shoulders worthy of shoving against a work-collar; but the neck tapered down small behind a short head, and the legs, for all their breadth at shoulder and hip, slipped away to small hoofs, and ankles which sloped sharply to the rear, the sure sign of the fine saddle-horse.

Yet the strong horse was winded by the burden he bore, a mighty figure, deep-chested, amply shouldered, an ideal cavalier for the days when youths rode out in armour-plate to seek adventures and when men of fifty still lifted the lance to run a "friendly" course or two in the lists.

At sight of him Logan so far bestirred himself as to uncoil his long legs, rise, and stand with one shoulder propped against the tree.

"Evening, Mr. Drew," he called.

"Hello, Logan. How's everything with you?"

He would have ridden on, but at Logan's reply he checked his horse to a slow walk.

"Busy. Lots of company lately, Mr. Drew."

"Company?"

"Yes, there's a young feller come along who says he wants to see you. He's over there by the creek now, fishin' I think. I told him I'd holler if I seen you, but I guess you wouldn't mind ridin' over that way yourself."

Drew brought his horse to a halt.

"What does he want of me?"

"Dunno. Something about wanting to hunt and fish on your streams here."

"Why didn't you tell him he was welcome to do what he liked? Must be an Easterner, Logan."

"Wants to bunk in the old house, too. Seems sort of interested in it."

"That so? What sort of a fellow is he?"

"All right. A bit talky. Green; but he rides damn well, an' he smokes good tobacco."

His hand automatically rose and touched his breast pocket.

"I'll go over to him," said Drew, and swung his horse to the left, but only to come again to a halt.

He called over his shoulder: "What sort of a looking fellow?"

"Pretty keen—dark," answered Logan, slipping down into his original position. "Thin face; black eyes."

"Ah, yes," murmured Drew, and started at a trot for the creek.

Once more he imitated the actions of Bard the day before, however, for no sooner had the trees screened him thoroughly from the eyes of Logan than he abandoned his direct course for the creek. He swung from the saddle with an ease surprising in a man of such age and bulk and tossed the reins over the head of the horse.

Then he commenced a cautious stalking through the woods, silent as an Indian, stealthy of foot, with eyes that glanced sharply in all directions. Once a twig snapped under foot, and after that he remained motionless through a long moment, shrinking against the trunk of a tree and scanning the forest anxiously in all directions. At length he ventured out again, grown doubly cautious. In this manner he worked his way up the course of the stream, always keeping the waters just within sight but never passing out on the banks, where the walking would have been tenfold easier. So he came in sight of a figure far off through the trees.

If he had been cautious before, he became now as still as night. Dropping to hands and knees, or crouching almost as prone, he moved from the shadow of one tree to the next, now and then venturing a glance to make sure that he was pursuing the right course, until he manœuvred to a point of vantage which commanded a clear view of Bard.

The latter was fishing, with his back to Drew; again and again he cast his fly out under an overhanging limb which shadowed a deep pool. The big grey man set his teeth and waited with the patience of a stalking beast of prey, or a cat which will sit half the day waiting for the mouse to show above the opening of its hole.

Apparently there was a bite at length. The pole bent almost double and the reel played back and forth rapidly as the fisher wore down his victim. Finally he came close to the edge of the stream, dipped his net into the water, and jerked it up at once bearing a twisting, shining trout enwrapped in the meshes. Swinging about as he did so, Drew caught his first full glimpse of Anthony's face. and knew him for the man who had ridden the wild horse at Madison Square Garden those weeks before.

Perhaps it was astonishment that moved the big man—surely it could not have been fear—yet he knelt there behind the sheltering tree grey-faced, wide, and blank of eye, as a man might look who dreamed and awoke to see his vision standing before him in full sunlit life. What his expression became then could not be said, for he buried his face in his hands and his great body shook with a tremor. If this was not fear it was something very like.

And very like a man in fear he stole back among the trees as cautiously as he had made his approach. Resuming his horse he rode straight for Logan.

"Couldn't find your young friend," he said, "along the creek."

"Why," said Logan, "I can reach him with a holler from here, I think."

"Never mind; just tell him that he's welcome to do what he pleases on the place; and he can bunk down at the house if he wants to. I'd like to know his name, though."

"That's easy. Anthony Bard."

"Ah," said Drew slowly, "Anthony Bard!"

"That's it," nodded Logan, and fixed a curious eye upon the big grey rider.

As if to escape from that inquiring scrutiny, Drew wheeled his horse and spurred at a sharp gallop up the hill, leaving Logan frowning behind.

"No stay over night," muttered the shepherd. "No fooling about that damned old shack of a house; what's wrong with Drew?"

He answered himself, for all shepherds are forced by the bitter loneliness of their work to talk with themselves. "The old boy's worried. Damned if he isn't! I'll keep an eye on this Bard feller."

And he loosened the revolver in its holster.

He might have been even more concerned had he seen the redoubled speed with which Drew galloped as soon as the hilltop was between him and Logan. Straight on he pushed his horse, not exactly like one who fled but rather more like one too busy with consuming thoughts to pay the slightest heed to the welfare of his mount. It was a spent horse on which he trotted late that night up to the big, yawning door of his barn.

"Where's Nash?" he asked of the man who took his horse.

"Playing a game with the boys in the bunk-house, sir."

So past the bunk-house Drew went on his way to his dwelling, knocked, and threw open the door.

Inside, a dozen men, seated at or standing around a table, looked up.

"Nash!"

"Here."

"On the jump, Nash. I'm in a hurry."

There rose a man of a build much prized in pugilistic circles. In those same circles he would have been described as a fellow with a fighting face and a heavy-weight above the hips and a light-weight below—a handsome fellow, except that his eyes were a little too small and his lips a trifle too thin. He rose now in the midst of a general groan of dismay, and scooped in a considerable stack of gold as well as several bright piles of silver; he was undoubtedly taking the glory of the game with him.

"Is this square?" growled one of the men clenching his fist on the edge of the table.

The sardonic smile hardened on the lips of Nash as he answered: "Before you've been here much longer, Pete, you'll find out that about everything I do is square. Sorry to leave you, boys, before you're broke, but orders is orders."

"But one more hand first," pleaded Pete.

"You poor fool," snarled Nash, "d'you think I'll take a chance on keepin' *him* waiting?"

The last of his winnings passed with a melodious

jingling into his pockets and he went hurriedly out of the bunk-house and up to the main building. There he found Drew in the room which the rancher used as an office, and stood at the door hat in hand.

"Come in; sit down," said "*him.*" "Been taking the money from the boys again, Steve? I thought I talked with you about that a month ago?"

"It's this way, Mr. Drew," explained Nash, "with me stayin' away from the cards is like a horse stayin' off its feed. Besides, I done the square thing by the lot of those short-horns."

"How's that?"

"I showed 'em my hand."

"Told them you were a professional gambler?"

"Sure. I explained they didn't have no chance against me."

"And of course that made them throw every cent they had against you?"

"Maybe."

"It can't go on, Nash."

"Look here, Mr. Drew. I told 'em that I wasn't a gambler but just a gold-digger."

The big man could not restrain his smile, though it came like a shadow of mirth rather than the sunlight.

"After all, they might as well lose it to you as to someone else."

"Sure," grinned Nash, "it keeps it in the family, eh?"

"But one of these days, Steve, crooked cards will be the end of you."

"I'm still pretty fast on the draw," said Steve sullenly.

"All right. That's your business. Now I want you to listen to some of mine."

"Real work?"

"Your own line."

"That," said Nash, with a smile of infinite meaning, "sounds like the dinner bell to me. Let her go, sir!"

CHAPTER XI

THE QUEST BEGINS

"You know the old place on the other side of the range?"

"Like a book. I got pet names for all the trees."

"There's a man there I want."

"Logan?"

"No. His name is Bard."

"H-m! Any relation of the old bird that was partners with you back about the year one?"

"I want Anthony Bard brought here," said Drew, entirely overlooking the question.

"Easy. I can make the trip in a buckboard and I'll dump him in the back of it."

"No. He's got to *ride* here, understand?"

"A dead man," said Nash calmly, "ain't much good on a hoss."

"Listen to me," said Drew, his voice lowering to a sort of musical thunder, "if you harm a hair of this lad's head I'll—I'll break you in two with my own hands."

And he made a significant gesture as if he were snapping a twig between his fingers. Nash moistened his lips, then his square, powerful jaw jutted out.

"Which the general idea is me doing baby talk and sort of hypnotizing this Bard feller into coming along?"

"More than that. He's got to be brought here alive, untouched, and placed in that chair tied so that he can't move hand or foot for ten minutes while I talk."

"Nice, quiet day you got planned for me, Mr. Drew."

The grey man considered thoughtfully.

"Now and then you've told me of a girl at Eldara—I think her name is Sally Fortune?"

"Right. She begins where the rest of the calico leaves off."

"H-m! that sounds familiar, somehow. Well, Steve, you've said that if you had a good start you think the girl would marry you."

"I think she *might.*"

"She pretty fond of you?"

"She knows that if I can't have her I'm fast enough to keep everyone else away."

"I see. A process of elimination with you as the eliminator. Rather an odd courtship, Steve?"

The cowpuncher grew deadly serious.

"You see, I love her. There ain't no way of bucking out of that. So do nine out of ten of all the boys that 've seen her. Which one will she pick? That's the question we all keep askin', because of all the contrary, freckle-faced devils with the heart of a man an' the smile of a woman, Sally has 'em all beat from the drop of the barrier. One feller has money; another has looks; another has a funny line of talk. But I've got the fastest gun. So Sally sees she's due for a complete outfit of black mournin' if she marries another man while I'm alive; an' that keeps her thinkin'. But if I had the price of a start in the world—why, maybe she'd take a long look at me."

"Would she call one thousand dollars in cash a start in the world—and your job as foreman of my place, with twice the salary you have now?"

Steve Nash wiped his forehead.

He said huskily: "A joke along this line don't bring no laugh from me, governor."

"I mean it, Steve. Get Anthony Bard tied hand and foot into this house so that I can talk to him safely for ten minutes, and you'll have everything I promise. Perhaps more. But that depends."

The blunt-fingered hand of Nash stole across the table.

"If it's a go, shake, Mr. Drew."

A mighty hand fell in his, and under the pressure he set his teeth. Afterward he covertly moved his fingers and sighed with relief to see that no permanent harm had been done.

"Me speakin' personal, Mr. Drew, I'd of give a lot to seen you when you was ridin' the range. This Bard—he'll be here before sunset to-morrow."

"Don't jump to conclusions, Steve. I've an idea that before you count your thousand you'll think that you've been underpaid. That's straight."

"This Bard is something of a man?"

"I can say that without stopping to think."

"Texas?"

"No. He's a tenderfoot, but he can ride a horse as if he was sewed to the skin, and I've an idea that he can do other things up to the same standard. If you can find two or three men who have silent tongues and strong hands, you'd better take them along. I'll pay their wages, and big ones. You can name your price."

But Nash was frowning.

"Now and then I talk to the cards a bit, Mr. Drew, and you'll hear fellers say some pretty rough things about me, but I've never asked for no odds against any man. I'm not going to start now."

"You're a hard man, Steve, but so am I; and hard men are the kind I take to. I know that you're the best foreman who ever rode this range and I know that when you start things you generally finish them. All that I ask is that you bring Bard to me in this house. The way you do it is your own problem. Drunk or drugged, I don't care how, but get him here unharmed. Understand?"

"Mr. Drew, you can start figurin' what you want to say to him now. I'll get him here—safe! And then Sally——"

"If money will buy her you'll have me behind you when you bid."

"When shall I start?"

"Now."

"So-long, then."

He rose and passed hastily from the room, leaning forward from the hips like a man who is making a start in a foot-race.

Straight up the stairs he went to his room, for the foreman lived in the big house of the rancher. There he took a quantity of equipment from a closet and flung it on the bed. Over three selections he lingered long.

The first was the cartridge belt, and he tried over several with conscientious care until he found the one which received the cartridges with the greatest ease. He could flip them out in the night, automatically as a pianist fingers the scale in the dark.

Next he examined lariats painfully, inch by inch, as though he were going out to rope the stanchest steer that ever roamed the range. Already he knew that those ropes were sound and true throughout, but he took no chances now. One of the ropes he discarded because one or two strands in it were, or might be, a trifle frayed. The others he took alternately and whirled with a broad loop, standing in the centre of the room. Of the set one was a little more supple, a little more durable, it seemed. This he selected and coiled swiftly.

Last of all he lingered—and longest—over his revolvers. Six in all, he set them in a row along the bed and without delay threw out two to begin with. Then he fingered the others, tried their weight and balance, slipped cartridges into the cylinders and extracted them again, whirled the cylinders, examined the minutest parts of the actions.

They were all such guns as an expert would have turned over with shining eyes, but finally he threw one aside into the discard; the cylinder revolved just a little too hard. Another was abandoned after much handling of the remaining three because to the delicate touch of Nash it seemed that the weight of the barrel was a gram more than in the other two; but after this selection it seemed that there was no possible choice between the final two.

So he stood in the centre of the room and went through a series of odd gymnastics. Each gun in turn he placed in the holster and then jerked it out, spinning it on the trigger guard around his second finger, while his left hand shot diagonally across his body and "fanned" the hammer. Still he could not make his choice, but he would not abandon the effort. It was an old maxim with him that there is in all the world one gun which is the best of all and with which even a novice can become a "killer."

He tried walking away, whirling as he made his draw, and levelling the gun on the door-knob. Then without moving his hand, he lowered his head and squinted down the sights. In each case the bead was drawn to a centre shot. Last of all he weighed each gun; one seemed a trifle lighter—the merest shade lighter than the other. This he slipped into the holster and carried the rest of his apparatus back to the closet from which he had taken it.

Still the preparation had not ended. Filling his cartridge belt, every cartridge was subject to a rigid inspection. A full half hour was wasted in this manner. Wasted, because he rejected not one of the many he examined. Yet he seemed happier after having made his selection, and went down the stairs, humming softly.

Out to the barn he went, lantern in hand. This time he made no comparison of horses but went directly to an ugly-headed roan, long of leg, vicious of eye, thin-shouldered, and with hips that slanted sharply down. No one with a knowledge of fine horse-flesh could have looked on this brute without aversion. It did not have even size in its favour. A wild, free spirit, perhaps, might be the reason; but the animal stood with hanging head and pendant lower lip. One eye was closed and the other only half opened. A blind affection, then, made him go to this horse first of all.

No, his greeting was to jerk his knee sharply into the ribs of the roan, which answered with a grunt and swung its head around with bared teeth, like an angry dog. "Damn your eyes!" roared the hoarse voice of Steve Nash, "stand still or I'll knock you for a goal!"

The ears of the mustang flattened close to its neck and a devil of hate came up in its eyes, but it stood quiet, while Nash went about at a judicious distance and examined all the vital points. The hoofs were sound, the backbone prominent, but not a high ridge from famine or much hard riding, and the indomitable hate in the eyes of the mustang seemed to please the cowpuncher.

It was a struggle to bridle the beast, which was accomplished only by grinding the points of his knuckles into a tender part of the jowl to make the locked teeth open.

In saddling, the knee came into play again, rapping the ribs of the brute repeatedly before the wind, which swelled out the chest to false proportions, was expelled in a sudden grunt, and the cinch whipped up taut. After that Nash dodged the flying heels, chose his time, and vaulted into the saddle.

The mustang trotted quietly out of the barn. Perhaps he had had his fill of bucking on that treacherous, slippery wooden floor, but once outside he turned loose the full assortment of the cattle-pony's tricks. It was only ten minutes, but while it lasted the cursing of Nash was loud and steady, mixed with the crack of his murderous quirt against the roan's flanks. The bucking ended as quickly as it had begun, and they started at a long canter over the trail.

CHAPTER XII

THE FIRST DAY

MILE after mile of the rough trail fell behind him, and still the pony shambled along at a loose trot or a swinging canter; the steep upgrades it took at a steady jog and where the slopes pitched sharply down, it wound among the rocks with a faultless sureness of foot.

Certainly the choice of Nash was well made. An Eastern horse of blood over a level course could have covered the same distance in half the time, but it would have broken down after ten miles of that hard trail.

Dawn came while they wound over the crest of the range, and with the sun in their faces they took the downgrade. It was well into the morning before Nash reached Logan. He forced from his eye the contempt which all cattlemen feel for sheepherders.

"I s'pose you're here askin' after Bard?" began Logan without the slightest prelude.

"Bard? Who's he?"

Logan considered the other with a sardonic smile.

"Maybe you been ridin' all night jest for fun?"

"If you start usin' your tongue on me, Logan you'll wear out the snapper on it. I'm on my way to the A Circle Y."

"Listen; I'm all for old man Drew. You know that. Tell me what Bard has on him?"

"Never heard the name before. Did he rustle a couple of your sheep?"

Logan went on patiently: "I knew something was wrong when Drew was here yesterday but I didn't think it was as bad as this."

"What did Drew do yesterday?"

"Came up as usual to potter around the old house, I guess, but when he heard about Bard bein' here he changed his mind sudden and went home."

"That's damn queer. What sort of a lookin' feller is this Bard?"

"I don't suppose you know, eh?" queried Logan ironically. "I don't suppose the old man described him before you started, maybe?"

"Logan, you poor old hornless maverick, d'you think I'm on somebody's trail? Don't you know

I've been through with that sort of game for a hell of a while?"

"When rocks turn into ham and eggs I'll trust you, Steve. I'll tell you what I done to Bard, anyway. Yesterday, after he found that Drew had been here and gone he seemed sort of upset; tried to keep it from me, but I'm too much used to judgin' changes of weather to be fooled by any tenderfoot that ever used school English. Then he hinted around about learnin' the way to Eldara, because he knows that town is pretty close to Drew's place, I guess. I told him; sure I did. He should of gone due west, but I sent him south. There *is* a south trail, only it takes about three days to get to Eldara."

"Maybe you think that interests me. It don't."

Logan overlooked this rejoinder, saying: "Is it his scalp you're after?"

"Your ideas are like nest-eggs, Logan, an' you set over 'em like a hen. They look like eggs; they feel like eggs; but they don't never hatch. That's the way with your ideas. They look all right; they sound all right; but they don't mean nothin'. So-long."

But Logan merely chuckled wisely. He had been long on the range.

As Nash turned his pony and trotted off in the

direction of the A Circle Y ranch, the sheepherder called after him: "What you say cuts both ways, Steve. This feller Bard looks like a tenderfoot; he sounds like a tenderfoot; but he ain't a tenderfoot."

Feeling that this parting shot gave him the honours of the meeting, he turned away whistling with such spirit that one of his dogs, overhearing, stood still and gazed at his master with his head cocked wisely to one side.

His eastern course Nash pursued for a mile or more, and then swung sharp to the south. He was weary, like his horse, and he made no attempt to start a sudden burst of speed. He let the pony go on at the same tireless jog, clinging like a bull-dog to the trail.

About midday he sighted a small house cuddled into a hollow of the hills and made toward it. As he dismounted, a tow-headed, spindling boy lounged out of the doorway and stood with his hands shoved carelessly into his little overall pockets.

"Hello, young feller."

"'Lo, stranger."

"What's the chance of bunking here for three or four hours and gettin' a good feed for the hoss?"

"Never better. Gimme the hoss; I'll put him up in the shed. Feed him grain?"

"No, you won't put him up. I'll tend to that."

"Looks like a bad 'un."

"That's it."

"But a sure goer, eh?"

"Yep.

He led the pony to the shed, unsaddled him, and gave him a small feed. The horse first rolled on the dirt floor and then started methodically on his fodder. Having made sure that his mount was not "off his feed," Nash rolled a cigarette and strolled back to the house with the boy.

"Where's the folks?" he asked.

"Ma's sick, a little, and didn't get up to-day. Pa's down to the corral, cussing mad. But I can cook you up some chow."

"All right son. I got a dollar here that'll buy you a pretty good store knife."

The boy flushed so red that by contrast his straw coloured hair seemed positively white.

"Maybe you want to pay me?" he suggested fiercely. "Maybe you think we're squatters that run a hotel?"

Recognizing the true Western breed even in this small edition, Nash grinned.

"Speakin' man to man, son, I didn't think that, but I thought I'd sort of feel my way."

"Which I'll say you're lucky you didn't try to feel your way with pa; not the way he's feelin' now."

In the shack of the house he placed the best chair for Nash and set about frying ham and making coffee. This with crackers, formed the meal. He watched Nash eat for a moment of solemn silence and then the foreman looked up to catch a meditative chuckle from the youngster.

"Let me in on the joke, son."

"Nothin'. I was just thinkin' of pa."

"What's he sore about? Come out short at poker lately?"

"No; he lost a hoss. Ha, ha, ha!"

He explained: "He's lost his only standin' joke, and now the laugh's on pa!"

Nash sipped his coffee and waited. On the mountain desert one does not draw out a narrator with questions.

"There was a feller come along early this mornin' on a lame hoss," the story began. "He was a sure enough tenderfoot—leastways he looked it an' he talked it, but he wasn't."

The familiarity of this description made Steve sit up a trifle straighter.

"Was he a ringer?"

"Maybe. I dunno. Pa meets him at the door and asks him in. What d'you think this feller comes back with?"

The boy paused to remember and then with twinkling eyes he mimicked: "'That's very good of you, sir, but I'll only stop to make a trade with you—this horse and some cash to boot for a durable mount out of your corral. The brute has gone lame, you see.'

"Pa waited and scratched his head while these here words sort of sunk in. Then says very smooth: 'I'll let you take the best hoss I've got, an' I won't ask much cash to boot.'

"I begin wonderin' what pa was drivin' at, but I didn't say nothin'—jest held myself together and waited.

"'Look over there to the corral,' says pa, and pointed. 'They's a hoss that ought to take you wherever you want to go. It's the best hoss I've ever had.'

"It *was* the best horse pa ever had, too. It was a piebald pinto called Jo, after my cousin Josiah, who's jest a plain bad un and raises hell when there's any excuse. The piebald, he didn't even need an excuse. You see, he's one of them hosses that likes company. When he leaves the corral he likes to have another hoss for a runnin' mate and he was jest as tame as anything. I could ride him; anybody could ride him. But if you took him outside the bars of the corral without company, first thing he done was to see if one of the other hosses was comin' out to join him. When he seen that he was all laid out to make a trip by himself he jest nacherally started in to raise hell. Which Jo can raise more hell for his size than any hoss I ever seen.

"He's what you call an eddicated bucker. He don't fool around with no pauses. He jest starts in and figgers out a situation and then he gets busy slidin' the gent that's on him off'n the saddle. An' he always used to win out. In fact, he was known for it all around these parts. He begun nice and easy, but he worked up like a fiddler playin' a favourite piece, and the end was the rider lyin' on the ground.

"Whenever the boys around here wanted any excitement they used to come over and try their hands with Jo. We used to keep a pile of arnica and stuff like that around to rub them up with and tame down the bruises after Jo laid 'em cold on the ground. There wasn't never anybody could ride that hoss when he was started out alone.

"Well, this tenderfoot, he looks over the hoss

in the corral and says: 'That's a pretty fine mount, it seems to me. What do you want to boot?'

"'Aw, twenty-five dollars is enough,' says pa.

"'All right,' says the tenderfoot, 'here's the money.'

"And he counts it out in pa's hand.

"He says: 'What a little beauty! It would be a treat to see him work on a polo field.'

"Pa says: 'It'd be a treat to see this hoss work anywhere.'

"Then he steps on my foot to make me wipe the grin off'n my face.

"Down goes the tenderfoot and takes his saddle and flops it on the piebald pinto, and the piebald was jest as nice as milk. Then he leads him out'n the corral and gets on.

"First the pinto takes a look over his shoulder like he was waiting for one of his pals among the hosses to come along, but he didn't see none. Then the circus started. An' b'lieve me, it was some circus. Jo hadn't had much action for some time, an' he must have used the wait thinkin' up new ways of raisin' hell.

"There ain't enough words in the Bible to describe what he done. Which maybe you sort of gather that he *had* to keep on performin', because the tenderfoot was still in the saddle. He was.

An' he never pulled leather. No, sir, he never touched the buckin' strap, but jest sat there with his teeth set and his lips twistin' back—the same smile he had when he got into the saddle. But pretty soon I s'pose Jo had a chance to figure out that it didn't do him no particular harm to be alone.

"The minute he seen that he stopped fightin' and started off at a gallop the way the tenderfoot wanted him to go, which was over there.

"'Damn my eyes!' says pa, an' couldn't do nuthin' but just stand there repeatin' that with variations because with Jo gone there wouldn't be no drawin' card to get the boys around the house no more. But you're lookin' sort of sleepy, stranger?"

"I am," answered Nash.

"Well, if you'd seen that show you wouldn't be thinkin' of sleep. Not for some time."

"Maybe not, but the point is I didn't see it. D' you mind if I turn in on that bunk over there?"

"Help yourself," said the boy. "What time d'you want me to wake you up?"

"Never mind; I wake up automatic. S'long, Bud."

He stretched out on the blankets and was instantly asleep.

CHAPTER XIII

A TOUCH OF CRIMSON

At the end of three hours he awoke as sharply as though an alarm were clamouring at his ear. There was no elaborate preparation for renewed activities. A single yawn and stretch and he was again on his feet. Since the boy was not in sight he cooked himself an enormous meal, devoured it, and went out to the mustang.

The roan greeted him with a volley from both heels that narrowly missed the head of Nash, but the cowpuncher merely smiled tolerantly.

"Feelin' fit agin, eh, damn your soul?" he said genially, and picking up a bit of board, fallen from the side of the shed, he smote the mustang mightily along the ribs. The mustang, as if it recognized the touch of the master, pricked up one ear and side-stepped. The brief rest had filled it with all the old, vicious energy.

For once more, as soon as they rode clear of the door, there ensued a furious struggle between man and beast. The man won, as always, and the roan, dropping both ears flat against its neck, trotted sullenly out across the hills.

In that monotony of landscape, one mile exactly like the other, no landmarks to guide him, no trail to follow, however faintly worn, it was strange to see the cowpuncher strike out through the vast distances of the mountain-desert with as much confidence as if he were travelling on a paved street in a city. He had not even a compass to direct him but he seemed to know his way as surely as the birds know the untracked paths of the air in the seasons of migration.

Straight on through the afternoon and during the long evening he kept his course at the same unvarying dog-trot until the flush of the sunset faded to a stern grey and the purple hills in the distance turned blue with shadows. Then, catch-ing the glimmer of a light on a hillside, he turned toward it to put up for the night.

In answer to his call a big man with a lantern came to the door and raised his light until it shone on a red, bald head and a portly figure. His wel-come was neither hearty nor cold; hospitality is expected in the mountain-desert. So Nash put up his horse in the shed and came back to the house.

The meal was half over, but two girls immediately set a plate heaped with fried potatoes and bacon and flanked by a mighty cup of jet-black coffee on one side and a pile of yellow biscuits on the other. He nodded to them, grunted by way of expressing thanks, and sat down to eat.

Beside the tall father and the rosy-faced mother, the family consisted of the two girls, one of them with her hair twisted severely close to her head, wearing a man's blue cotton shirt with the sleeves rolled up to a pair of brown elbows. Evidently she was the boy of the family and to her fell the duty of performing the innumerable chores of the ranch, for her hands were thick with work and the tips of the fingers blunted. Also she had that calm, self-satisfied eye which belongs to the workingman who knows that he has earned his meal.

Her sister monopolized all the beauty and the grace, not that she was either very pretty or extremely graceful, but she was instinct with the challenge of femininity like a rare scent. It lingered about her, it enveloped her ways; it gave a light to her eyes and made her smile exquisite. Her clothes were not of much finer material than her sister's, but they were cut to fit, and a bow of crimson ribbon at her throat was as effective in that environment as the most costly orchids on an evening gown.

She was armed in pride this night, talking only to her mother, and then in monosyllables alone. At first it occurred to Steve that his coming had made her self-conscious, but he soon discovered that her pride was directed at the third man at the table. She at least maintained a pretence of eating, but he made not even a sham, sitting miserably, his mouth hard set, his eyes shadowed by a tremendous frown. At length he shoved back his chair with such violence that the table trembled.

"Well," he rumbled, "I guess this lets me out. S'long."

And he strode heavily from the room; a moment later his cursing came back to them as he rode into the night.

"Takes it kind of hard, don't he?" said the father.

And the mother murmured: "Poor Ralph!"

"So you went an' done it?" said the mannish girl to her sister.

"What of it?" snapped the other.

"He's too good for you, that's what of it."

"Girls!" exclaimed the mother anxiously. "Remember we got a guest!"

"Oh," said she of the strong brown arms, "I guess we can't tell him nothin'; I guess he had eyes to be seein' what's happened."

She turned calmly to Steve.

"Lizzie turned down Ralph Boardman—poor feller!"

"Sue!" cried the other girl.

"Well, after you done it, are you ashamed to have it talked about? You make me sore, I'll tell a man!"

"That's enough, Sue," growled the father.

"What's enough?"

"We ain't goin' to have no more show about this. I've had my supper spoiled by it already."

"I say it's a rotten shame," broke out Sue, and she repeated, "Ralph's too good for her. All because of a city dude—a tenderfoot!"

In the extremity of her scorn her voice drawled in a harsh murmur.

"Then take him yourself, if you can get him!" cried Lizzie. "I'm sure I don't want him!"

Their eyes blazed at each other across the table, and Lizzie, having scored an unexpected point, struck again.

"I think you've always had a sort of hankerin' after Ralph—oh, I've seen your eyes rollin' at him."

The other girl coloured hotly through her tan.

"If I was fond of him I wouldn't be ashamed to

8

let him know, you can tell the world that. And I wouldn't keep him trottin' about like a little pet dog till I got tired of him and give him up for the sake of a greenhorn who"—her voice lowered to a spiteful hiss—"kissed you the first time he even seen you!"

In vain Lizzie fought for her control; her lip trembled and her voice shook.

"I hate you, Sue!"

"Sue, ain't you ashamed of yourself?" pleaded the mother.

"No, I ain't! Think of it; here's Ralph been sweet on Liz for two years an' now she gives him the go-by for a skinny, affected dude like that feller that was here. And *he's* forgot you already, Liz, the minute he stopped laughing at you for bein' so easy."

"Ma, are you goin' to let Sue talk like this— right before a stranger?"

"Sue, you shut up!" commanded the father.

"I don't see nobody that can make me," she said, surly as a grown boy. "I can't make any more of a fool out of Liz than that tenderfoot made her!"

"Did he," asked Steve, "ride a piebald mustang?"

"D'you know him?" breathed Lizzie, forgetting

the tears of shame which had been gathering in her eyes.

"Nope. Jest heard a little about him along the road."

"What's his name?"

Then she coloured, even before Sue could say spitefully: "Didn't he even have to tell you his name before he kissed you?"

"He did! His name is—Tony!"

"Tony!"—in deep disgust. "Well, he's dark enough to be a dago! Maybe he's a foreign count, or something, Liz, and he'll take you back to live in some castle or other."

But the girl queried, in spite of this badinage: "Do you know his name?"

"His name," said Nash, thinking that it could do no harm to betray as much as this, "is Anthony Bard, I think."

"And you don't know him?"

"All I know is that the feller who used to own that piebald mustang is pretty mad and cusses every time he thinks of him."

"He didn't steal the hoss?"

This with more bated breath than if the question had been: "He didn't kill a man?" for indeed horse-stealing was the greater crime.

Even Nash would not make such an accusation

directly, and therefore he fell back on an innuendo almost as deadly.

"I dunno," he said non-committally, and shrugged his shoulders.

With all his soul he was concentrating on the picture of the man who conquered a fighting horse and flirted successfully with a pretty girl the same day; each time riding on swiftly from his conquest. The clues on this trail were surely thick enough, but they were of such a nature that the pleasant mind of Steve grew more and more thoughtful.

CHAPTER XIV

LEMONADE

In fact, so thoughtful had Nash become, that he slept with extraordinary lightness that night and was up at the first hint of day. Sue appeared on the scene just in time to witness the last act of the usual drama of bucking on the part of the roan, before it settled down to the mechanical dog-trot with which it would wear out the ceaseless miles of the mountain-desert all day and far into the night, if need be.

Nash now swung more to the right, cutting across the hills, for he presumed that by this time the tenderfoot must have gotten his bearings and would head straight for Eldara. It was a stiff two-day journey, now, the whole first day's riding having been a worse than useless detour; so the bulldog jaw set harder and harder, and the keen eyes squinted as if to look into the dim future.

Once each day, about noon, when the heat made even the desert and the men of the desert drowsy, he allowed his imagination to roam freely, counting the thousand dollars over and over again, and tasting again the joys of a double salary. Yet even his hardy imagination rarely rose to the height of Sally Fortune. That hour of dreaming, however, made the day of labour almost pleasant.

This time, in the very middle of his dream, he reached the cross-roads saloon and general merchandise store of Flanders; so he banished his visions with a compelling shrug of the shoulders and rode for it at a gallop, a hot dryness growing in his throat at every stride. Quick service he was sure to get, for there were not more than half a dozen cattle-ponies standing in front of the little building with its rickety walls guiltless of paint save for the one great sign inscribed with uncertain letters.

He swung from the saddle, tossed the reins over the head of the mustang, made a stride forward— and then checked himself with a soft curse and reached for his gun.

For the door of the bar dashed open and down the steps rushed a tall man with light yellow moustache, so long that it literally blew on either side over his shoulders as he ran; in either hand he carried a revolver—a two-gun man, fleeing, perhaps, from another murder.

For Nash recognized in him a character notorious through a thousand miles of the range, Sandy Ferguson, nicknamed by the colour of that famous moustache, which was envied and dreaded so far and so wide. It was not fear that made Nash halt, for otherwise he would have finished the motion and whipped out his gun; but at least it was something closely akin to fear.

For that matter, there were unmistakable signs in Sandy himself of what would have been called arrant terror in any other man. His face was so bloodless that the pallor showed even through the leathery tan; one eye stared wildly, the other being sheltered under a clumsy patch which could not quite conceal the ugly bruise beneath. Under his great moustache his lips were as puffed and swollen as the lips of a negro.

Staggering in his haste, he whirled a few paces from the house and turned, his guns levelled. At the same moment the door opened and the perspiring figure of little fat Flanders appeared. Scorn and anger rather than hate or any bloodlust appeared in his face. His right arm, hanging loosely at his side, held a revolver, and he seemed to have the greatest unconcern for the levelled weapons of the gunman.

He made a gesture with that armed hand, and

Sandy winced as though a whiplash had flicked him.

"Steady up, damn your eyes!" bellowed Flanders, "and put them guns away. Put 'em up; hear me?"

To the mortal astonishment of Nash, Sandy obeyed, keeping the while a fascinated eye upon the little Dutchman.

"Now climb your hoss and beat it, and if I ever find you in reach again, I'll send my kid out to rope you and give you a hoss-whippin'."

The gun fighter lost no time. A single leap carried him into his saddle and he was off over the sand with a sharp rattle of the beating hoofs.

"Well," breathed Nash, "I'll be hanged."

"Sure you will," suggested Flanders, at once changing his frown for a smile of somewhat professional good nature, as one who greeted an old customer, "sure you will unless you come in an' have a drink on the house. I want something myself to forget what I been doin'. I feel like the dog-catcher."

Steve, deeply meditative, strode into the room.

"Partner," he said gravely to Flanders, "I've always prided myself on having eyes a little better than the next one, but just now I guess I must of been seein' double. Seemed to me that that was

Sandy Ferguson that you hot-footed out of that door—or has Sandy got a double?"

"Nope," said the bartender, wiping the last of the perspiration from his forehead, "that's Sandy, all right."

"Then gimme a big drink. I need it."

The bottle spun expertly across the bar, and the glasses tinkled after.

"Funny about him, all right," nodded Flanders, "but then it's happened the same way with others I could tell about. As long as he was winnin' Sandy was the king of any roost. The minute he lost a fight he wasn't worth so many pounds of salt pork. Take a hoss; a fine hoss is often jest the same. Long as it wins nothin' can touch some of them blooded boys. But let 'em go under the wire second, maybe jest because they's packing twenty pounds too much weight, and they're never any good any more. Any second-rater can lick 'em. I lost five hundred iron boys on a hoss that laid down like that."

"All of which means," suggested Nash, "that Sandy has been licked?"

"Licked? No, he ain't been licked, but he's been plumb annihilated, washed off the map, cleaned out, faded, rubbed into the dirt; if there was some stronger way of puttin' it, I would.

Only last night, at that, but now look at him. A girl that never seen a man before could tell that he wasn't any more dangerous now than if he was made of putty; but if the fool keeps packin' them guns he's sure to get into trouble."

He raised his glass.

"So here's to the man that Sandy was and ain't no more."

They drank solemnly.

"Maybe you took the fall out of him yourself, Flanders?"

"Nope. I ain't no fighter, Steve. You know that. The feller that downed Sandy was—a tenderfoot. Yep, a greenhorn."

"Ah-h-h," drawled Nash softly, "I thought so."

"You did?"

"Anyway, let's hear the story. Another drink—on me, Flanders."

"It was like this. Along about evening of yesterday Sandy was in here with a couple of other boys. He was pretty well lighted—the glow was circulatin' promiscuous, in fact—when in comes a feller about your height, Steve, but lighter. Good-lookin', thin face, big dark eyes like a girl. He carried the signs of a long ride on him. Well, sir, he walks up to the bar and says: 'Can you make me a very sour lemonade, Mr. Bartender?'

"I grabbed the edge of the bar and hung tight.

"'A which?' says I.

"'Lemonade, if you please.'

"I rolled an eye at Sandy, who was standin' there with his jaw falling, and then I got busy with lemons and the squeezer, but pretty soon Ferguson walks up to the stranger.

"'Are you English?' he asks.

"I knew by his tone what was comin', so I slid the gun I keep behind the bar closer and got prepared for a lot of damaged crockery.

"'I?' says the tenderfoot. 'Why, no. What makes you ask?'

"'Your damned funny way of talkin',' says Sandy.

"'Oh,' says the greenhorn, nodding as if he was thinkin' this over and discovering a little truth in it. 'I suppose the way I talk is a little unusual.'

"'A little rotten,' says Sandy. 'Did I hear you askin' for a lemonade?'

"'You did.'

"'Would I seem to be askin' too many questions,' says Sandy, terrible polite, 'if I inquires if bar whisky ain't good enough for you?'

"The tenderfoot, he stands there jest as easy as you an' me stand here now, and he laughed.

"He says: 'The bar whisky I've tasted around

this country is not very good for any one, unless, perhaps, after a snake has bitten you. Then it works on the principle of poison fight poison, eh?'

"Sandy says after a minute: 'I'm the most quietest, gentle, innercent cowpuncher that ever rode the range, but I'd tell a man that it riles me to hear good bar whisky insulted like this. Look at me! Do I look as if whisky ain't good for a man?'

"'Why,' says the tenderfoot, 'you look sort of funny to me.'

"He said it as easy as if he was passin' the morning with Ferguson, but I seen that it was the last straw with Sandy. He hefted out both guns and trained 'em on the greenhorn.

"I yelled: 'Sandy, for God's sake, don't be killin' a tenderfoot!'

"'If whisky will kill him he's goin' to die,' says Sandy. 'Flanders, pour out a drink of rye for this gent.'

"I did it, though my hand was shaking a lot, and the chap takes the glass and raises it polite, and looks at the colour of it. I thought he was goin' to drink, and starts wipin' the sweat off'n my forehead.

"But this chap, he sets down the glass and smiles over to Sandy.

"'Listen,' he says, still grinnin', 'in the old days I suppose this would have been a pretty bluff, but it won't work with me now. You want me to drink this glass of very bad whisky, but I'm sure that you don't want it badly enough to shoot me.

"'There are many reasons. In the old days a man shot down another and then rode off on his horse and was forgotten, but in these days the telegraph is faster than any horse that was ever foaled. They'd be sure to get you, sir, though you might dodge them for a while. And I believe that for a crime such as you threaten, they have recently installed a little electric chair which is a perfectly good inducer of sleep—in fact, it is better than a cradle. Taking these things all into consideration, I take it for granted that you are bluffing, my friend, and one of my favourite occupations is calling a bluff. You look dangerous, but I've an idea that you are as yellow as your moustache.'

"Sandy, he sort of swelled up all over like a poisoned dog.

"He says: 'I begin to see your style. You want a clean man-handlin', which suits me uncommon well.'

"With that, he lays down his guns, soft and

careful, and puts up his fists, and goes for the other gent.

"He makes his pass, which should have sent the other gent into kingdom come. But it didn't. No, sir, the tenderfoot, he seemed to evaporate. He wasn't there when the fist of Ferguson come along. Ferguson, he checked up short and wheeled around and charged again like a bull. And he missed again. And so they kept on playin' a sort of a game of tag over the place, the stranger jest side-steppin' like a prize-fighter, the prettiest you ever seen, and not developin' when Sandy started on one of his swings.

"At last one of Sandy's fists grazed him on the shoulder and sort of peeved him, it looked like. He ducks under Sandy's next punch, steps in, and wallops Sandy over the eye—that punch didn't travel more'n six inches. But it slammed Sandy down in a corner like he's been shot.

"He was too surprised to be much hurt, though, and drags himself up to his feet, makin' a pass at his pocket at the same time. Then he came again, silent and thinkin' of blood, I s'pose, with a knife in his hand.

"This time the tenderfoot didn't wait. He went in with a sort of hitch step, like a dancer. Ferguson's knife carved the air beside the tenderfoot's head, and then the skinny boy jerked up his right and his left—one, two—into Sandy's mouth. Down he goes again—slumps down as if all the bones in his body was busted—right down on his face. The other feller grabs his shoulder and jerks him over on his back.

"He stands lookin' down at him for a moment, and then he says, sort of thoughtful: 'He isn't badly hurt, but I suppose I shouldn't have hit him twice.'

"Can you beat that, Steve? You can't!

"When Sandy come to he got up to his feet, wobbling—seen his guns—went over and scooped 'em up, with the eye of the tenderfoot on him all the time—scooped 'em up—stood with 'em all poised—and so he backed out through the door. It wasn't any pretty thing to see. The tenderfoot, he turned to the bar again.

"'If you don't mind,' he says, 'I think I'll switch my order and take that whisky instead. I seem to need it.'

"'Son!' says I, 'there ain't nothin' in the house you can't have for the askin'. Try some of this!'

"And I pulled out a bottle of my private stock— you know the stuff; I've had it twenty-five years, and it was ten years old when I got it. That ain't as much of a lie as it sounds.

"He takes a glass of it and sips it, sort of suspicious, like a wolf scentin' the wind for an elk in winter. Then his face lighted up like a lantern had been flashed on it. You'd of thought that he was lookin' his long-lost brother in the eye from the way he smiled at me. He holds the glass up and lets the light come through it, showin' the little traces and bubbles of oil.

"'May I know your name?' he says.

"It made me feel like Rockerbilt, hearin' him say that, in *that* special voice.

"'Me,' says I, 'I'm Flanders.'

"'It's an honour to know you, Mr. Flanders,' he says. 'My name is Anthony Bard.'

"We shook hands, and his grip was three fourths man, I'll tell the world.

"'Good liquor,' says he, 'is like a fine lady. Only a gentleman can appreciate it. I drink to you, sir.'

"So that's how Sandy Ferguson went under the sod. To-day? Well, I couldn't let Ferguson stand in a barroom where a gentleman had been, could I?"

CHAPTER XV

THE DARKNESS IN ELDARA

EVEN the stout roan grew weary during the third day, and when they topped the last rise of hills, and looked down to darker shadows in Eldara in the black heart of the hollow, the mustang stood with hanging head, and one ear flopped forward. Cruel indeed had been the pace which Nash maintained, yet they had never been able to overhaul the flying piebald of Anthony Bard.

As they trotted down the slope, Nash looked to his equipment, handled his revolver, felt the strands of the lariat, and resting only his toes in the stirrups, eased all his muscles to make sure that they were uncramped from the long journey. He was fit; there was no doubt of that.

Coming down the main street—for Eldara boasted no fewer than three thoroughfares—the first houses which Nash passed showed no lights. As far as he could see, the blinds were all drawn;

not even the glimmer of a candle showed, and the voices which he heard were muffled and low.

He thought of plague or some other disaster which might have overtaken the little village and wiped out nine tenths of the populace in a day. Only such a thing could account for silence in Eldara. There should have been bursts and roars of laughter here and there, and now and then a harsh stream of cursing. There should have been clatter of kitchen tins; there should have been neighing of horses; there should have been the quiver and tingle of children's voices at play in the dusty streets. But there was none of this. The silence was as thick and oppressive as the unbroken dark of the night. Even Butler's saloon was closed!

This, however, was something which he would not believe, no matter what testimony his eyes gave him. He rode up to a shuttered window and kicked it with his heel.

Only the echoes of that racket replied to him from the interior of the place. He swore, somewhat touched with awe, and kicked again.

A faint voice called: "Who's there?"

"Steve Nash. What the devil's happened to Eldara?"

The boards of the shutter stirred, opened, so that the man within could look out.

"Is it Steve, honest?"

"Damn it, Butler, don't you know my voice? What's turned Eldara into a cemetery?"

"Cemetery's right. 'Butch' Conklin and his gang are going to raid the place to-night."

"Butch Conklin?"

And Nash whistled long and low.

"But why the devil don't the boys get together if they know Butch is coming with his gunmen?"

"That's what they've done. Every able-bodied man in town is out in the hills trying to surprise Conklin's gang before they hit town with their guns going."

Butler was a one-legged man, so Nash kept back the question which naturally formed in his mind.

"How do they know Conklin is coming? Who gave the tip?"

"Conklin himself."

"What? Has he been in town?"

"Right. Came in roaring drunk."

"Why'd they let him get away again?"

"Because the sheriff's a bonehead and because our marshal is solid ivory. That's why."

"What happened?"

"Butch came in drunk, as I was saying, which he generally is, but he wasn't giving no trouble at all, and nobody felt particular called on to cross him and ask questions. He was real sociable, in fact, and that's how the mess was started."

"Go on. I don't get your drift."

"Everybody was treatin' Butch like he was the king of the earth and not passin' out any back-talk, all except one tenderfoot——"

But here a stream of tremendous profanity burst from Nash. It rose, it rushed on, it seemed an exhaustless vocabulary built up by long practice on mustangs and cattle.

At length: "Is that damned fool in Eldara?"

"D' you know him?"

"No. Anyway, go on. What happened?"

"I was sayin' that Butch was feelin' pretty sociable. It went all right in the bars. He was in here and didn't do nothin' wrong. Even paid for all the drinks for everybody in the house, which nobody could ask more even from a white man. But then Butch got hungry and went up the street to Sally Fortune's place."

A snarl came from Nash.

"Did they let that swine go in there?"

"Who'd stop him? Would you?"

"I'd try my damnedest."

"Anyway, in he went and got the centre table and called for ten dollars' worth of bacon and eggs—which there hasn't been an egg in Eldara this week. Sally, she told him, not being afraid even of Butch. He got pretty sore at that and said that it was a frame-up and everyone was ag'in' him. But finally he allowed that if she'd sit down to the table and keep him company he'd manage to make out on whatever her cook had ready to eat."

"And Sally done it?" groaned Nash.

"Sure; it was like a dare—and you know Sally. She'd risk her whole place any time for the sake of a bet."

"I know it, but don't rub it in."

"She fetched out a steak and served Butch as if he'd been a king and then sat down beside him and started kiddin' him along, with all the gang of us sittin' or standin' around and laughin' fit to bust, but not loud for fear Butch would get annoyed.

"Then two things come in together and spoiled the prettiest little party that was ever started in Eldara. First was that player piano which Sally got shipped in and paid God-knows-how-much for; the second was this greenhorn I was tellin' you about."

"Go on," said Nash, the little snarl coming back in his voice. "Tell me how the tenderfoot walked up and kicked Butch out of the place."

"Somebody been tellin' you?"

"No; I just been readin' the mind of Eldara."

"It was a nice play, though. This Bard—we found out later that was his name—walks in, takes a table, and not being served none too quick, he walks over and slips a nickel in the slot of the piano. Out she starts with a piece of rippin' ragtime—you know how loud it plays? Butch, he kept on talkin' for a minute, but couldn't hear himself think. Finally he bellers: 'Who turned that damned tin-pan loose?'

"This Bard walks up and bows. He says: 'Sir, I came here to find food, and since I can't get service, I'll take music as a substitute.'

"Them was the words he used, Steve, honest to God. Used them to Butch!

"Well, Conklin was too flabbergasted to budge, and Bard, he leaned over and says to Sally: 'This floor is fairly smooth. Suppose you and I dance till I get a chance to eat?'

"We didn't know whether to laugh or to cheer, but most of us compromised by keeping an eye on Butch's gun.

"Sally says, 'Sure I'll dance,' and gets up.

"'Wait!' hollers Butch; 'are you leavin' me for this wall-eyed galoot?'

"There ain't nothin' Sally loves more'n a fight—we all know that. But this time I guess she took pity on the poor tenderfoot, or maybe she jest didn't want to get her floor all messed up.

"'Keep your hat on, Butch,' she says, 'all I want to do is to give him some motherly advice.'

"'If you're acting that part,' says Bard, calm as you please, 'I've got to tell mother that she's been keeping some pretty bad company.'

"'Some what?' bellers Butch, not believin' his ears.

"And young Bard, he steps around the girl and stands over Butch.

"'Bad company is what I said,' he repeats, 'but maybe I can be convinced.'

"'Easy,' says Butch, and reaches for his gun.

"We all dived for the door, but me being held up on account of my missing leg, I was slow an' couldn't help seein' what happened. Butch was fast, but the young feller was faster. He had Butch by the wrist before the gun came clear—just gave a little twist—and there he stood with the gun in his hand pointin' into Butch's face, and Butch sittin' there like a feller in a trance or wakin' up out of a bad dream.

"Then he gets up, slow and dignified, though he had enough liquor in him to float a ship.

"'I been mobbed,' he says, 'it's easy to see that. I come here peaceful and quiet, and here I been mobbed. But I'm comin' back, boys, and I ain't comin' alone.'

"There was our chance to get him, while he was walking out of that place without a gun, but somehow nobody moved for him. He didn't look none too easy, even without his shootin' irons. Out he goes into the night, and we stood around starin' at each other. Everybody was upset, except Sally and Bard.

"He says: 'Miss Fortune, this is our dance, I think.'

"'Excuse me,' says Sally, 'I almost forgot about it.'

"And they started to dance to the piano, waltzin' around among the tables; the rest of us lit out for home because we knew that Butch would be on his way with his gang before we got very far under cover. But hey, Steve, where you goin'?"

"I'm going to get in on that dance," called Nash, and was gone at a racing gallop down the street.

CHAPTER XVI

BLUFF

HE found no dance in progress, however, but in the otherwise empty eating place, which Sally owned and ran with her two capable hands and the assistance of a cook, sat Sally herself dining at the same table with the tenderfoot, the flirt, the horse-breaker, the tamer of gun-fighters.

Nash stood in the shadow of the doorway watching that lean, handsome face with the suggestion of mockery in the eyes and the trace of sternness around the thin lips. Not a formidable fig. ure by any means, but since his experiences of the past few days, Nash was grown extremely thoughtful.

What he finally thought he caught in this most unusual tenderfoot was a certain alertness of a more or less hair-trigger variety. Even now as he sat at ease at the table, one elbow resting lightly upon it, apparently enwrapped in the converse of Sally Fortune, Nash had a consciousness that the other might be on his feet and in the most distant part of the room within a second.

What he noted in the second instant of his observation was that Sally was not at all loath to waste her time on the stranger. She was eating with a truly formidable conventionality of manner, and a certain grace with which she raised the ponderous coffee cup, made of crockery guaranteed to resist all falls, struck awe through the heart of the cowpuncher. She was bent on another conquest, beyond all doubt, and that she would not make it never entered the thoughts of Nash. He set his face to banish a natural scowl and advanced with a good-natured smile into the room.

"Hello!" he called.

"It's old Steve!" sang out Sally, and whirling from her chair, she advanced almost at a run to meet him, caught him by both hands, and led him to a table next to that at which she had been sitting.

It was as gracefully done as if she had been welcoming a brother, but Nash, knowing Sally, understood perfectly that it was only a play to impress the eye of Bard. Nevertheless he was forced to accept it in good part.

"My old pal, Steve Nash," said Sally, "and this is Mr. Anthony Bard."

Just the faintest accent fell on the "Mr.," but

it made Steve wince. He rose and shook hands gravely with the tenderfoot.

"I stopped at Butler's place down the street," he said, "and been hearin' a pile about a little play you made a while ago. It was about time for some-body to call old Butch's bluff."

"Bluff?" cried Sally indignantly.

"Bluff?" queried Bard, with a slight raising of the eyebrows.

"Sure—bluff. Butch wasn't any more danger-ous than a cat with trimmed claws. But I guess you seen that?"

He settled down easily in his chair just as Sally resumed her place opposite Bard.

"Steve," she said, with a quiet venom, "that bluff of his has been as good as four-of-a-kind with you for a long time. I never seen you make any play at Butch."

He returned amiably: "Like to sit here and have a nice social chat, Sally, but I got to be gettin' back to the ranch, and in the meantime, I'm sure hungry."

At the reminder of business a green light came in the fine blue eyes of Sally. They were her only really fine features, for the nose tilted an engaging trifle, the mouth was a little too generous, the chin so strong that it gave, in moments of passivity, an air of sternness to her face. That sternness was exaggerated as she rose, keeping her glare fixed upon Nash; a thing impossible for him to bear, so he lowered his eyes and engaged in rolling a cigarette. She turned back toward Bard.

"Sorry I got to go—before I finished eating—but business is business."

"And sometimes," suggested Bard, "a bore."

It was an excellent opening for a quarrel, but Nash was remembering religiously a certain thousand dollars, and also a gesture of William Drew when he seemed to be breaking an imaginary twig. So he merely lighted his cigarette and seemed to have heard nothing.

"The whole town," he remarked casually, "seems scared stiff by this Butch; but of course he ain't comin' back to-night."

"I suppose," said the tenderfoot, after a cold pause, "that he will not."

But the coldness reacted like the most genial warmth upon Nash. He had chosen a part detestable to him but necessary to his business. He must be a "gabber" for the nonce, a free talker, a chatterer, who would cover up all pauses.

"Kind of strange to ride into a dark town like this," he began, "but I could tell you a story about——"

"Oh, Steve," called the voice of Sally from the kitchen.

He rose and nodded to Bard.

"'Scuse me, I'll be back in a minute."

"Thanks," answered the other, with a somewhat grim emphasis.

In the kitchen Sally spoke without prelude. "What deviltry are you up to now, Steve?"

"Me?" he repeated with eyes widened by innocence. "What d'you mean, Sally?"

"Don't four-flush me, Steve."

"Is eating in your place deviltry?"

"Am I blind?" she answered hotly. "Have I got spring-halt, maybe? You're too polite, Steve; I can always tell when you're on the way to a little hell of your own making, by the way you get sort of kind and warmed up. What is it now?"

"Kiss me, Sally, and I'll tell you why I came to town."

She said with a touch of colour: "I'll see you—" and then changing quickly, she slipped inside his ready arms with a smile and tilted up her face.

"Now what is it, Steve?"

"This," he answered.

"What d'you mean?"

"You know me, Sally. I've worn out the other

ways of raising hell, so I thought I'd start a little by coming to Eldara to kiss you."

Her open hand cracked sharply twice on his lean face and she was out of his arms. He followed, laughing, but she armed herself with a red-hot frying pan and defied him.

"You ain't even a good sport, Steve. I'm done with you! Kiss you?"

He said calmly: "I see the hell is startin', all right."

But she changed at once, and smiled up to him.

"I can't stay mad at you, Steve. I s'pose it's because of your nerve. I want you to do something for me."

"What?"

"Is that a way to take it? I've asked you a favour, Steve."

He said suspiciously: "It's got something to do with the tenderfoot in the room out there?"

It was a palpable hit, for she coloured sharply. Then she took the bull by the horns.

"What if it is?"

"Sally, d'you mean to say you've fallen for that cheap line of lingo he passes out?"

"Steve, don't try to kid me."

"Why, you know who he is, don't you?"

"Sure; Anthony Bard."

"And do you know who Anthony Bard is?"

"Well?" she asked with some anxiety.

"Well, if you don't know you can find out. That's what the last girl done."

She wavered, and then blinked her eyes as if she were resolved to shut out the truth.

"I asked you to do me a favour, Steve."

"And I will. You know that."

"I want you to see that Bard gets safe out of this town."

"Sure. Nothing I'd rather do."

She tilted her head a little to one side and regarded him wistfully.

"Are you double-crossin' me, Steve?"

"Why d'you suspect me? Haven't I said I'd do it?"

"But you said it too easy."

The gentleness died in her face. She said sternly: "If you do double-cross me, you'll find I'm about as hard as any man on the range. Get me?"

"Shake."

Their hands met. After all, he did not guarantee what would happen to the tenderfoot after they were clear of the town. But perhaps this was a distinction a little too fine for the downright mind of the girl. A sea of troubles besieged the mind of Nash.

And to let that sea subside he wandered back to the eating room and found the tenderfoot finishing his coffee. The latter kept an eye of frank suspicion upon him. So the silence held for a brooding moment, until Bard asked: "D'you know the way to the ranch of William Drew?"

It was a puzzler to Nash. Was not that his job, to go out and bring the man to Drew's place? Here he was already on the way. He remembered just in time that the manner of bringing was decidedly qualified.

He said aloud: "The way? Sure; I work on Drew's place."

"Really!"

"Yep; foreman."

"You don't happen to be going back that way to-night?"

"Not all the way; part of it."

"Mind if I went along?"

"Nobody to keep you from it," said the cowpuncher without enthusiasm.

"By the way, what sort of a man is Drew?"

"Don't you know him?"

"No. The reason I want to see him is because I want to get the right to do some—er—fishing and hunting on a place of his on the other side of the range."

"The place with the old house on it; the place Logan is?"

"Exactly. Also I wish to see Logan again. I've got several little things I'd like to have him explain."

"H-m!" grunted Nash without apparent interest.

"And Drew?"

"He's a big feller; big and grey."

"Ah-h-h," said the other, and drew in his breath, as though he were drinking.

It seemed to Nash that he had never seen such an unpleasant smile.

"You'll get what you want out of Drew. He's generous."

"I hope so," nodded the other, with far-off eyes. "I've got a lot to ask of him."

10

CHAPTER XVII

HE reminded Nash of some big puma cub warming itself at a hearth like a common tabby cat, a tame puma thrusting out its claws and turning its yellow eyes up to its owner—tame, but with infinite possibilities of danger. For the information which Nash had given seemed to remove all his distrust of the moment before and he became instantly genial, pleasant. In fact, he voiced this sentiment with a disarming frankness immediately.

"Perhaps I've seemed to be carrying a chip on my shoulder, Mr. Nash. You see, I'm not long in the West, and the people I've met seem to be ready to fight first and ask questions afterward. So I've caught the habit, I suppose."

"Which a habit like that ain't uncommon. The graveyards are full of fellers that had that habit and they're going to be fuller still of the same kind."

Here Sally entered, carrying the meal of the

146

cowpuncher, arranged it, and then sat on the edge of Bard's table, turning from one to the other as a bird on a spray of leaves turns from sunlight to shadow and cannot make a choice.

"Bard," stated Nash, "is going out to the ranch with me to-night."

"Long ride for to-night, isn't it?"

"Yes, but we'll bunk on the way and finish up early in the morning."

"Then you'll have a chance to teach him Western manners on the way, Steve."

"Manners?" queried the Easterner, smiling up to the girl.

She turned, caught him beneath the chin with one hand, tilting his face, and raised the lessoning forefinger of the other while she stared down at him with a half frown and a half smile like a schoolteacher about to discipline a recalcitrant boy.

"Western manners," she said, "mean first not to doubt a man till he tries to double-cross you, and not to trust him till he saves your life; to keep your gun inside the leather till you're backed up against the wall, and then to start shootin' as soon as the muzzle is past the holster. Then the thing to remember is that the fast shootin' is fine, but sure shootin' is a lot better. D'you get me?"

"That's a fine sermon," smiled Bard, "but

you're too young to make a convincing preacher, Miss Fortune."

"Misfortune," said the girl quickly, "don't have to be old to do a lot of teachin'."

She sat back and regarded him with something of a frown and with folded arms.

He said with a sudden earnestness: "You seem to take it for granted that I'm due for a lot of trouble."

But she shook her head gloomily.

"I know what you're due for; I can see it in your eyes; I can hear it in your way of talkin'. If you was to ride the range with a sheriff on one side of you and a marshal on the other you couldn't help fallin' into trouble."

"As a fortune-teller," remarked Nash, "you'd make a good undertaker, Sally."

"Shut up, Steve. I've seen this bird in action and I know what I'm talking about. When you coming back this way, Bard?"

He said thoughtfully: "Perhaps to-morrow night —perhaps——"

"It ought to be to-morrow night," she said pointedly, her eyes on Nash.

The latter had pushed his chair back a trifle and sat now with downward head and his right hand resting lightly on his thigh. Only the place in which they sat was illumined by the two lamps, and the forward part of the room, nearer the street, was a seat of shadows, wavering when the wind stirred the flame in one of the lamps or sent it smoking up the chimney. Sally and Bard sat with their backs to the door, and Nash half facing it.

"Steve," she said, with a sudden low tenseness of voice that sent a chill up Bard's spinal cord, "Steve, what's wrong?"

"This," answered the cowboy calmly, and whirling in his chair, his gun flashed and exploded.

They sprang up in time to see the bulky form of Butch Conklin rise out of the shadows in the front part of the room with outstretched arms, from one of which a revolver dropped clattering to the floor. Backward he reeled as though a hand were pulling him from behind, and then measured his length with a crash on the floor.

Bard, standing erect, quite forgot to touch his weapon, but Sally had produced a ponderous forty-five with mysterious speed and now crouched behind a table with the gun poised. Nash, bending low, ran forward to the fallen man.

"Nicked, but not done for," he called.

"Thank God!" cried Sally, and the two joined Nash about the prostrate body.

That bullet had had very certain intentions,

but by a freak of chance it had been deflected on the angle of the skull and merely ploughed a bloody furrow through the mat of hair from forehead to the back of the skull. He was stunned, but hardly more seriously hurt than if he had been knocked down by a club.

"I've an idea," said the Easterner calmly, "that I owe my life to you, Mr. Nash."

"Let that drop," answered the other.

"A quarter of an inch lower," said the girl, who was examining the wound, "and Butch would have kissed the world good-bye."

Not till then did the full horror of the thing dawn on Bard. The girl was no more excited than one of her Eastern cousins would have been over a game of bridge, and the man in the most matter-of-fact manner, was slipping another cartridge into the cylinder of the revolver, which he then restored to the holster.

It still seemed incredible that the man could have drawn his gun and fired it in that flash of time. He recalled his adventure with Butch earlier that evening and with Sandy Ferguson before; for the first time he realized what he had done and a cold horror possessed him like the man who has nerves to walk the tight rope across the chasm and faints when he looks back on the gorge from the safety of the other side. The girl took command.

"Steve, run down to the marshal's office; Deputy Glendin is there."

She took the wet cloth and made a deft bandage for the head of Conklin. With his shaggy hair covered, and all his face sagging with lines of weariness, the gun-fighter seemed no more than a middle-aged man asleep, worn out by trouble.

"Is there a doctor?" asked Bard anxiously.

"That ain't a case for a doctor—look here; you're in a blue faint. What is the matter?"

"I don't know; I'm thinking of that quarter of an inch which would have meant the difference to poor Conklin."

"'Poor' Conklin? Why, you fish, he was sneakin' in here to try his hand on you. He found out he couldn't get his gang into town, so he slipped in by himself. He'll get ten years for this —and a thousand if they hold him up for the other things he's done."

"I know—and this fellow Nash was as quiet as the strike of a snake. If he'd been a fraction of a second slower I might be where Conklin is now. I'll never forget Nash for this."

She said pointedly: "No, he's a bad one to for-

get; keep an eye on him. You spoke of a snake—
that's how smooth Steve is."

"Remember your own motto, Miss Fortune.
He saved my life; therefore I must trust him."

She answered sullenly: "You're your own boss."

"What's wrong with Nash?"

"Find out for yourself."

"Are all these fellows something other than
they seem?"

"What about yourself?"

"How do you mean that?"

"What trail are you on, Bard? Don't look so
innocent. Oh, I seen you was after something a
long time ago."

"I am. After excitement, you know."

"Ain't you finding enough?"

"I've got two things ahead of me."

"Well?"

"This trip, and when I come back I think
making love to you would be more exciting than
gun-plays."

They regarded each other with bantering smiles.

"A tenderfoot like you make love to *me?* That
would be exciting, all right, if it wasn't so funny."

"As for the competition," he said serenely,
"that would be simply a good background."

"Hate yourself, don't you, Bard?" she grinned.

"The rest of these boys are all very well, but they don't see that what you want is the velvet touch."

"What's that?"

She was as frankly curious as some boy hearing a new game described.

"You've only been loved in one way. These rough-handed fellows come in and throw an arm around you and ask you to marry them; isn't that it? What you really need, is an old, simple, but very effective method."

Though her eyes were shining, she yawned.

"It don't interest me, Bard."

"On the contrary, you're getting quite excited."

"So does a horse before it gets ready to buck."

"Exactly. If I thought it would be easy I wouldn't be tempted."

"Well, if you like fighting you've sure mapped out a nice sizeable quarrel with me, Bud."

"Good. I'm certainly coming back to Eldara. Now about this method of mine——"

"Throwing your cards on the table, eh? What you got, Bard, a royal flush?"

"Right again. It's a very simple method but you couldn't beat it."

"Bud, you ain't half old enough to kid me."

"What you need," he persisted calmly, "is

someone who would sit down and simply talk good, plain English to you."

"Let 'er go."

"In the first place I will call attention to your method of dressing."

"Anything wrong with it?"

"I knew you'd be interested."

She slipped into a chair and sat cross-legged in it, her elbows on her knees and her chin cupped in both her hands.

"Sure I'm interested. If there's a new way fixin' ham-and, serve it out."

"I would begin," he went on judiciously, "by saying that you dressed in five minutes in the dark."

"It's generally dark at 5 A.M.," she admitted.

"You look, on the whole, as if you'd fallen into your clothes."

The wounded man stirred and groaned faintly. She called: "Lie down, Butch; I'm busy. Go on, Bard."

"If you keep a mirror it's a wall decoration—not for personal use."

"Maybe this is an old method, Bard; but around this place it'd be a quick way of gettin' shot."

"Angry?"

"You'd peeve a mule."

"This was only an introduction. The next thing is to sit close beside you and shift the lamp so that the light would shine on your face; then take your hand——"

He suited his action to his word.

"Let go my hand, Bard. It's like the rest of me—not a decoration but for use."

"Afraid of me, Sally?"

"Not of a regiment like you."

"Then of my method?"

"Go on; I'm game."

"But this is all there is to it."

"What d'you mean?"

"Just what I say. Having observed that you haven't set off any of your advantages, I will sit here and look into your face in silence, which is as much as to say that no matter how you dress you can't spoil a very excellent figure, Sally. I suppose you've heard that before?"

"Lots of times," she muttered.

"But you wouldn't hear it from me. All I would do would be to sit and stare and let you imagine what I'm thinking. And you'd begin to see that in spite of the way you do your hair you can't spoil its colour nor its texture."

He raised his other hand and touched it.

"Like silk, Sally."

He studied her closely, noting the flush which began to touch her cheeks.

"Part of the game is for you to keep looking me in the eye."

"Well, I'll be— Go on, I'm game."

"Is it hard to sit like this—silently? Do I do it badly?"

"No, you show lots of practice. How many have you tried this method on, Bard?"

He made a vague gesture and then, smiling: "Millions, Sally, and they all liked it."

"So do I."

And they laughed together, and grew serious at the same instant.

"All silence—like this?" she queried.

"No; after a while I would say: 'You are beautiful.'"

"You don't get a blue ribbon for that, Bard."

"Not for the words, but the way they're said, which shows I mean them."

She blinked as though to clear her eyes and then met his stare again.

"You know you *are* beautiful, Sally."

"With a pug nose—freckles—and all that?"

"Just a tip-tilt in the nose, Sally. Why, it's charming. And you have everything else—young, strong, graceful, clear."

"What d' you mean by that?"

"Clear? Fresh and colourful like the sunset over the desert. Do you understand?"

Her eyes went down to consider.

"I s'pose I do."

"With a touch of awe in it, because the silence and the night are coming, and the stars walk down, one by one—one by one. And the wind is low, soft, musical, whispering, as you do now— What if this were not a game of suppose, Sally?"

She wrenched herself suddenly away, rising.

"I'm tired of supposing!" she cried.

"Then we'll call it all real. What of that?"

That colour was unmistakably high now; it ran down from her cheeks and even stained the pure white of the throat where the flap of the shirt was open. He was excited as a hunter who has tracked some new and dangerous animal and at last driven it to bay, holding his gun poised, and not knowing whether or not it will prove vulnerable.

He stepped close, eager, prepared for any wild burst of temper; but she let him take her hands, let him draw her close, bend back her head; hold her closer still, till the warmth and softness of her body reached him, but when his lips came close she said quietly: "Are you a rotter, Bard?"

He stiffened and the smile went out on his lips. He stepped back.

She repeated: "Are you a rotter?"

He raised the one hand which he still retained and touched it to his lips.

"I am very sorry," said Anthony, "will you forgive me?"

And with her eyes large and grave upon him she answered: "I wonder if I can!"

Butch Conklin looked up, raising his bandaged head slowly, like a white flag of truce, with a stain of red growing through the cloth. He stared at the two, raised a hand to his head as though to rub away the dream, found a pain too real for a dream, and then, like a crab which has grown almost too old to walk, waddled on hands and knees, slowly, from the room and melted silently into the dark beyond.

CHAPTER XVIII

FOOLISH HABITS

A SHARP noise of running feet leaped from the dust of the street and clattered through the doorway; the two turned. A swarthy man, broad of shoulder, was the first, and afterward appeared Nash.

"Conklin?" called Deputy Glendin, and swept the room with his startled glance. "Where's Conklin?"

He was not there; only a red stain remained on the floor to show where he had lain.

"Where's Conklin?" called Nash.

"I'm afraid," whispered Bard quickly to the girl, "that it was more than a game of suppose."

He said easily to the other two: "He had enough. His share of trouble came to-night; I let him go."

"Young feller," growled Glendin, "you ain't been in town a long while, but I've heard a pile too much about you already. What you mean by takin' the law into your own hands?"

"Wait," said Nash, his keen eyes on the two, "I guess I understand."

"Let's have it, then."

Still the steady eyes of Nash passed from Sally Fortune to Bard and back again.

"This feller bein' a tenderfoot, he don't understand our ways; maybe he thinks the range is a bit freer than it is."

"That's the trouble," answered Glendin, "he thinks too damned much."

"And does quite a pile besides thinkin'," murmured Nash, but too low for the others to hear it.

He hesitated, and then, as if making up his mind by a great effort: "There ain't no use blamin' him; better let it drop, Glendin."

"Nothin' else to do, Steve; but it's funny Sally let him do it."

"It is," said Nash with emphasis, "but then women is pretty funny in lots of ways. Ready to start, Bard?"

"All ready."

"S'long, Sally."

"Good-night, Miss Fortune."

"Evenin', boys. We'll be lookin' for you back in Eldara to-morrow night, Bard."

And her eyes fixed with meaning on Nash.

"Certainly," answered the other, "my business ought not to take longer than that."

"I'll take him by the shortest cut," said Nash, and the two went out to their horses.

They had difficulty in riding the trail side by side, for though the roan was somewhat rested by the delay at Eldara it was impossible to keep him up with Bard's prancing piebald, which side-stepped at every shadow. Yet the tenderfoot never allowed his mount to pass entirely ahead of the man, but kept checking him back hard, turning toward Nash with an apology each time he surged ahead. It might have been merely that he did not wish to precede the cowpuncher on a trail which he did not know. It might have been something quite other than this which made him consistently keep to the rear; Nash felt certain that the second possibility was the truth.

In that case his work would be doubly hard. From all that he had seen the man was dangerous —the image of the tame puma returned to him again and again. He could not see him plainly through the dark of the night, but he caught the sway of the body and recognized a perfect horsemanship, not a Western style of riding, but a good one no matter where it was learned. He rode as if he were sewed to the back of the horse, and, as old

11

William Drew had suggested, he probably did
other things up to the same standard. It would
have been hard to fulfil his promise to Drew under
any circumstances with such a man as this; but
with Bard apparently forewarned and suspicious
the thing became almost impossible.

Almost, but not entirely so. He set himself
calmly to the problem; on the horn of his saddle
the lariat hung loose; if the Easterner should turn
his back for a single instant during all the time
they were together old Drew should not be disappointed, and one thousand cash would be de-
posited for the mutual interest of Sally Fortune
and himself. That is to say, if Sally would consent
to become interested. To the silent persuasion of
money, however, Nash trusted many things.

The roan jogged sullenly ahead, giving all the
strength of his gallant, ugly body to the work; the
piebald mustang pranced like a dancing master
beside and behind with a continual jingling of the
tossed bridle.

The masters were to a degree like the horses
they rode, for Nash kept steadily leaning to the
front, his bulldog jaw thrusting out; and Bard
was forever shifting in the saddle, settling his hat,
humming a tune, whistling, talking to the piebald,
or asking idle questions of the things they passed,

like a boy starting out for a vacation. So they reached the old house of which Nash had spoken—a mere, shapeless, black heap huddling through the night.

In the shed to the rear they tied the horses and unsaddled. In the single room of the shanty, afterward, Nash lighted a candle, which he produced from his pack, placed it in the centre of the floor, and they unrolled their blankets on the two bunks which were built against the wall on either side of the narrow apartment.

Truly it was a crazy shack—such a building as two men, having the materials at hand, might put together in a single day. It was hardly based on a foundation, but rather set on the slope side of the hill, and accordingly had settled down on the lower side toward the door. Not an old place, but the wind had pried and the rain warped generous cracks between the boards through which the rising storm whistled and sang and through which the chill mist of the coming rain cut at them.

Now and then a feeling came to Anthony that the gale might lift the tottering old shack and roll it on down the hillside to the floor of the valley, for it rocked and swayed under the breath of the storm. In a way it was as if the night was giving a loud voice to the silent struggle of the two men, who continued pleasant, careless with each other.

But when Nash stepped across the room behind Bard, the latter turned and was busy with the folding of his blankets at the foot of his bunk, his face toward the cowpuncher and when Bard, slipping off his belt, fumbled at his holster, Nash was instantly busy with the cleaning of his own gun.

The cattleman, having removed his boots, his hat, and his belt, was ready for bed, and slipped his legs under the blankets. He stooped and picked up his lariat, which lay coiled on the floor beside him.

"People gets into foolish habits on the range," he said, thumbing the strong rope curiously, and so doing, spreading out the noose.

"Yes?" smiled Bard, and he also sat up in his bunk.

"It's like a kid. Give him a new toy and he wants to take it to bed with him. Ever notice?"

"Surely."

"That's the way with me. When I go to bed nothin' matters with me except that I have my lariat around. I generally like to have it hangin' on a nail at the head of my bunk. The fellers always laugh at me, but I can't help it; makes me feel more at home."

And with that, still smiling at his own folly in a rather shamefaced way, he turned in the blankets and dropped the big coil of the lariat over a nail which projected from the boards just over the head of his bunk. The noose was outermost and could be disengaged from the nail by a single twist of the cowpuncher's hand as he lay passive in the bunk.

On this noose Bard cast a curious eye. To city-folk a piece of rope is a harmless thing with which one may make a trunk secure or on occasion construct a clothes line on the roof of the apartment building, or in the kitchen on rainy Mondays.

To a sailor the rope is nothing and everything at once. Give a seaman even a piece of string and he will amuse himself all evening making lashings and knots. A piece of rope calls up in his mind the stout lines which hold the masts steady and the yards true in the gale, the comfortable cable which moors the ship at the end of the dreary voyage, and a thousand things between.

To the Westerner a rope is a different thing. It is not so much a useful material as a weapon. An Italian, fighting man to man, would choose a knife; a Westerner would take in preference that same harmless piece of rope. In his hands it takes on life, it gains a strange and sinister quality. One instant it lies passive, or slowly whirled in a careless circle—the next its noose darts out like the head of a striking cobra, the coil falls and fastens, and then it draws tighter and tighter, remorselessly as a boa constrictor, paralyzing life.

Something of all this went through the mind of Bard as he lay watching the limp noose of the cowboy's lariat, and then he nodded smiling.

"I suppose that seems an odd habit to some men, but I sympathize with it. I have it myself, in fact. And whenever I'm out in the wilds and carry a gun I like to have it under my head when I sleep. That's even queerer than your fancy, isn't it?"

And he slipped his revolver under the blankets at the head of his bunk.

CHAPTER XIX

THE CANDLE

"YES," said Nash, "that's a queer stunt, because when you're lyin' like that with your head right over the gun and the blankets in between, it'd take you a couple of seconds to get it out."

"Not when you're used to it. You'd be surprised to see how quickly a man can get the gun out from under."

"That so?"

"Yes, and shooting while you're lying on your back is pretty easy, too, when you've had practice."

"Sure, with a rifle, but not with a revolver."

"Well, do you see that bit of paper in the corner there up on the rafter?"

"Yes."

The hand of Bard whipped under his head, there was a gleam and whirl of steel, an explosion, and the bit of paper came fluttering slowly down from the rafter, like a wounded bird struggling to keep up in the air. A draft caught the paper just before it landed and whirled it through the doorless entrance and out into the night.

He was yawning as he restored the gun beneath the blanket, but from the corner of his eye he saw the hardening of Nash's face, a brief change which came and went like the passing of a shadow.

"That's something I'll remember," drawled the cowpuncher.

"You ought to," answered the other quickly, "it comes in handy now and then."

"Feel sleepy?"

The candle guttered and flickered on the floor midway between the two bunks, and Bard, glancing to it, was about to move from his bed and snuff it; but at the thought of so doing it seemed to him as if he could almost sense with prophetic mind the upward dart of the noose about his shoulders. He edged a little lower in the blankets.

"Not a bit. How about you?"

"Me? I most generally lie awake a while and gab after I hit the hay. Makes me sleep better afterward."

"I do the same thing when I've any one who listens to me—or talks to me."

"Queer how many habits we got the same, eh?"

"It is. But after all, most of us are more alike than we care to imagine."

"Yes, there ain't much difference; sometimes the difference ain't as much as a split-second watch would catch, but it may mean that one feller passes out and the other goes on."

They lay half facing each other, each with his head pillowed on an arm.

"By Jove! lucky we reached this shelter before the rain came."

"Yep. A couple of hours of this and the rivers will be up—may take up all day to get back to the ranch if we have to ride up to the ford on the Saverack."

"Then we'll swim 'em."

The other smiled drily.

"Swim the Saverack when she's up? No, lad, we won't do that."

"Then I'll have to work it alone, I suppose. You see, I have that date in Eldara for to-morrow night."

Nash set his teeth, to choke back the cough. He produced papers and tobacco, rolled a cigarette with lightning speed, lighted it, and inhaled a long puff.

"Sure, you ought to keep that date, but maybe Sally would wait till the night after."

"She impressed me, on the whole, as not being of the waiting kind."

"H-m! A little delay does 'em good; gives 'em a chance to think."

"Why, every man has his own way with women, I suppose, but my idea is, keep them busy—never give them a chance to think. If you do, they generally waste the chance and forget you altogether."

Another coughing spell overtook Nash and left him frowning down at the glowing end of his butt.

"She ain't like the rest."

"I wonder?" mused the Easterner.

He had an infinite advantage in this duel of words, for he could watch from under the shadow of his long, dark lashes the effect of his speeches on the cowboy, yet never seem to be looking. For he was wondering whether the enmity of Nash, which he felt as one feels an unknown eye upon him in the dark, came from their rivalry about the girl, or from some deeper cause. He was inclined to think that the girl was the bottom of everything, but he left his mind open on the subject.

And Nash, pondering darkly and silently, measured the strength of the slender stranger and felt that if he were the club the other was the knife which made less sound but might prove more deadly. Above all he was conscious of the Easterner's superiority of language, which might turn the balance against him in the ear of Sally Fortune. He dropped the subject of the girl.

"You was huntin' over on the old place on the other side of the range?"

"Yes."

"Pretty fair run of game?"

"Rather."

"I think you said something about Logan?"

"Did I? I've been thinking a good deal about him. He gave me the wrong tip about the way to Eldara. When I get back to the old place——"

"Well?"

The other smiled unpleasantly and made a gesture as if he were snapping a twig between his hands.

"I'll break him in two."

The eyes of Nash grew wide with astonishment; he was remembering that same phrase on the lips of the big, grey man, Drew.

He murmured: "That may give you a little trouble. Logan's a peaceable chap, but he has his record before he got down as low as sheepherdin'."

"I like trouble—now and then."

A pause.

"Odd old shack over there."

"Drew's old house?"

"Yes. There's a grave in front of it."

"And there's quite a yarn inside the grave."

The cowpuncher was aware that the other stirred—not much, but as if he winced from a drop of cold water; he felt that he was close on the trail of the real reason why the Easterner wished to see Drew.

"A story about Drew's wife?"

"You read the writing on the headstone, eh?"

"'Joan, she chose this place for rest,'" quoted Bard.

"That was all before my time; it was before the time of any others in these parts, but a few of the grey-beards know a bit about the story and I've gathered a little of it from Drew, though he ain't much of a talker."

"I'd like to hear it."

Sensitively aware of Bard, as a photographic plate is aware of light on exposures, the cowpuncher went on with the tale.

And Bard, his glance probing among the shadowy rafters of the room, seemed to be searching there for the secret on whose trail he rode. Through the interims the rain crashed and volleyed on the roof above them; the cold spray whipped down on them through the cracks; the wind shook and rattled the crazy house; and the drawling voice of Nash went on and on.

CHAPTER XX

JOAN

"THEM were the days when this was a man's country, which a man could climb on his hoss with a gun and a rope and touch heaven and hell in one day's ridin'. Them good old days ain't no more. I've heard the old man tell about 'em. Now they've got everybody stamped and branded with law an' order, herded together like cattle, ticketed, done for. That's the way the range is now. The marshals have us by the throat. In the old days a sheriff that outlived his term was probably crooked and runnin' hand in hand with the long-riders."

"Long-riders?" queried Bard.

"Fellers that got tired of workin' and took to ridin' for their livin'. Mostly they worked in little gangs of five and six. They was called long-riders, I guess, partly because they was in the saddle all the time, and partly because they done their jobs so far apart. They'd ride into Eldara and blow up the safe in the bank one day, for instance, and five days later they'd be two hundred and fifty miles away stoppin' a train at Lewis Station.

"They never hung around no one part of the country and that made it hard as hell to run 'em down—that and because they had the best hosses that money could buy. They had friends, too, strung out all over—squatters and the like of that. They'd drop in on these little fellers and pass 'em a couple of twenties and make themselves solid for life. Afterward they used 'em for stoppin' places.

"They'd pull off a couple of hold-ups, then they'd ride off to one of these squatter places and lay up for ten days, maybe, drinkin' and feedin' up themselves and their hosses. That was the only way they was ever caught. They was killed off by each other, fighting about the split-up, or something like that.

"But now and then a gang held together long enough to raise so much hell that they got known from one end of the range to the other. Mostly they held together because they had a leader who knew how to handle 'em and who kept 'em under his thumb. That was the way with old Piotto.

"He had five men under him. They was all hell-benders who had ridden the range alone and

had their share of fights and killings, which there
wasn't one of 'em that wouldn't have been good
enough to go leader in any other crew, but they
had to knuckle under to old Piotto. He was a
great gunman and he was pretty good in scheming
up ways of dodging the law and picking the best
booty. He had these five men, and then he had
his daughter, Joan. She was better'n two ordinary
men herself.

"Three years that gang held together and got
rich—fair rich. They made it so fast they couldn't
even gamble the stuff away. About a thousand
times, I guess posses went out after Piotto, but
they never came back with a trace of 'em; they
never got within shootin' distance. Finally Piotto
got so confident that he started raidin' ranches
and carryin' off members of well-off ranchers to
hold for ransom. That was the easiest way of
makin' money; it was also pretty damned dangerous.

"One time they held up a stage and picked off
of it two kids who was comin' out from the East
to try their hands in the cattle business. They
was young, they looked like gentlemen, they was
dressed nifty, and they packed big rolls. So wise
old Piotto took 'em off into the hills and held 'em
till their folks back East could wire out the money

to save 'em. That was easy money for Piotto, but that was the beginnin' of the end for him; because while they was waitin', them two kids seen Joan and seen her good.

"I been telling you she was better 'n two common men. She was. Which means she was equal to about ten ordinary girls. There's still a legend about how beautiful Joan Piotto was—tall and straight and big black eyes and terrible handy with her gun. She could ride anything that walked and she didn't know what fear meant.

"These two kids seen her. One of 'em was William Drew; one of 'em was John Bard."

He turned to Anthony and saw that the latter was stern of face. He had surely scored his point.

"Same name as yours, eh?" he asked, to explain his turning.

"It's a common enough name," murmured Bard.

"Well, them two had come out to be partners, and there they was, fallin' in love with the same girl. So when they got free they put their heads together—bein' uncommon wise kids—and figured it out this way. Neither of 'em had a chance workin' alone to get Joan way from her father's gang, but workin' together they might have a ghost of a show. So they decided to stay on the trail of Piotto till they got Joan. Then they'd give her a choice between the two of 'em and the one that lost would simply back off the boards.

"They done what they agreed. For six months they stuck on the trail of old Piotto and never got in hailin' distance of him. Then they come on the gang while they were restin' up in the house of a squatter.

"That was a pretty night. Drew and Bard went through that gang. It sounds like a nice fairy-story, all right, but I know old fellers who'll swear it's true. They killed three of the men with their guns; they knifed another one, an' they killed Riley with their bare hands. It wasn't no pretty sight to see—the inside of that house. And last of all they got Piotto, fightin' like an old wild-cat, into a corner with his daughter; and William Drew, he took Piotto into his arms and busted his back. That don't sound possible, but when you see Drew you'll know how it was done.

"The girl, she'd been knocked cold before this happened. So while Bard and Drew sat together bindin' up each other's wounds—because they was shot pretty near to pieces—they talked it over and they seen pretty clear that the girl would never marry the man that had killed her father. Of course, old Bill Drew, he'd done the killing, but that wasn't any reason why he had to take the blame.

"They made up their minds that right there and then with the dead men lyin' all around 'em, they'd match coins to see which one would take the blame of havin' killed Piotto—meanin' that the other one would get the girl—if he could.

"And Bard lost. So he had to take the credit of havin' killed old Piotto. I'd of give something to have seen the two of 'em sittin' there—oozin' blood—after that marchin' was decided. Because they tell me that Bard was as big as Drew and looked pretty much the same.

"Then Bard, he asked Drew to let him have one chance at the girl, lettin' her know first what he'd done, but jest trustin' to his power of talk. Which, of course, didn't give him no show. While he was makin' love to the girl she outs with a knife and tries to stick him—nice, pleasant sort she must have been—and Drew, he had to pry the two of 'em apart.

"That made the girl look sort of kind on Drew and she swore that sooner or later she'd have the blood of Bard for what he'd done—either have it herself or else send someone after him to the end of the world. She was a wild one, all right.

"She was so wild that Drew, after they got married, took her over on the far side of the range and built that old house that's rottin' there now.

Bard, he left the range and wasn't never seen again, far as I know."

It was clear to Anthony, bitterly clear. His father had had a grim scene in parting with Drew and had placed the continent between them. And in the Eastern states he had met that black-eyed girl, his mother, and loved her because she was so much like the wild daughter of Piotto. The girl Joan in dying had probably extracted from Drew a promise that he would kill Bard, and that promise he had lived to fulfil.

"So Joan died?" he queried.

"Yep, and was buried under them two trees in front of the house. I don't think she lived long after they was married, but about that nobody knows. They was clear off by themselves and there isn't any one can tell about their life after they was married. All we know is that Drew didn't get over her dyin'. He ain't over it yet, and goes out to the old place every month or so to potter around the grave and keep the grass and the weeds off of it and clean the head-stone."

The candle guttered wildly on the floor. It had burnt almost to the wood and now the remnant of the wick stood in a little sprawling pool of grease white at the outer edges.

Bard yawned, and patted idly the blanket where

it touched on the shape of the revolver beneath. In another moment that candle would gutter out and they would be left in darkness.

He said: "That's the best yarn I've heard in a good many days; it's enough to make any one sleepy—so here goes."

And he turned deliberately on his side.

Nash, his eyes staring with incredulity, sat up slowly among his blankets and his hand stole up toward the noose of the lariat. A light snore reached him, hardly a snore so much as the heavy intake of breath of a very weary, sleeping man; yet the hand of Nash froze on the lariat.

"By God," he whispered faintly to himself, "he ain't asleep!"

And the candle flared wildly, leaped and shook out.

CHAPTER XXI

THE SWIMMING OF THE SAVERACK

OVER the face of Nash the darkness passed like a cold hand and a colder sense of failure touched his heart; but men who have ridden the range have one great power surpassing all others—the power of patience. As soundlessly as he had pushed himself up the moment before, he now slipped down in the blankets and resigned himself to sleep.

He knew that he would wake at the first hint of grey light and trusted that after the long ride of the day before his companion would still be fast asleep. That half light would be enough for his work; but when he roused while the room was still scarcely more visible than if it were filled with a grey fog, he found Bard already up and pulling on his boots.

"How'd you sleep?" he growled, following the example of the tenderfoot.

"Not very well," said the other cheerily. "You see, that story of yours was so vivid in my mind that I stayed awake about all night, I guess, thinking it over."

"I knew it," murmured Nash to himself. "He was awake all the time. And still——"

If that thrown noose of the lariat had settled over the head and shoulders of the sham sleeper it would have made no difference whether he waked or slept—in the end he would have sat before William Drew tied hand and foot. If that noose had not settled? The picture of the little piece of paper fluttering to the floor came back with a strange vividness to the mind of Nash, and he had to shrug his shoulders to shake the thought away.

They were in the saddle a very few moments after they awoke and started out, breakfastless. The rain long ago had ceased, and there was only the solemn silence of the brown hills around them —silence, and a faint, crinkling sound as if the thirsty soil still drank. It had been a heavy fall of rain, they could see, for whenever they passed a bare spot where no grass grew, it was crossed by a thick tracery of the rivulets which had washed down the slopes during the night.

Soon they reached a little creek whose current, barely knee deep, foamed up around the shoulders of the horses and set them staggering.

"The Saverack will be hell," said Nash, "and we'd better cut straight for the ford."

"How long will it take?"

"Add about three hours to the trip."

"Can't do it; remember that little date back in Eldara to-night."

"Then look for yourself and make up your mind for yourself," said Nash drily, for they topped a hill, and below them saw a mighty yellow flood pouring down the valley. It went leaping and shouting as if it rejoiced in some destruction it had worked and was still working, and the muddy torrent was threaded with many a ridge of white and swirling with bubbles.

"The Saverack," said Nash. "Now what d'you think about fording it?"

"If we can't ford it, we can swim it," declared Bard. "Look at that tree-trunk. If that will float I will float, and if I can float I can swim, and if I can swim I'll reach the other bank of that little creek. Won't we, boy?"

And he slapped the proud neck of the mustang.

"Swim it?" said Nash incredulously. "Does that date mean as much as that to you?"

"It isn't the date; it's the promise I gave," answered the other, watching the current with a cool eye, "besides, when I was a youngster I used to do things like this for the sport of it."

They rode down to the edge of the stream.

"How about it, Nash, will you take the chance with me?"

And the other, looking down: "Try the current, I'll stay here on the shore and if it gets too strong for you I'll throw out a rope, eh? But if you can make it, I'll follow suit."

The other cast a somewhat wistful eye of doubt upon the cowpuncher.

"How far is it to the ford?" he asked.

"About eight miles," answered Nash, doubling the distance on the spot.

"Eight miles?" repeated the other ruefully. "Too far. Then here goes, Nash."

Still never turning his back on the cowpuncher, who was now uncoiling his lariat and preparing it for a cast, Bard edged the piebald into the current. He felt the mustang stagger as the water came knee-deep, and he checked the horse, casting his eye from shore to shore and summing up the chances.

If it had been simply water against which he had to contend, he would not have hesitated, but here and there along the course sharp pointed rocks and broad-backed boulders loomed, and now and then, with a mighty splashing and crashing one of these was overbalanced by the force of the current and rolled another step toward the far-off sea.

That rush of water would carry him far downstream and the chances were hardly more than even that he would not strike against one of these murderous obstructions about which the current foamed.

An impulse made him turn and wave a hand to Nash.

He shouted: "Give me luck?"

"Luck?" roared the cowboy, and his voice came as if faint with distance over the thunder of the stream.

He touched the piebald with the spurs, and the gallant little horse floundered forward, lost footing and struck into water beyond its depth. At the same instant Bard swung clear of the saddle and let his body trail out behind, holding with his left hand to the tail of the struggling horse and kicking to aid the progress.

Immersed to the chin, and sometimes covered by a more violent wave, the sound of the river grew at once strangely dim, but he felt the force of the current tugging at him like a thousand invisible hands. He began to wish that he had taken off his boots before entering, for they weighted his feet so that it made him leg-weary to kick. Nevertheless he trusted in the brave heart of the mustang. There was no wavering in the wild horse. Only his head showed over the water, but the ears were pricking straight and high, and it never once swerved back toward the nearer shore.

Their progress at first was good, but as they neared the central portion of the water they were swept many yards downstream for one that they made in a transverse direction. Twice they missed projecting rocks by the narrowest margin, and then something like an exceedingly thin and exceedingly strong arm caught Anthony around the shoulders. It tugged back, stopped all their forward progress, and let them sweep rapidly down the stream and back toward the shore.

Turning his head he caught a glimpse of Nash sitting calmly in his saddle, holding the rope in both hands—and laughing. The next instant he saw no more, for the current placed a taller rock between him and the bank. On that rock the line of the lariat caught, hooking the swimmers sharply in toward the bank. He would have cut the rope, but it would be almost impossible to get out a knife and open a blade with his teeth, still clinging to the tail of the swimming horse with one hand.

He reached down through the water, pulled out the colt, and with an effort swung himself about. Close at hand he could not reach the rope, and therefore he fired not directly at the rope itself, but at the edge of the rock around which the lariat bent at a sharp angle. The splash of that bullet from the strong face of the rock sliced the rope like a knife. It snapped free, and the brave little mustang straightened out again for the far shore.

An instant more Bard swam with the revolver poised above the water, but he caught no glimpse of Nash; so he restored it with some difficulty to the holster, and gave all his attention and strength to helping the horse through the water, swimming with one hand and kicking vigorously with his feet.

Perhaps they would not have made it, for now through exhaustion the ears of the mustang were drooping back. He shouted, and at the faint sound of his cheer the piebald pricked a single weary ear. He shouted again, and this time not for encouragement, but from exultation; a swerving current had caught them and was bearing them swiftly toward the desired bank.

It failed them when they were almost touching bottom and swung sharply out toward the centre again, but the mustang, as though it realized that this was the last chance, fought furiously. Anthony gave the rest of his strength, and they edged through, inch by inch, and horse and man staggered up the bank and stood trembling with fatigue.

Glancing back, he saw Nash in the act of throwing his lariat to the ground, wild with anger, and before he could understand the meaning of this burst of temper over a mere spoiled lariat, the gun whipped from the side of the cowboy, exploded, and the little piebald, with ears pricked sharply forward as though in vague curiosity, crumpled to the ground. The suddenness of it took all power of action from Bard for the instant. He stood staring stupidly down at the dying horse and then whirled, gun in hand, frantic with anger and grief.

Nash was galloping furiously up the far bank of the Saverack, already safely out of range, and speeding toward the ford.

CHAPTER XXII

DREW SMILES

WHEN the cattleman felt the rope snap back to his hand he could not realize at first just what had happened. The crack of the gun had been no louder than the snapping of a twig in that storming of the river, and the only explanation he could find was that the rope had struck some superlatively sharp edge of the rock and been sawed in two. But examining the cut end he found it severed as cleanly as if a knife had slashed across it, and then it was he knew and threw the lariat to the ground.

When he saw Bard scramble up the opposite bank he knew that his game was lost and all the tables reversed, for the Easterner was a full two hours closer to the home of Drew than he was, with the necessary detour up to the ford. The Easterner might be delayed by the unknown country for a time, but not very long. He was sure to meet someone who would point the way. It was then that Nash drew his gun and shot down the piebald mustang.

The next instant he was racing straight up the river toward the ford. The roan was not spared this day, for there were many chances that Bard might secure a fresh mount to speed him on the way to the Drew ranch, and now it was all important that the big grey man be warned; for there was a danger in that meeting, as Nash was beginning to feel.

By noon he reached the house and went straight to the owner, a desperate figure, spattered with mud to the eyes, a three days' growth of whiskers blackening his face, and that face gaunt with the long, hard riding. He found the imperturbable Drew deep in a book in his office. While he was drawing breath, the rancher examined him with a faint smile.

"I thought this would be the end of it," he announced.

"The devil and all hell plays on the side of Bard," answered the foreman. "I had him safe—almost tied hand and foot. He got away."

"Got away?"

"Shot the rope in two."

The other placed a book-mark, closed the volume, and looked up with the utmost serenity.

"Try again," he said quietly. "Take half a dozen men with you, surprise him in the night——"

"Surprise a wolf," growled Nash. "It's just the same."

The shaggy eyebrows stirred.

"How far is he away?"

"Two or three miles—maybe half a dozen—I don't know. He'll be here before night."

The big man changed colour and gripped the edge of the desk. Nash had never dreamed that it would be possible to so stir him.

"Coming here?"

"Yes."

"Nash—you infernal fool! Did you let him know where you were taking him?"

"No. He was already on the way here."

Once more Drew winced. He rose now and strode across the room and back; from the wall the heavy echo of his footfall came sharply back. And he paused in front of Nash, looming above his foreman like some primitive monster, or as the Grecian heroes loomed above the rank and file at the siege of Troy. He was like a relic of some earlier period when bigger men were needed for a greater physical labour.

"What does he want?"

"I don't know. Says he wants to ask for the

right of hunting on your old place on the other side of the range. Which I'd tell a man it's jest a lie. He knows he can hunt there if he wants to."

"Does he know me?"

"Just your name."

"Did he ask many questions about me?"

"Wanted to know what you looked like."

"And you told him?"

"A lot of things. Said you were big and grey. And I told him that story about you and John Bard."

Drew slumped into a chair and ground the knuckles of his right hand across his forehead. The white marks remained as he looked up again.

"What was that?"

"Why, how you happened to marry Joan Piotto and how Bard left the country."

"That was all?"

"Is there any more, sir?"

The other stared into the distance, overlooking the question.

"Tell me what you've found out about him."

"I been after him these three days. Logan tipped him wrong, and he started the south trail for Eldara. I got on his trail three times and couldn't catch him till we hit Eldara."

"I thought your roan was the most durable

horse on the range, Steve. You've often told me so."

"He is."

"But you couldn't catch—Bard?"

"He was on a faster horse than mine—for a while."

"Well? Isn't he now?'

"I killed the horse."

"You showed your hand, then? He knows you were sent after him?"

"No, he thinks it's because of a woman."

"Is he tangling himself up with some girl?" frowned the rancher.

"He's cutting in on me with Sally Fortune— damn his heart!"

And Nash paled visibly, even through whiskers and mud. The other almost smiled.

"So soon, Nash?"

"With hosses and women, he don't lose no time."

"What's he done?"

"The first trace I caught of him was at a shack of an old ranchhouse where he'd traded his lame hoss in. They gave him the wildest mustang they had—a hoss that was saddle-shy and that hadn't never been ridden. He busted that hoss in—a little piebald mustang, tougher 'n iron—and that was why I didn't catch him till we hit Eldara."

The smile was growing more palpable on the face of Drew, and he nodded for the story to continue.

"Then I come to a house which was all busted up because Bard had come along and flirted with the girl, and she's got too proud for the feller she was engaged to—begun thinkin' of millionaires right away, I s'pose.

"Next I tracked him to Flanders's saloon, where he'd showed up Sandy Ferguson the day before and licked him bad. I seen Ferguson. It was sure some lickin'."

"Ferguson? The gun-fighter? The two-gun man?"

"Him."

"Ah-h-h!" drawled the big man.

The colour was back in his face. He seemed to be enjoying the recountal hugely.

"Then I hit Eldara and found all the lights out."

"Because of Bard?"

"H-m! He'd had a run-in with Butch Conklin, and Butch threatened to come back with all his gang and wipe Eldara off the map. He stuck around and while he was waitin' for Butch and his gang, he started flirtin' with Sally—Fortune."

The name seemed to stick in his throat and he had to bring it out with a grimace.

"So now you want his blood, Nash?"

"I'll have it," said the cowpuncher quietly, "I've got gambler's luck. In the end I'm sure to win."

"You're not going to win here, Nash."

"No?" queried the younger man, with a dangerous intonation.

"No. I know the blood behind that chap. You won't win here. Blood will out."

He smote his great fist on the desk-top and his laugh was a thunder which reverberated through the room.

"Blood will out? The blood of John Bard?" asked Nash.

Drew started.

"Who said John Bard?"

He grew grey again, the flush dying swiftly. He started to his feet and repeated in a great voice, sweeping the room with a wild glance: "Who said John Bard?"

"I thought maybe this was his son," answered Nash.

"You're a fool! Does he look like John Bard? No, there's only one person in the world he looks like."

He strode again up and down the room, repeating in a deep monotone: "John Bard!"

Coming to a sharp halt he said: "I don't want the rest of your story. The point is that the boy will be here within—an hour—two hours. We've got work to do before that time."

"Listen to me," answered the foreman, "don't let him get inside this house. I'd rather take part of hell into a house of mine. Besides, if he sees me——"

"He's coming here, but he's not going to see either of us—my mind is made up—neither of us until I have him helpless."

CHAPTER XXIII

THE COMEDY SETTING

"DEAD, you mean," broke in Nash, "because otherwise he'll never be helpless."

"I tell you, Nash," said the other solemnly, "I can make him helpless with one minute of talk. My problem is to keep that wild devil harmless while he listens to me talk. Another thing—if he ever sees me, nothing *but* death will stop him from coming at my throat."

"Speakin' personal," said the other coldly, "I never take no chances on fellers that might come at my throat."

"I know; you're for the quick draw and the quick finish. But I'd rather die myself than have a hair of his head hurt. I mean that!"

Nash, his thoughts spinning, stood staring blankly.

"I give up tryin' to figure it out; but if he's comin' here and you want to keep him safe I'd better take a fresh hoss and get twenty miles away before night."

"You'll do nothing of the kind; you'll stay here with me."

"And face him without a gun?" asked the other incredulously.

"Leave gun talk out of this. I think one of the boys looks a little like me. Lawlor—isn't that his name?"

"Him? Yes; a little bit like you—but he's got his thickness through the stomach and not through the chest."

"Never mind. He's big, and he's grey. Send for him, and get the rest of the boys in here. They're around now for noon. Get *every* one. Understand? And make it fast."

In ten minutes they came to the office in a troop —rough men, smooth men, little and big, fat and thin, but good cattlemen, every one.

"Boys," said Drew, "a tenderfoot is coming to the ranch to-day. I'm going to play a few jokes on him. First of all, I want you to know that until the stranger leaves the house, Lawlor is going to take my place. He is going to be Drew. Understand?"

"Lawlor?" broke out several of them, and turned in surprise to a big, cheerful man—grey, plump, with monstrous white whiskers.

"Because he looks a bit like me. First, you'll have to crop those whiskers, Lawlor."

He clutched at the threatened whiskers with both hands.

"Crop 'em? Chief, you ain't maybe runnin' me a bit?"

"Not a bit," said Drew, smiling faintly. "I'll make it worth your while."

"It took me thirty years to raise them whiskers," said the cattleman, stern with rebuke. "D'you think I could be *hired* to give 'em up? It's like givin' up some of myself."

"Let them go, then. You can play the part, whiskers and all. The rest of you remember that Lawlor is the boss."

"And brand that deep," growled Lawlor, looking about with a frown.

He had already stepped into his part; the others laughed loudly.

"Steady there!" called Drew. "Lawlor starts as boss right now. Cut out the laughing. I'll tell the rest of you what you're to do later on. In the meantime just step out and I'll have a talk with Lawlor on his part. We haven't much time to get ready. But remember—if one of you grins when Lawlor gives an order—I'm done with that man—that's all."

They filed out of the room, looking serious, and Drew concentrated on Lawlor.

"This sounds like a joke," he began, "but there's something serious about it. If you carry it through safely, there's a hundred in it for you. If you fall down, why, you fall out of an easy place on this ranch."

The big cattleman wiped a growing perspiration from his forehead and considered his boss with plaintive eyes.

"This tenderfoot who's coming is green to the range, but he's a hard man; a fine horseman, a sure shot, and a natural fighter. More than that, he's coming here looking for trouble; and he'll expect to get the trouble from you."

Lawlor brushed his moustache anxiously.

"Let someone else take the job—that's all. A hundred ain't to be picked up every week, but I'll do without it. In my day I've done my share of brawlin' around, but I'm too stiff in the joints to make a fast draw and getaway now. Let Nash take this job. He's gun-fighter enough to handle this bad-man for you."

"No," said Drew, "not even Nash can handle this one."

"Then"—with a mighty and explosive emphasis—"there ain't no possible use of me lingering around the job. S'-long."

"Wait. This young chap isn't going to murder

you. I'll tell you this much. The man he wants is
I; but he knows my face, not my name. He's been
on the trail of that face for some time, and now
he's tracking it to the right house; but when he
sees you and hears you called Drew, he'll be thrown
off again."

The other nodded gloomily.

"I'm by way of a lightning rod. This tenderfoot
with the hard hand, he strikes and I sort of conduct
the shock away from anything that'll burn, eh?"

Drew overlooked the comment.

"There are certain things about me you will
have to know." And he explained carefully the
story which Nash had told to Bard.

"This Bard," asked the cautious Lawlor, "is he
any relation of old John Bard?"

"Even if he were, it wouldn't make your position dangerous. The man he wants is I. He knows
my face—not my name. Until he sees me he'll
be perfectly reasonable, unless he's crossed. You
must seem frank and above board. If you tell
more lies than are necessary he may get suspicious,
and if he grows suspicious the game is up and will
have to be finished with a gun play. Remember
that. He'll want to know about Nash. Tell him
that Nash is a bad one and that you've fixed him;
he mustn't expect to find Nash here."

Lawlor rubbed his hands, like one coming from the cold outdoors to a warm fire.

"I'm beginning to see light. Lemme at this Bard. I'm going to get enough fun out of this to keep me laughin' the rest of my life."

"Good; but keep that laugh up your sleeve. If he asks questions you'll have some solemn things to say."

"Chief, when the time comes, there's going to be about a gallon of tears in my eyes."

So Drew left him to complete the other arrangements. If Bard reached the house he must be requested to stay, and if he stayed he must be fed and entertained. The difficulty in the way of this was that the servants in the big ranchhouse were two Chinese boys. They could never be trusted to help in the deception, so Drew summoned two of his men, "Shorty" Kilrain and "Calamity" Ben.

Calamity had no other name than Ben, as far as any one on the range had ever been able to learn. His nickname was derived from the most dolorous face between Eldara and Twin Rivers. Two pale-blue eyes, set close together, stared out with an endless and wistful pathos; a long nose dropped below them, and his mouth curled down at the sides. He was hopelessly round-shouldered from much and careless riding, and in attempting to straighten he only succeeded in throwing back his head, so that his lean neck generally was in a V-shape with the Adam's apple as the apex of the wedge.

Shorty Kilrain received his early education at sea and learned there a general handiness which stood him in stead when he came to the mountain-desert. There was nothing which Shorty could not do with his hands, from making a knot to throwing a knife, and he was equally ready to oblige with either accomplishment. Drew proposed that he take charge of the kitchen with Calamity Ben as an assistant. Shorty glowered on the rancher.

"Me!" he said. "Me go into the galley to wait on a blasted tenderfoot?"

"After he leaves you'll have a month off with full pay and some over, Shorty."

"Don't want the month off."

Drew considered him thoughtfully, following the precept of Walpole that every man has his price.

"What *do* you want, Shorty?"

The ex-sailor scratched his head and then rolled his eyes up with a dawning smile, as one who sees a vision of ultimate bliss.

"Let one of the other boys catch my hoss out of the corral every morning and saddle him for me for a month."

"It's a bargain. What'll you do with that time?"

"Sit on the fence and roll a cigarette like a blasted gentleman and damn the eyes of the feller that's catchin' my hoss."

"And me," said Calamity Ben, "what do I get?"

"You get orders," answered Kilrain, "from me."

Calamity regarded him, uncertain whether or not to fight out the point, but apparently decided that the effort was not worth while.

"There ain't going to be no luck come out of this," he said darkly. "Before this tenderfoot gets out of the house, we're all going to wish he was in hell."

CHAPTER XXIV

"SAM'L HALL"

BUT with the stage set and the curtain ready to rise on the farce, the audience did not arrive until the shadow of the evening blotted the windows of the office where big Lawlor waited impatiently, rehearsing his part; but when the lamp had been lighted, as though that were a signal for which the tenderfoot had waited, came a knock at the door of the room, and then it was jerked open and the head of one of the cowpunchers was inserted.

"He's coming!"

The head disappeared; the door slammed. Lawlor stretched both arms wide, shifted his belt, loosened his gun in the holster for the fiftieth time, and exhaled a long breath. Once more the door jerked open, and this time it was the head and sullen face of Nash, enlivened now by a peculiarly unpleasant smile.

"He's here!"

As the door closed the grim realization came to

Lawlor that he could not face the tenderfoot—
his staring eyes and his pallor would betray him
even if the jerking of his hands did not. He swung
about in the comfortable chair, seized a book and
whisking it open bowed his head to read. All that
he saw was a dance of irregular black lines: voices
sounded through the hall outside.

"Sure, he'll see you," Calamity Ben was saying.
"And if you want to put up for the night there
ain't nobody more hospital than the Chief. Right
in here, son."

The door yawned. He could not see, for his
back was resolutely toward it and he was gripping
the cover of the book hard to steady his hands;
but he felt a breath of colder air from the outer
hall; he felt above all a new presence peering in
upon him, like a winter-starved lynx that might
flatten its round face against the window and peer
in at the lazy warmth and comfort of the humans
around the hearth inside. Some such feeling sent
a chill through Lawlor's blood.

"Hello!" called Calamity Ben.

"Humph!" grunted Lawlor.

"Got a visitor, Mr. Drew."

"Bring him in."

And Lawlor cleared his throat.

"All right, here he is."

The door closed, and Lawlor snapped the book shut.

"Drew!" said a low voice.

The cowpuncher turned in his chair. He had intended to rise, but at the sound of that controlled menace he knew that his legs were too weak to answer that purpose. What he saw was a slender fellow, who stood with his head somewhat lowered while his eyes peered down from under contracted brows, as though the light were hurting them. His feet were braced apart and his hands dropped lightly on his hips—the very picture of a man ready to spring into action.

Under the great brush of his moustache, Lawlor set his teeth, but he was instantly at ease; for if the sight of the stranger shook him to the very centre, the other was even more obviously shocked by what he saw. The hands dropped limp from his hips and dangled idly at his sides; his body straightened almost with a jerk, as though he had been struck violently, and now, instead of that searching look, he was blinking down at his host. Lawlor rose and extended a broad hand and an even broader smile; he was proud of the strength which had suddenly returned to his legs.

"H'ware ye, stranger? Sure glad to see you."

The other accepted the proffered hand automatically, like one moving in a dream.

"Are you Drew?"

"Sure am."

"William Drew?"

He still held the hand as if he were fearful of the vision escaping without that sensible bondage.

"William Drew is right. Sit down. Make yourself to home."

"Thanks!" breathed the other and as if that breath expelled with it all his strength he slumped into a chair and sat with a fascinated eye glued to his host.

Lawlor had time to mark now the signs of long and severe travelling which the other bore, streaks of mud that disfigured him from heel to shoulder; and his face was somewhat drawn like a man who has gone to work fasting.

"William Drew!" he repeated, more to himself than to Lawlor, and the latter formed a silent prayer of gratitude that he was *not* William Drew.

"I'm forgetting myself," went on the tenderfoot, with a ghost of a smile. "My name is Bard—Anthony Bard."

His glance narrowed again, and this time Lawlor, remembering his part, pretended to start with surprise.

"Bard?"

"Yes. Anthony Bard."

"Glad to know you. You ain't by any chance related to a John Bard?"

"Why?"

"Had a partner once by that name. Good old John Bard!"

He shook his head, as though overcome by recollections.

"I've heard something about you and your partner, Mr. Drew."

"Yes?"

"In fact, it seems to be a rather unusual story."

"Well, it ain't common. John Bard! I'll tell the world there was a man."

"Yes, he was."

"What's that?"

"He must have been," answered Anthony, "from all that I've heard of him. I'm interested in what I scrape together about him. You see, he carries the same name."

"That's nacheral. How long since you ate?"

"Last night."

"The hell! Starved?"

"Rather."

"It's near chow-time. Will you eat now or wait for the reg'lar spread?"

14

"I think I can wait, thank you."

"A little drink right now to help you along, eh?"

He strode over and opened the door.

"Hey! Shorty!"

For answer there came only the wail of an old pirate song.

> "Oh, my name's Sam'l Hall—Sam'l Hall;
> My name's Sam'l Hall—Sam'l Hall.
> My name is Sam'l Hall,
> And I hate you one an' all,
> You're a gang of muckers all—
>   Damn your eyes!"

"Listen!" said Lawlor, turning to his guest with a deprecating wave of the hand. "A cook what sings! Which in the old days I wouldn't have had a bum like that around my place, but there ain't no choosin' now."

The voice from the kitchen rolled out louder:

> "I killed a man, they said, so they said;
> I killed a man, they said, so they said.
> I killed a man they said,
> For I hit 'im on the head,
> And I left him there for dead—
>   Damn your eyes!"

"Hey! Shorty Kilrain!" bellowed the aggravated host.

He turned to Bard.

"What'd you do with a bum like that for a cook?"

"Pay him wages and keep him around to sing songs. I like this one. Listen!"

> "They put me in the quad—in the quad;
> They put me in the quad—in the quad.
> They put me in the quad,
> They chained me to a rod,
> And they left me there, by God—
>   Damn your eyes!"

"Kilrain, come here and make it fast or I'll damn *your* eyes!"

He explained to Bard: "Got to be hard with these fellers or you never get nowhere with 'em."

"Yo ho!" answered the voice of the singer, and approached booming:

> "The parson he did come, he did come;
> The parson he did come—did come.
> The parson he did come,
> He looked almighty glum,
> He talked of kingdom come—
>   Damn your eyes!"

Shorty loomed in the doorway and caught his hand to his forehead in a nautical salute. He had one bad eye, and now it squinted as villainously as if he were the real *Sam'l Hall*.

"Righto sir. What'll you have, mate?"

"Don't mate me, you igner'nt sweepin' of the South Sea, but trot up some red-eye—and gallop."

The ex-sailor shifted his quid so that it stuck far out in the opposite cheek with such violence of pressure that a little spot of white appeared through the tan of the skin. He regarded Lawlor for a silent moment with bodeful eyes.

"What the hell are you lookin' at?" roared the other. "On your way!"

The features of Kilrain twitched spasmodically. "Righto, sir."

Another salute, and he was off, his voice coming back less and less distinctly.

"So up the rope I'll go, I will go;
So up the rope I'll go—I'll go.
So up the rope I'll go
With the crowd all down below
Yelling, 'Sam, I told you so!'
Damn their eyes!"

CHAPTER XXV

HAIR LIKE THE SUNSHINE

"WELL," grumbled Lawlor, settling back comfortably into his chair, "one of these days I'm goin' to clean out my whole gang and put in a new one. They maybe won't be any better but they can't be any wuss."

Nevertheless, he did not seem in the least downhearted, but apparently had some difficulty in restraining his broad grin.

The voice of the grim cook returned:

"I'll see Nelly in the crowd, in the crowd;
I'll see Nelly in the crowd, in the crowd;
I'll see Nelly in the crowd,
And I'll holler to her loud:
'Hey, Nelly, ain't you proud—
Damn your eyes?'"

"I ask you," cried Lawlor, with freshly risen wrath, "is that any way to go around talkin' about women?"

213

"Not talking. He's singing," answered Bard. "Let him alone."

The thunder of their burly Ganymede's singing rose and echoed about them.

> "And this shall be my knell, be my knell;
> And this shall be my knell—my knell.
> And this shall be my knell:
> 'Sam, I hope you go to hell,
> Sam, I hope you sizzle well—
>   Damn your eyes!'"

Shorty Kilrain appeared in the doorway, his mouth wide on the last, long, wailing note.

"Shorty," said Lawlor, with a sort of hopeless sadness, "ain't you never been educated to sing no better songs than that?"

"Why, you old, grey-headed—" began Shorty, and then stopped short and hitched his trousers violently.

Lawlor pushed the bottle of whisky and glass toward Bard.

"Help yourself." And to Kilrain, who was leaving the room: "Come back here."

"Well?" snarled the sailor, half turning at the door.

"While I'm runnin' this here ranch you're goin' to have manners, see?"

"If manners was like your whiskers," said the unabashed Shorty, "it'd take me nigh onto thirty years to get 'em."

And he winked at Bard for sympathy.

Lawlor smashed his fist on the table.

"What I say is, are you running this ranch or am I?"

"Well?" growled Kilrain.

"If you was a kid you'd have your mouth washed out with soap."

The eyes of Shorty bulged.

"It ought to be done now, but there ain't no one I'd give such dirty work to. What you're going to do is stand right here and show us you know how to sing a decent song in a decent way. That there song of yours didn't leave nothin' sacred untouched, from parsons and jails to women and the gallows. Stand over there and sing."

The eyes of the sailor filmed over with cold hate.

"Was I hired to punch cattle," he said, "or make a blasted, roarin' fool out of myself?"

"You was hired," answered Lawlor softly, as he filled his glass to the brim with the old rye whisky, "to be a cook, and you're the rottenest hash-slinger that ever served cold dough for biscuits; a blasted, roarin' fool you've already made out of yourself by singin' that song. I want another one to get the sound of that out of my ears. Tune up!"

Thoughts of murder, ill-concealed, whitened the face of the sailor.

"Some day—" he began hoarsely, and then stopped. For a vision came to him of blithe mornings when he should sit on the top of the corral fence rolling a cigarette, while some other puncher went into the herd and roped and saddled his horse.

"D'you mean this—Drew?" he asked, with an odd emphasis.

"D'you think I'm talking for fun?"

"What'll I sing?" he asked in a voice which was reduced to a faint whisper by rage.

"I dunno," mused Lawlor, "but maybe it ought to lie between 'Alice, Ben Bolt,' and 'Annie Laurie.' What d'you choose, partner?"

He turned to Bard.

"'Alice, Ben Bolt,' by all means. I don't think he could manage the Scotch."

"Start!" commanded Lawlor.

The sailor closed his eyes, tilted back his head, twisted his face to a hideous grimace, and then opening his shapeless mouth emitted a tremendous wail which took shape in the following words:

"Oh, don't you remember sweet Alice, Ben Bolt,
Sweet Alice, with hair like the sunshine—"

"Shut up!" roared Lawlor.

It required a moment for Shorty to unkink the congested muscles of his face.

"What the hell's the matter now?" he inquired.

"Whoever heard of 'hair like the sunshine'? There ain't no such thing possible. 'Hair so brown,' that's what the song says. Shorty, we got more feelin' for our ears than to let you go on singin' an' showin' your ignerance. G'wan back to the kitchen!"

Kilrain drew a long breath, regarded Lawlor again with that considerate, expectant eye, and then turned on his heel and strode from the room. Back to Bard came fragments of tremendous cursing of an epic breadth and a world-wide inclusiveness.

"Got to do things like this once in a while to keep 'em under my thumb," Lawlor explained genially.

With all his might Bard was struggling to reconcile this big-handed vulgarian with his mental picture of the man who could write for an epitaph:

"Here sleeps Joan, the wife of William Drew. She chose this place for rest." But the two ideas were not inclusive.

He said aloud: "Aren't you afraid that that black-eyed fellow will run a knife between your ribs one of these dark nights?"

"Who? My ribs?" exclaimed Lawlor, nevertheless stirring somewhat uneasily in his chair. "Nope, they know that I'm William Drew. They may be hard, but they know I'm harder."

"Oh," drawled the other, and his eyes held with uncomfortable steadiness on the rosy face of Lawlor. "I understand."

To cover his confusion Lawlor seized his glass. "Here's to you—drinkin' deep."

And he tossed off the mighty potion. Bard had poured only a few drops into his glass; he had too much sympathy for his empty stomach to do more. His host leaned back, coughing, with tears of pleasure in his eyes.

"Damn me!" he breathed reverently. "I ain't touched stuff like this in ten years."

"Is this a new stock?" inquired Bard, apparently puzzled.

"This?" said Lawlor, recalling his position with a start. "Sure it is; brand new. Yep, stuff ain't been in more'n five days. Smooth, ain't it? Medicine, that's what I call it; a gentleman's drink—goes down like water."

Observing a rather quizzical light in the eyes of Bard, he felt that he had probably been making a few missteps, and being warmed greatly at the heart by the whisky, he launched forth in a new phase of the conversation.

CHAPTER XXVI

"THE CRITIQUE OF PURE REASON"

"SPEAKIN' of hard cattlemen," he said, "I could maybe tell you a few things, son."

"No doubt of it," smiled Anthony. "I presume it would take a *very* hard man to handle this crowd."

"Fairly hard," nodded the redoubtable Lawlor, "but they ain't nothin' to the men that used to ride the range in the old days."

"No?"

"Nope. One of them men—why, he'd eat a dozen like Kilrain and think nothin' of it. Them was the sort I learned to ride the range with."

"I've heard something about a fight which you and John Bard had against the Piotto gang. Care to tell me anything of it?"

Lawlor lolled easily back in his chair and balanced a second large drink between thumb and forefinger.

"There ain't no harm in talk, son; sure I'll tell you about it. What d'you want to know?"

"The way Bard fought—the way you both fought."

"Lemme see."

He closed his eyes like one who strives to recollect; he was, in fact, carefully recalling the skeleton of facts which Drew had told him earlier in the day.

"Six months, me and Bard had been trailin' Piotto, damn his old soul! Bard—he'd of quit cold a couple of times, but I kept him at it."

"John Bard would have quit?" asked Anthony softly.

"Sure. He was a big man, was Bard, but he didn't have none too much endurance."

"Go on," nodded Anthony.

"Six months, I say, we was ridin' day and night and wearin' out a hoss about every week of that time. Then we got jest a hint from a bartender that maybe the Piottos was nearby in that section.

"It didn't need no more than a hint for us to get busy on the trail. We hit a circle through the mountains—it was over near Twin Rivers where the ground ain't got a level stretch of a hundred yards in a whole day's ridin'. And along about evenin' of the second day we come to the house of Tom Shaw, a squatter.

"Bard would of passed the house up, because he knew Shaw and said there wasn't nothin' crooked about him, but I didn't trust nobody in them days—and I ain't changed a pile since."

"That," remarked Anthony, "is an example I think I shall follow."

"Eh?" said Lawlor, somewhat blankly. "Well, we rode up on the blind side of the house—from the north, see, got off, and sneaked around to the east end of the shack. The windows was covered with cloths on the inside, which didn't make me none too sure about Shaw havin' no dealin's with crooks. It ain't ordinary for a feller to be so savin' on light. Pretty soon we found a tear in one of the cloths, and lookin' through that we seen old Piotto sittin' beside Tom Shaw with his daughter on the other side.

"We went back to the north side of the house and figured out different ways of tacklin' the job. There was only the two of us, see, and the fellers inside that house was all cut out for man-killers. How would you have gone after 'em, son?"

"Opened the door, I suppose, and started shooting," said Bard, "if I had the courage."

The other stared at him.

"You heard this story before?"

"Not this part."

"Well, that was jest what we done. First off, it sounds like a fool way of tacklin' them; but when you think twice it was the best of all. They never was expectin' anybody fool enough to walk right into that room and start fightin'. We went back and had a look at the door.

"It wasn't none too husky. John Bard, he tried the latch, soft, but the thing was locked, and when he pulled there was a snap.

"'Who's there?' hollers someone inside.

"We froze ag'in' the side of the house, lookin' at each other pretty sick.

"'Nobody's there,' sings out the voice of old Piotto. 'We can trust Tom Shaw, jest because he knows that if he double-crossed us he'd be the first man to die.'

"And we heard Tom say, sort of quaverin': 'God's sake, boys, what d'you think I am?'

"'Now,' says Bard, and we put our shoulders to the door, and takes our guns in our hands—we each had two.

"The door went down like nothin', because we was both husky fellers in them days, and as she smashed in the fall upset two of the boys sittin' closest and gave 'em no chance on a quick draw.

The rest of 'em was too paralyzed at first, except old Piotto. He pulled his gun, but what he shot was Tom Shaw, who jest leaned forward in his chair and crumpled up dead.

"We went at 'em, pumpin' lead. It wasn't no fight at first and half of 'em was down before they had their guns workin'. But when the real hell started it wasn't no fireside story, I'll tell a man. We had the jump on 'em, but they meant business. I dropped to the floor and lay on my side, shootin'; Bard, he followered suit. They went down like tenpins till our guns were empty. Then we up and rushed what was left of 'em—Piotto and his daughter. Bard makes a pass to knock the gun out of the hand of Joan and wallops her on the head instead. Down she goes. I finished Piotto with my bare hands."

"Broke his back, eh?"

"Me? Whoever heard of breakin' a man's back? Ha, ha, ha! You been hearin' fairy tales, son. Nope, I choked the old rat."

"Were you badly hurt?"

Lawlor searched his memory hastily; there was no information on this important point.

"Couple of grazes," he said, dismissing the subject with a tolerant wave of the hand. "Nothin' worth talkin' of."

"I see," nodded Bard.

It occurred to Lawlor that his guest was taking the narrative in a remarkably philosophic spirit. He reviewed his telling of the story hastily and could find nothing that jarred.

He concluded: "That was the way of livin' in them days. They ain't no more—they ain't no more!"

"And now," said Anthony, "the only excitement you get is out of books—and running the labourers?"

He had picked up the book which Lawlor had just laid down.

"Oh, I read a bit now and then," said the cow-puncher easily, "but I ain't much on book-learnin'."

Bard was turning the pages slowly. The title, whose meaning dawned slowly on his astonished mind as a sunset comes in winter over a grey landscape, was *The Critique of Pure Reason*. He turned the book over and over in his hands. It was well thumbed.

He asked, controlling his voice: "Are you fond of Kant?"

"Eh?" queried the other.

"Fond of this book?"

"Yep, that's one of my favourites. But I ain't much on any books."

15

"However," said Bard, "the story of this is interesting."

"It is. There's some great stuff in it," mumbled Lawlor, trying to squint at the title, which he had quite overlooked during the daze in which he first picked it up.

Bard laid the book aside and out of sight.

"And I like the characters, don't you? Some very close work done with them."

"Yep, there's a lot of narrow escapes."

"Exactly. I'm glad that we agree about books."

"So'm I. Feller can kill a lot of time chinning about books."

"Yes, I suppose a good many people have killed time over this book."

And as he smiled genially upon the cowpuncher, Bard felt a great relief sweep over him, a mighty gladness that this was *not* Drew—that this loose-lipped gabbler was not the man who had written the epitaph over the tomb of Joan Piotto. He lied about the book; he had lied about it all. And knowing that this was not Drew, he felt suddenly as if someone were watching him from behind, someone large and grey and stern of eye, like the giant who had spoken to him so long before in the arena at Madison Square Garden.

A game was being played with him, and behind

that game must be Drew himself; all Bard could do was to wait for developments.

The familiar, booming voice of Shorty Kilrain echoed through the house: "Supper!"

And the loud clangour of a bell supported the invitation.

"Chow-time," breathed Lawlor heavily, like one relieved at the end of a hard shift of work. "I figure you ain't sorry, son?"

"No," answered Bard, "but it's too bad to break off this talk. I've learned a lot."

CHAPTER XXVII

THE STAGE

"You first," said Lawlor at the door.

"I've been taught to let an older man go first," said Bard, smiling pleasantly. "After you, sir."

"Any way you want it, Bard," answered Lawlor, but as he led the way down the hall he was saying to himself, through his stiffly mumbling lips: "He knows! Calamity was right; there's going to be hell poppin' before long."

He lengthened his stride going down the long hall to the dining-room, and entering, he found the cowpunchers about to take their places around the big table. Straight toward the head to the big chair he stalked, and paused an instant beside little Duffy. Their interchange of whispers was like a muffled rapid-fire, for they had to finish before young Bard, now just entering the room, could reach them and take his designated chair at the right of Lawlor.

"He knows," muttered Lawlor.

"Hell! Then it's all up?"

"No; keep bluffin'; wait. How's everything?"

"Gregory ain't come in, but Drew may put him wise before he gets inside the house."

"You done all I could expect," said Lawlor aloud as Bard came up, "but to-morrow go back on the same job and try to get something definite."

To Bard: "Here's your place, partner. Just been tellin' Duffy, there on your right, about some work. Some of the doggies have been rustled lately and we're on their trail."

They took their places, and Bard surveyed the room carefully, as an actor who stands in the wings and surveys the stage on which he is soon to step and play a great part; for in Anthony there was a gathering sense of impending disaster and action. What he saw was a long, low apartment, the bare rafters overhead browned by the kitchen smoke, which even now was rolling in from the wide door at the end of the room—the thick, oily smoke of burnt meat mingled with steam and the nameless vapours of a great oven.

There was no semblance of a decoration on the walls; the boards were not even painted. It was strictly a place for use, not pleasure. The food itself which Shorty Kilrain and Calamity Ben now brought on was distinctly utilitarian rather than appetizing. The *pièce de resistance* was a monstrous platter heaped high with beefsteak, not the inviting meat of a restaurant in a civilized city, but thin, brown slabs, fried dry throughout. The real nourishment was in the gravy in which the steak swam. In a dish of even more amazing proportions was a vast heap of potatoes boiled with their jackets on. Lawlor commenced loading the stack of plates before him, each with a slab and a potato or two.

Meantime from a number of big coffee pots a stream of a liquid, bitter as lye and black as night, was poured into the tin cups. Yet the cattlemen about the table settled themselves for the meal with a pleasant expectation fully equal to that of the most seasoned gourmand in a Manhattan restaurant.

The peculiar cowboy's squint—a frowning of the brow and a compression of the thin lips—relaxed. That frown came from the steady effort to shade the eyes from the white-hot sunlight; the compression of the lips was due to a determination to admit none of the air, laden with alkali dust, except through the nostrils. It grew in time into a perpetual grimace, so that the expression of an old range rider is that of a man steeling himself to pass through some grim ordeal.

Now as they relaxed, Anthony perceived first of all that most of the grimness passed away from the narrowed eyes and they lighted instead with good-humoured banter, though of a weary nature. One by one, they cast off ten years of age; the lines rubbed out; the jaws which had thrust out grew normal; the leaning heads straightened and went back.

They paid not the slightest attention to the newcomer, talking easily among themselves, but Anthony was certain that at least some of them were thinking of him. If they said nothing, their thoughts were the more.

In fact, in the meantime little Duffy had passed on to the next man, in a side mutter, the significant phrase: "He knows!" It went from lip to lip like a watchword passing along a line of sentinels. Each man heard it imperturbably, completed the sentence he was speaking before, or maintained his original silence through a pause, and then repeated it to his right-hand neighbour. Their demeanour did not alter perceptibly, except that the laughter, perhaps, became a little more uproarious, and they were sitting straighter in their chairs, their eyes brighter.

All they knew was that Drew had impressed on them that Bard must not leave that room in command of his six-shooter or even of his hands. He must be bound securely. The working out of the details of execution he had left to their own ingenuity. It might have seemed a little thing to do to greener fellows, but every one of these men was an experienced cowpuncher, and like all old hands on the range they were perfectly familiar with the amount of damage which a single armed man can do.

The thing could be done, of course, but the point was to do it with the minimum of danger. So they waited, and talked, and ate and always from the corners of their eyes were conscious of the slightly built, inoffensive man who sat beside Lawlor near the head of the table. In appearance he was surely most innocuous, but Nash had spoken, and in such matters they were all willing to take his word with a childlike faith.

So the meal went on, and the only sign, to the most experienced eye, was that the chairs were placed a little far back from the edge of the table, a most necessary condition when men may have to rise rapidly or get at their holsters for a quick draw.

Calamity Ben bearing a mighty dish of bread pudding, passed directly behind the chair of the stranger. The whole table watched with a sudden keenness, and they saw Bard turn, ever so slightly, just as Calamity passed behind the chair.

"I say," he said, "may I have a bit of hot water to put in this coffee?"

"Sure," said Calamity, and went on, but the whole table knew that the stranger was on his guard.

The mutual suspicion gave a tenseness to the atmosphere, as if it were charged with the electricity of a coming storm, a tingling waiting which made the men prone to become silent and then talk again in fitful outbursts. Or it might be said that it was like a glass full of precipitate which only waits for the injection of a single unusual substance before it settles to the bottom and leaves the remaining liquid clear. It was for the unusual, then, that the entire assembly waited, feeling momentarily that it must be coming, for the strain could not endure.

As for Bard, he stuck by his original apparent indifference. For he still felt sure that the real William Drew was behind this elaborate deception and the thing for which he waited was some revelation of the hand of the master. The trumps which he felt he held was in being forewarned; he could not see that the others knew his hand.

He said to Lawlor: "I think a man named Nash

works on this ranch. I expected to see him at supper here."

"Nash?" answered Lawlor. "Sure, he used to be foreman here. Ain't no more. Nope—I couldn't stand for his lip. Didn't mind him getting fresh till he tried to ride me. Then I turned him loose. Where did you meet him?"

"While I was riding in this direction."

"Want to see him bad?"

The other moistened his lips.

"Rather! He killed my horse."

A silence fell on these who were within hearing. They would not have given equal attention to the story of the killing of a man.

"How'd he get away with it?"

"The Saverack was between us. Before I could get my gun out he was riding out of range. I'll meet him and have another talk some day."

"Well, the range ain't very small."

"But my dear fellow, it's not nearly as big as my certainty of meeting this—cur."

There is something in a low, slow voice more thrilling than the thunder of actual rage. Those who heard glanced to one another with thoughtful eyes. They were thinking of Nash, and thinking of him with sympathy.

Little Duffy, squat and thick-set, felt inspiration descend on him. He turned to Bard on his left.

"That ain't a full-size forty-five, is it— that one you're packin'?"

"Doesn't it look it?" answered Bard.

"Nope. Holster seems pretty small to me."

"It's the usual gun, I'm sure," said Bard, and pulled the weapon from the leather.

Holding the butt loosely, his trigger finger hooked clear around the far side of the guard, he showed the gun.

"I was wrong," nodded Duffy unabashed, "that's the regular kind. Let's have a look at it."

And he stretched out his hand. No one would ever have guessed how closely the table followed what now happened, for each man began talking in a voice even louder than before. It was as if they sought to cover the stratagem of Duffy with their noise.

"There's nothing unusual about the gun," said Bard, "but I'd be glad to let you have it except that I've formed a habit of never letting a six-shooter get away from me. It's a foolish habit, I know, but I can't lose it. If there's any part you'd like to see, just name it."

"Thanks," answered Duffy. "I guess I've seen all I want of it."

Calamity had failed; Duffy had failed. It began to look as if force of downright numbers must settle the affair.

CHAPTER XXVIII

SALLY BREAKS A MIRROR

As Sally had remarked the night before, one does not pay much attention to a toilet when one rises at 5 A.M. At least that is the rule, but Sally, turning out with a groan in the chill, dark room, shut off the alarm, lighted her lamp, and set about the serious task of dressing. A woman, after all, is much like a diplomatic statesman; a hint along certain lines is more to her than a sworn statement.

She had secured a large mirror, and in front of this she laboured patiently for a full ten minutes, twisting her hair this way and that, and using the comb and brush vigorously. Now and then, as she worked, she became aware that a fluff of hair rolling down low over her forehead did amazing things to her face and brought her from Sally Fortune into the strange dignity of a "lady." But she could not complete any of the manœuvres, no matter how promisingly they started. In the end she dashed a handful of hairpins on the floor and wound the hair about her head with a few swift turns.

She studied the sullen, boyish visage which looked back at her. After all, she would be unmercifully joked if she were to appear with her hair grown suddenly fluffy and womanly—it would become impossible for her to run the eating-place without the assistance of a man, and a fighting man at that. So what was the use? She threw the mirror crashing on the floor; it splintered in a thousand pieces.

"After all," she murmured aloud, "do I *want* to be a woman?"

The sullen mouth undoubtedly answered "No"; the wistful eyes undoubtedly replied in another key. She shrugged the question away and stepped out of her room toward the kitchen, whistling a tune to raise her spirits.

"Late, Sally," said the cook, tossing another hot cake on the growing pile which surmounted the warmer.

"Sure; I busted my mirror," said Sally.

The cook stared at her in such astonishment that he allowed a quantity of dough to fall from the dish cupped in the hollow of his arm; it overflowed the griddle-iron.

"Blockhead!" shouted Sally. "Watch your step!"

She resumed, when the dough had been rescued by somewhat questionable means: "D'you think a girl can dress in the dark?"

But the cook had had too much experience with his employer to press what seemed a tender point. He confined his attention to the pancakes.

"There ain't no fool worse than a he-fool," continued Sally bitterly. "Which maybe you think a girl can dress without a mirror?"

Since this taunt brought no response from her victim, she went on into the eating-room. It was already filling, and the duties of her strenuous day began.

They continued without interruption hour after hour, for the popularity of her restaurant had driven all competition out of Eldara, a result which filled the pocket-book and fattened the bank account of Sally Fortune, but loaded unnumbered burdens onto her strong shoulders. For she could not hire a waiter to take her place; every man who came into the eating-room expected to be served by the slim hands of Sally herself, and he expected also some trifling repartee which would make him pay his bill with a grin.

The repartee dragged with Sally to-day, almost to sullenness, and when she began to grow weary in the early afternoon, there was no reserve strength on which she could fall back. She suddenly became aware that she wanted support, aid, comfort. Finally she spilled a great armful of "empties" down on the long drain-board of the sink, turned to the wall, and buried her face in her hands. The cook, Bert, though he cast a startled glance at her would not have dared to speak, after that encounter of the morning, but a rather explosive sniff was too eloquent an appeal to his manliness.

His left sleeve having fallen, he rolled it back, tied the strings of the apron tighter about his plump middle, and advanced to the battle. His hand touched the shoulder of the girl.

"Sally!"

"Shut your face!" moaned a stifled voice.

But he took his courage between his teeth and persisted.

"Sally, somethin' is wrong."

"Nothin' you can right, Fatty," said the same woe-stricken voice.

"Sally, if somebody's been gettin' fresh with you——"

Her arms jerked down; she whirled and faced

him with clenched fists; her eyes shining more brightly for the mist which was in them.

"Fresh with me? Why, you poor, one-horned yearling, d'you think there's anybody in Eldara man enough to get fresh with *me?*"

Bert retreated a step; caution was a moving element in his nature. From a vantage point behind a table, however, he ventured: "Then what *is* wrong?"

Her woe, apparently, was greater than her wrath.

She said sadly: "I dunno, Bert. I ain't the man I used to be—I mean, the woman."

He waited, his small eyes gentle. What woman can altogether resist sympathy, even from a fat man and a cook? Not even the redoubtable soul of a Sally.

She confessed: "I feel sort of hollow and gone— around the stomach, Fatty."

"Eat," suggested the cook. "I just took out a pie that would——"

"But it *ain't* the stomach. It's like bein' hungry and wantin' no food. Fatty, d'you think I'm sick?"

"You look kind of whitish."

"Fatty, I feel——"

She hesitated, as though too great a confession

were at her lips, but she stumbled on: "I feel as if I was afraid of somethin', or someone."

"That," said Bert confidently, "ain't possible. It's the stomach, Sally. Something ain't agreed with you."

She turned from him with a vague gesture of despair.

"If this here feelin' is goin' to keep up—why, I wisht I was dead—I wisht I was dead!"

She went on to the swinging door, paused there to dab her eyes swiftly, started to whistle a tune, and in this fashion marched back to the eating-room. Fatty, turning back to the stove, shook his head; he was more than ever convinced in his secret theory that all women are crazy.

Sally found that a new man had entered, one whom she could not remember having seen before. She went to him at once, for it seemed to her that she would die, indeed, if she had to look much longer on the familiar, unshaven faces of the other men in the room.

"Anything you got," said the stranger, who was broad of hands and thick of neck and he cast an anxious eye on her. "I hear you seen something of a thinnish, dark feller named Bard."

"What d' *you* want with him?" asked Sally with dangerous calm.

"I was aimin' to meet up with him. That's all."

"Partner, if you want to stand in solid around here, don't let out that you're a friend of his. He ain't none too popular; that's straight and puttin' it nice and easy."

"Which who said I was his friend?" said the other with heat.

She turned away to the kitchen and reappeared shortly, bearing his meal. The frown with which she departed had disappeared, and she was smiling as brightly as ever while she arranged the dishes in front of him. He paid no attention to the food.

"Now," she said, resting both hands on the table and leaning so that she could look him directly in the eye: "What's Bard done now? Horse—gun-fighter—woman; which?"

The other loosened the bandanna which circled his bull neck.

"Woman," he said hoarsely, and the blood swelled his throat and face with veins of purple.

"Ah-h-h," drawled the girl, and straightening, she dropped both hands on her hips. It was a struggle, but she managed to summon another smile.

"Wife—sister—sweetheart?"

The man stared dubiously on her, and Sally, mother to five hundred wild rangers, knew the symptoms of a man eager for a confidant. She slipped into the opposite chair.

"It might be any of the three," she went on gently, "and I know because I've seen him work."

"Damn his soul!" growled the other by way of a prefix to his story. "It ain't any of the three with me. This Bard—maybe he tried his hand with *you?*"

Whether it was rage or scorn that made her start and redden he could not tell.

"Me?" she repeated. "A tenderfoot get fresh with me? Stranger, you ain't been long in Eldara or you wouldn't pull a bonehead like that."

"'Scuse me. I was hopin' that maybe you took a fall out of him, that's all."

He studied the blue eyes. They had been tinted with ugly green a moment before, but now they were clear, deep, dark, guileless blue. He could not resist. The very nearness of the woman was like a gentle, cool hand caressing his forehead and rubbing away the troubles.

"It was like this," he began. "Me and Lizzie had been thick for a couple of years and was jest waitin' till I'd corralled enough cash for a start. Then the other day along comes this feller Bard with a queer way of talkin' school language. Made you feel like you was readin' a bit out of a dictionary jest to listen to him for a minute. Liz, she never heard nothin' like it, I figure. She got all eyes and sat still and listened. Bein' like that he plumb made a fool out of Liz. Kidded her along and wound up by kissing her good-bye. I didn't see none of this; I jest heard about it later. When I come up and started talkin' jest friendly with Liz she got sore and passed me the frosty stare. I didn't think she could be doin' more than kiddin' me a bit, so I kept right on and it ended up with Liz sayin' that all was over between us.''

He paused on his tragedy, set his teeth over a sigh, and went on: "The feller ain't no good. I know that from a chap that come to the house a few hours after Bard left. Nash was his name——"

"What!"

"Nash. Feller built husky around the shoulders —looks like a fighter. Know him?"

"Pretty well. D'you say he come to your house right after Bard left it?"

"Yep. Why?"

"How long ago was this?"

"About three days."

"Three days?"

"What's wrong?"

"Nothin'."

"You look like you was goin' to murder some one, lady."

Her laughter ended with a jerk and jar.

"Maybe I am. G'wan! Tell me some more about what Nash said."

"Why, he didn't say much. Hinted around that maybe Bard had walked off with the piebald hoss he was ridin'."

"That's a lie."

"Lady," said the other a little coldly, "you say that like you was a friend of Bard's."

"Me? There ain't nobody around these parts man enough to say to my face that I'm a friend of that tenderfoot."

"I'm glad of that. My name's Ralph Boardman."

"I'm Sally Fortune."

"Sure; I've heard of you—a lot. Say, you couldn't tip me off where I could hit the trail of Bard?"

"Dunno. Wait; lemme see."

She studied, with closed eyes. What she was thinking was that if Nash had been so close to Bard three days before he was surely on the trail of the tenderfoot and certainly that meeting in her place had not been a casual one. She set her teeth, thinking of the promise Nash had given to her.

Undoubtedly he had laughed at it afterward. And now Bard probably lay stretched on his back somewhere among the silent hills looking up to the pitiless brightness of the sky with eyes which could never shut.

The hollow feeling of which Sally had complained to Bert grew to a positive ache, and the tears stood up closer to her eyes.

"Wait around town," she said in a changed voice. "I think I heard him say something of riding out, but he'll be back before long. That's the only tip I can give you, partner."

So she rose and hurried back to the kitchen.

"Bert," she said, "I'm off for the rest of the day. You got to handle the place."

He panted: "But the heavy rush—it ain't started yet."

"It's started for me."

"What d'you mean?"

"Nothin'. I'm on my way. S'long, Bert. Back in the mornin' bright and early."

If she could not find Bard at least she could find Nash at the ranch of Drew, and in that direction she headed her racing horse.

CHAPTER XXIX

THE SHOW

JANSEN, the big Swede, was the first to finish his meal in Drew's dining-room. For that matter, he was always first. He ate with astonishing expedition, lowering his head till that tremendous, shapeless mouth was close to the plate and then working knife and fork alternately with an unfaltering industry. To-night, spurred on by a desire to pass through this mechanical effort and be prepared for the coming action, his speed was something truly marvellous. He did not appear to eat; the food simply vanished from the plate; it was absorbed like a mist before the wind. While the others were barely growing settled in their places, Jansen was already through.

He wiped his mouth on the back of his hand, produced Durham and papers, and proceeded to light up. Lawlor, struggling still to re-establish himself in the eyes of Bard as the real William Drew, seized the opportunity to exert a show of authority. He smashed his big fist on the table.

"Jansen!" he roared.

"Eh?" grunted the Swede.

"Where was you raised?"

"Me?"

"You, square-head."

"Elvaruheimarstadhaven."

"Are you sneezin' or talkin' English?"

Jansen, irritated, bellowed: "Elvaruheimarstad-haven! That's where I was born."

"That's where you was born? Elvaru—damn such a language! No wonder you Swedes don't know nothin'. It takes all your time learnin' how to talk your lingo. But if you ain't never had no special trainin' in manners, I'm goin' to make a late start with you now. Put out that cigarette!"

The pale eyes of Jansen stared, fascinated; the vast mouth fell agape.

"Maybe," he began, and then finished weakly: "I be damned!"

"There ain't no reasonable way of doubtin' that unless you put out that smoke. Hear me?"

Shorty Kilrain, coming from the kitchen, grinned broadly. Having felt the lash of discipline himself, he was glad to see it fall in another place.

He continued his gleeful course around that side' of the table.

And big Jansen slowly, imperturbably, raised the cigarette and inhaled a mighty cloud of smoke which issued at once in a rushing, fine blue mist, impelled by a snort.

"Maybe," he rumbled, completing his thought, "maybe you're one damn fool!"

"I'm going to learn you who's boss in these parts," boomed Lawlor. "Put out that cigarette! Don't you know no better than to smoke at the table?"

Jansen pushed back his chair and started to rise. There was no doubt as to his intentions; they were advertised in the dull and growing red which flamed in his face. But Kilrain, as though he had known such a moment would come, caught the Swede by the shoulders and forced him back into the chair. As he did so he whispered something in the ear of Jansen.

"Let him go!" bellowed Lawlor. "Let him come on. Don't hold him. I ain't had work for my hands for five years. I need exercise, I do."

The mouth of Jansen stirred, but no words came. A hopeless yearning was in his eyes. But he dropped the cigarette and ground it under his heel.

"I thought," growled Lawlor, "that you knew your master, but don't make no mistake again. Speakin' personal, I don't think no more of knockin' down a Swede than I do of flickin' the ashes off'n a cigar."

He indulged in a side glance at Bard to see if the latter were properly impressed, but Anthony was staring blankly straight before him, unable, to all appearances, to see anything of what was happening.

"Kilrain," went on Lawlor, "trot out some cigars. You know where they're kept."

Kilrain falling to the temptation, asked: "Where's the key to the cabinet?"

For Drew kept his tobacco in a small cabinet, locked because of long experience with tobacco-loving employees. Lawlor started to speak, checked himself, fumbled through his pockets, and then roared: "Smash the door open. I misplaced the key."

No semblance of a smile altered the faces of the cowpunchers around the table, but glances of vague meaning were interchanged. Kilrain reappeared almost at once, bearing a large box of cigars under each arm.

"The eats bein' over," announced Lawlor, "we can now light up. Open them boxes, Shorty.

Am I goin' to work on you the rest of my life teachin' you how to serve cigars?"

Kilrain sighed deeply, but obeyed, presenting the open boxes in turn to Bard, who thanked him, and to Lawlor, who bit off the end of his smoke continued: "A match, Kilrain."

And he waited, swelling with pleasure, his eyes fixed upon space. Kilrain lighted a match and held it for the two in turn. Two rows of waiting, expectant eyes were turned from the whole length, of the table, toward the cigars.

"Shall I pass on the cigars?" suggested Bard.

"*These* smokes?" breathed Lawlor. "Waste 'em on common hands? Partner, you ain't serious, are you?"

A breath like the faint sighing of wind reached them; the cowpunchers were resigned, and started now to roll their Durham. But it seemed as if a chuckle came from above; it was only some sound in the gasoline lamp, a big fixture which hung suspended by a slender chain from the centre of the ceiling and immediately above the table.

"Civilizin' cowpunchers," went on Lawlor, tilting back in his chair and bracing his feet against the edge of the table, "civilizin' cowpunchers is worse'n breakin' mustangs. They's some that say it can't be done. But look at this crew. Do they look like rough uns?"

A stir had passed among the cowpunchers and solemn stares of hate transfixed Lawlor, but he went on: "I'm askin' you, do these look rough?"

"I should say," answered Bard courteously, "that you have a pretty experienced lot of cattlemen."

"Experienced? Well, they'll pass. They've had experience with bar whisky and talkin' to their cards at poker, but aside from bein' pretty much drunks and crookin' the cards, they ain't anything uncommon. But when I got 'em they was wild, they was. Why, if I'd talked like this in front of 'em they'd of been guns pulled. But look at 'em now. I ask you: Look at 'em now! Ain't they tame? They hear me call 'em what they are, but they don't even bat an eye. Yes, sir, I've tamed 'em. They took a lot of lickin', but now they're tamed. Hello!"

For through the door stalked a newcomer. He paused and cast a curious eye up the table to Lawlor.

"What the hell!" he remarked naïvely. "Where's the chief?"

"Fired!" bellowed Lawlor without a moment of hesitation.

"Who fired him?" asked the new man, with an expectant smile, like one who waits for the point of a joke, but he caught a series of strange signals from men at the table and many a broad wink.

"I fired him, Gregory," answered Lawlor. "I fired Nash!"

He turned to Bard.

"You see," he said rather weakly, "the boys is used to callin' Nash 'the chief.'"

"Ah, yes," said Bard, "I understand."

And Lawlor felt that he *did* understand, and too well.

Gregory, in the meantime, silenced by the mysterious signs from his fellow cowpunchers, took his place and began eating without another word. No one spoke to him, but as if he caught the tenseness of the situation, his eyes finally turned and glanced up the table to Bard.

It was easy for Anthony to understand that glance. It is the sort of look which the curious turn on the man accused of a great crime and sitting in the court room guilty. His trial in silence had continued until he was found guilty. Apparently, he was now to be both judged and executed at the same time.

There could not be long delay. The entrance of Gregory had almost been the precipitant of action, and though it had been smoothed over to an extent, still the air was each moment more charged with suspense. The men were lighting their second cigarette. With each second it grew clearer that they were waiting for something. And as if thoughtful of the work before them, they no longer talked so fluently.

Finally there was no talk at all, save for sporadic outbursts, and the blue smoke and the brown curled up slowly in undisturbed drifts toward the ceiling until a bright halo formed around the gasoline lamp. A childish thought came to Bard that where the smoke was so thick the fire could not be long delayed.

A second form appeared in the doorway, lithe, graceful, and the light made her hair almost golden.

"Ev'nin', fellers," called Sally jauntily. "Hello, Lawlor; what you doin' at the head of the table?"

CHAPTER XXX

THE LAMP

THE bluff was ended. It was as if the wind blew a cloud suddenly from the face of the sun and let the yellow sunlight pour brightly over the world; so everyone in the room at the voice of Sally knew that the time had come for action. There was no vocal answer to her, but each man rose slowly in his place, his gun naked in his hand, and every face was turned to Bard.

"Gentlemen," he said in his soft voice, "I see that my friend Lawlor has not wasted his lessons in manners. At least you know enough to rise when a lady enters the room."

His gun, held at the hip, pointed straight down the table to the burly form of Jansen, but his eyes, like those of a pugilist, seemed to be taking in every face at the table, and each man felt in some subtle manner that the danger would fall first on him. They did not answer, but hands were tightening around revolver butts.

256

Lawlor moved back, pace by pace, his revolver shaking in his hand.

"But," went on Bard, "you are all facing me. Is it possible?"

He laughed.

"I knew that Mr. Drew was very anxious to receive me with courtesy; I did not dream that he would be able to induce so many men to take care of me."

And Sally Fortune, bracing herself against the wall with one hand, and in the capable grasp of the other a six-gun balanced, stared in growing amazement on the scene, and shuddered at the silences.

"Bard," she called, "what have I done?"

"You've started a game," he answered, "which I presume we've all been waiting to play. What about it, boys? I hope you're well paid; I'd hate to die a cheap death."

A voice, deep and ringing, sounded close at hand, almost within the room, and from a direction which Bard could not locate.

"Don't harm him if you can help it. But keep him in that room!"

Bard stepped back a pace till his shoulders touched the wall.

"Sirs," he said, "if you keep me here you will most certainly have to harm me."

A figure ran around the edge of the crowd and stood beside him.

"Stand clear of me, Sally," he muttered, much moved. "Stand away. This is a man's work."

"The work of a pack of coyotes!" she cried shrilly. "What d'ye mean?"

She turned on them fiercely.

"Are you goin' to murder a tenderfoot among you? One that ain't done no real harm? I don't believe my eyes. You, there, Shorty Kilrain, I've waited on you with my own hands. You've played the man with me. Are you goin' to play the dog now? Jansen, you was tellin' me about a blue-eyed girl in Sweden; have you forgot about her now? And Calamity Ben! My God, ain't there a man among you to step over here and join the two of us?"

They were shaken, but the memory of Drew quelled them.

"They's no harm intended him, on my honour, Sally," said Lawlor. "All he's got to do is give up his gun—and—and"—he finished weakly—"let his hands be tied."

"Is that all?" said Sally scornfully.

"Don't follow me, Sally," said Bard. "Stay out of this. Boys, you may have been paid high, but I don't think you've been paid high enough to

risk taking a chance with me. If you put me out
with the first shot that ends it, of course, but the
chances are that I'll be alive when I hit the floor,
and if I am, I'll have my gun working—and I won't
miss. One or two of you are going to drop."

He surveyed them with a quick glance which
seemed to linger on each face.

"I don't know who'll go first. But now I'm
going to walk straight for that door, and I'm going
out of it."

He moved slowly, deliberately toward the door,
around the table. Still they did not shoot.

"Bard!" commanded the voice which had
spoken from nowhere before. "Stop where you
are. Are you fool enough to think that I'll let
you go?"

"Are you William Drew?"

"I am, and you are——"

"The son of John Bard. Are you in this house?"

"I am; Bard, listen to me for thirty seconds——"

"Not for three. Sally, go out of this room and
through that door.

There was a grim command in his voice. It
started her moving against her will. She paused
and looked back with an imploring gesture.

"Go on," he repeated.

And she passed out of the door and stood there,

a glimmering figure against the night. Still there was not a shot fired, though all those guns were trained on Bard.

"You've got me Drew," he called, "but I've got you, and your hirelings—all of you, and I'm going to take you to hell with me—to hell!"

He jerked his gun up and fired, not at a man, for the bullet struck the thin chain which held the gasoline lamp suspended, struck it with a clang, and it rushed down to the table. It struck, but not with the loud explosion which Bard had expected. There was a dull report, as of a shot fired at a great distance, the scream of Sally from the door, and then liquid fire spurted from the lamp across the table, whipped in a flare to the ceiling, and licked against the walls. It shot to all sides but it shot high, and every man was down on his face.

Anthony, scarcely believing that he was still alive, rushed for the door, with a cry of agony ringing in his ears from the voice beyond the room. One man in all that crowd was near enough or had the courage to obey the master even to the uttermost. The gaunt form of Calamity Ben blocked the doorway in front of Bard, blocked it with poised revolver.

"Halt!" he yelled.

But the other rushed on. Calamity whipped down the gun and fired, but even before the trigger was pulled he was sagging toward the floor, for Bard had shot to kill. Over the prostrate form of the cowpuncher he leaped, and into the night, where the white face of Sally greeted him.

Outside the red inferno of that room, as if the taste of blood had maddened him, he raised his arms and shouted, like one crying a wild prayer: "William Drew! William Drew! Come out to me!"

Small, strong hands gripped his wrists and turned him away from the house

"You fool!" cried Sally. "Ride for it! You've raised your hell at last—I knew you would!"

Red light flared in all the windows of the dining-room; shouts and groans and cursing poured out of them. Bard turned and followed her out toward the stable on the run, and he heard her moaning as she ran: "I knew! I knew!"

She mounted her horse, which was tethered near the barn. He chose at random the first horse he reached, a grey, threw on his back the saddle which hung from the peg behind, mounted, and they were off through the night. No thought, no direction; but only in blind speed there seemed to be the hope of a salvation.

A mile, two miles dropped behind them, and then in an open stretch, for he had outridden her somewhat, Anthony reined back, caught the bridle of her horse, and pulled it down to a sharp trot.

"Why have you come?"

Their faces were so close that even through the night he could see the grim set of her lips.

"Ain't you raised your hell—the hell you was hungry to raise? Don't you need help?"

"What I've done is my own doing. I'll take the burden of it."

"You'll take a halter for it, that's what you'll take. The whole range'll rise for this. You're marked already. Everywhere you've gone you've made an enemy. They'll be out to get you—Nash —Boardman—the whole gang."

"Let 'em come. I'd do this all over again."

"Born gunman, eh? Bard, you ain't got a week to live."

It was fierceness; it was a reproach rather than sorrow.

"Then let me go my own way. Why do you follow, Sally?"

"D'you know these mountains?"

"No, but——"

"Then they'd run you down in twelve hours. Where'll you head for?"

He said, as the first thought entered his mind:
"I'll go for the old house that Drew has on the
other side of the range."

"That ain't bad. Know the short cut?"

"What cut?"

"You can make it in five hours over one trail.
But of course you don't know. Nobody but old
Dan and me ever knowed it. Let go my bridle
and ride like hell."

She jerked the reins away from him and galloped
off at full speed. He followed.

"Sally!" he called.

But she kept straight ahead, and he followed,
shouting, imploring her to go back. Finally he
settled to the chase, resolved on overtaking her.
It was no easy task, for she rode like a centaur,
and she knew the way.

CHAPTER XXXI

NASH STARTS THE FINISH

THROUGH the windows and the door the cow-punchers fled from the red spurt of the flames, each man for himself, except Shorty Kilrain, who stooped, gathered the lanky frame of Calamity Ben into his arms, and staggered out with his burden. The great form of William Drew loomed through the night.

His hand on the shoulder of Shorty, he cried: "Is he badly burned?"

"Shot," said Kilrain bitterly, "by the tender-foot; done for."

It was strange to hear the big voice go shrill with pain.

"Shot? By Anthony? Give him to me."

Kilrain lowered his burden to the ground.

"You've got him murdered. Ain't you through with him? Calamity, he was my pal!"

But the big man thrust him aside and knelt by the stricken cowpuncher.

He commanded: "Gather the boys; form a line of buckets from the pump; fight that fire. It hasn't a hold on the house yet."

The habit of obedience persisted in Kilrain. Under the glow of the fire, excited by the red light, the other man stood irresolute, eager for action, but not knowing what to do. A picture came back to him of a ship labouring in a storm; the huddling men on the deck; the mate on the bridge, shrieking his orders through a megaphone. He cupped his hands at his mouth and began to bark orders.

They obeyed on the run. Some rushed for the kitchen and secured buckets; two manned the big pump and started a great gush of water; in a moment a steady stream was being flung by the foremost men of the line against the smoking walls and even the ceiling of the dining-room. So far it was the oil itself, which had made most of the flame and smoke, and now, although the big table was on fire, the main structure of the house was hardly touched.

They caught it in time and worked with a cheer, swinging the buckets from hand to hand, shouting as the flames fell little by little until the floor of the room was awash, the walls gave back clouds of steam, and the only fire was that which smouldered along the ruined table. Even this went out, hissing, at last, and they came back with blackened, singed faces to Calamity and Drew.

The rancher had torn away the coat and shirt of the wounded man, and now, with much labour, was twisting a tight bandage around his chest. At every turn Calamity groaned feebly. Kilrain dropped beside his partner, taking the head between his hands.

"Calamity—pal," he said, "how'd you let a tenderfoot, a damned tenderfoot, do this?"

The other sighed: "I dunno. I had him covered. I should have sent him to hell. But sure shootin' is better'n fast shootin'. He nailed me fair and square while I was blockin' him at the door."

"How d'you feel?"

"Done for, Shorty, but damned glad that——"

His voice died away in a horrible whisper and bubbles of red foam rose to his lips.

"God!" groaned Shorty, and then called loudly, as if the strength of his voice might recall the other, "Calamity!"

The eyes of Calamity rolled up; the wide lips twisted over formless words; there was no sound from his mouth. Someone was holding a lantern whose light fell full on the silent struggle. It was Nash, his habitual sneer grown more malevolent than ever.

"What of the feller that done it, Shorty?" he suggested.

"So help me God," said the cattleman, with surprising softness, "the range ain't big enough to keep him away from me."

Drew, completing his bandage, said: "That's enough of such talk, Nash. Let it drop there. Here, Kilrain, take his feet; help me into the house with him."

They moved in, the rest trailing behind like sheep after a bell-wether, and it was astonishing to see the care with which big Drew handled his burden, placing it at last on his own four-poster bed.

"The old man's all busted up," said little Duffy to Nash. "I'd never of guessed he was so fond of Calamity."

"You're a fool," answered Nash. "It ain't Calamity he cares about."

"Then what the devil is it?"

"I dunno. We're goin' to see some queer things around here."

Drew, having disposed of the wounded man, carefully raising his head on a pillow, turned to the others.

"Who saw Ben shot?"

"I did," said Kilrain, who was making his way to the door.

"Come back here. Are you sure you saw the shot fired?"

"I seen the tenderfoot—damn his eyes!—whip up his gun and take a snap shot while he was runnin' for the door where Calamity stood."

Nash raised his lantern high, so that the light fell full on the face of Drew. The rancher was more grey than ever.

He said, with almost an appeal in his voice: "Mightn't it have been one of the other boys, shooting at random?"

The tone of Kilrain raised and grew ugly.

"Are you tryin' to cover the tenderfoot, Drew?"

The big man made a fierce gesture.

"Why should I cover him?"

"Because you been actin' damned queer," answered Nash.

"Ah, you're here again, Nash? I know you hate Bard because he was too much for you."

"He got the start of me, but I'll do a lot of finishing."

"Kilrain," called Drew, "you're Calamity's best friend. Ride for Eldara and bring back Dr. Young. Quick! We're going to pull Ben through."

"Jest a waste of time," said Nash coolly. "He's got one foot in hell already."

"You've said too much, Nash. Kilrain, are you going?"

"I'll stop for the doctor at Eldara, but then I'll keep on riding."

"What do you mean?"

"Nothin'."

"I'll go with you," said Nash, and turned with the other.

"Stop!" called Drew. "Boys, I know what you have planned; but let the law take care of this. Remember that we were the aggressors against young Bard. He came peaceably into this house and I tried to hold him here. What would you have done in his place?"

"They's a dozen men know how peaceable he is," said Nash drily. "Wherever he's gone on the range he's raised hell. He's cut out for a killer, and Glendin in Eldara knows it."

"I'll talk to Glendin. In the meantime you fellows keep your hands off Bard. In the first place because if you take the law into your own hands you'll have me against you—understand?"

Kilrain and Nash glowered at him a moment, and then backed through the door.

As they hurried for the barn Kilrain asked: "What makes the chief act soft to that hell-raiser?"

"If you have a feller cut out for your own meat," answered Nash, "d'you want to have any one else step in and take your meal away?"

"But you and me, Steve, we'll get this bird."

"We'll get Glendin behind us first."

"Why him?"

"Play safe. Glendin can swear us in as deputies to—'apprehend,' as he calls it, this Bard. Apprehendin' a feller like Bard simply means to shoot him down and ask him to come along afterward, see?"

"Nash, you got a great head. You ought to be one of these lawyers. There ain't nothin' you can't find a way out of. But will Glendin do it?"

"He'll do what I ask him to do."

"Friend of yours?"

"Better'n a friend."

"Got something on him?"

"These here questions, they ain't polite, Shorty," grinned Nash.

"All right. You do the leadin' in this game and I'll jest follow suit. But lay your course with nothin' but the tops'ls flyin', because I've got an idea we're goin' to hit a hell of a storm before we get back to port, Steve."

"For my part," answered Nash, "I'm gettin' used to rough weather."

They saddled their horses and cut across the hills straight for Eldara. Kilrain spurred viciously, and the roan had hard work keeping up.

"Hold in," called Nash after a time; "save your hoss, Shorty. This ain't no short trail. D'you notice the hosses when we was in the barn?"

"Nope."

"Bard took Duffy's grey, and the grey can go like the devil. Hoss-liftin'? That's another little mark on Bard's score."

CHAPTER XXXII

TO "APPREHEND" A MAN

As if to make up for its silence of the blast when the two reached it late the night before, Eldara was going full that evening. Kilrain went straight for Doc Young, to bring him later to join Nash at the house of Deputy Glendin.

The front of the deputy's house was utterly dark, but Nash, unabashed, knocked loudly on the door, and went immediately to the rear of the place. He was in time to see a light wink out at an upper window of the two-story shack. He, slipped back, chuckling, among the trees, and waited until the back door slammed and a dark figure ran noiselessly down the steps and out into the night. Then he returned, still chuckling, to the front of the house, and banged again on the door.

A window above him raised at length and a drawling voice, apparently overcome with sleep, called down: "What's up in Eldara?"

Nash answered: "Everything's wrong. Deputy Glendin, he sits up in a back room playin' poker and hittin' the redeye. No wonder Eldara's goin' to hell!"

A muffled cursing rolled down to the cowpuncher, and then a sharp challenge: "Who's there?"

"Nash, you blockhead!"

"Nash!" cried a relieved voice, "come in; confound you. I thought—no matter what I thought. Come in!"

Nash opened the door and went up the stairs. The deputy met him, clad in a bathrobe and carrying a lamp. Under the bathrobe he was fully dressed.

"Thought your game was called, eh?" grinned the cattleman.

"Sure. I had a tidy little thing in black-jack running and was pulling in the iron boys, one after another. Why didn't you tip me off? You could have sat in with us."

"Nope; I'm here on business."

"Let's have it."

He led the way into a back room and placed the lamp on a table littered with cards and a black bottle looming in the centre.

"Drink?"

18

"Nope. I said I came on business."

"What kind?"

"Bard."

"I thought so."

"I want a posse."

"What's he done?"

"Killed Calamity Ben at Drew's place, started a fire that near burned the house, and lifted Duffy's hoss."

Glendin whistled softly.

"Nice little start."

"Sure; and it's just a beginnin' for this Bard."

"I'll go out to Drew's place and see what he's done."

"And then start after him with a gang?"

"Sure."

"By that time he'll be a thousand miles away."

"Well?"

"I'm running this little party. Let me get a gang together; you can swear 'em in and put me in charge. I'll guarantee to get him before morning."

Glendin shook his head.

"It ain't legal, Steve. You know that."

"The hell with legality."

"That's what you say; but I got to hold my job."

"You'll do your part by goin' to Drew's place with Doc Young. He'll be here with Shorty Kilrain in a minute."

"And let you go after Bard?"

"Right."

"Far's I know, you may jest shoot him down and then come back and say you done it because he resisted arrest."

"Well?"

"You admit that's what you want, Steve?"

"Absolute."

"Well, partner, it can't be done. That ain't apprehendin' a man. It's jest plain murder."

"D'you think you could ever catch that bird alive?"

"Dunno, I'd try."

"Never in a thousand years."

"He don't know the country. He'll travel in a circle and I'll ride him down."

"He's got somebody with him that knows the country better'n you or me."

"Who?"

The face of Nash twisted into an ugly grimace.

"Sally Fortune."

"The hell!"

"It is; but it's true."

"It ain't possible. Sally ain't the kind to make

a fool of herself about any man, let alone a gun-fighter."

"That's what I thought, but I seen her back up this Bard ag'in' a roomful of men. And she'll keep on backin' him till he's got his toes turned up."

"That's another reason for you to get Bard, eh? Well, I can't send you after him, Nash. That's final."

"Not a bit. I know too much about you, Glendin."

The glance of the other raised slowly, fixed on Nash, and then lowered to the floor. He produced papers and Durham, rolled and lighted his cigarette, and inhaled a long puff.

"So that's the game, Steve?"

"I hate to do it."

"Let that go. You'll run the limit on this?"

"Listen, Glendin. I've got to get this Bard. He's out-ridden me, out-shot me, out-gamed me, out-lucked me, out-guessed me—and taken Sally. He's mine. He b'longs all to me. D'you see that?"

"I'm only seein' one thing just now."

"I know. You think I'm double-crossin' you. Maybe I am, but I'm desperate, Glendin."

"After all," mused the deputy, "you'd be simply

doin' work I'd have to do later. You're right about this Bard. He'll never be taken alive."

"Good ol' Glendin. I knew you'd see light. I'll go out and get the boys I want in ten minutes. Wait here. Shorty and Doc Young will come in a minute. One thing more: when you get to Drew's place you'll find him actin' queer."

"What about?"

"I dunno why. It's a bad mess. You see, he's after this Bard himself, the way I figure it, and he wants him left alone. He'd raise hell if he knew a posse was after the tenderfoot."

"Drew's a bad one to get against me."

"I know. You think I'm double-crossin'?"

"I'll do it. But this squares all scores between us, Steve?"

"Right. It leaves the debt on my side, and you know I've never dodged an I. O. U. Drew may talk queer. He'll tell you that Bard done all that work in self-defence."

"Did he?"

"The point is he killed a man and stole a hoss. No matter what comes of it, he's got to be arrested, don't he?"

"And shot down while 'resistin' arrest'? Steve, I'd hate to have you out for me like this."

"But you won't listen to Drew?"

"Not this one time. But, Lord, man, I hate to face him if he's on the warpath. Who'll you take with you?"

"Shorty, of course. He was Calamity Ben's pal. The rest will be—don't laugh—Butch Conklin and his gang."

"Butch!"

"Hold yourself together. That's what I mean—Butch Conklin."

"After you dropped him the other night?"

"Self-defence, and he knows it. I can find Butch, and I can make him go with me. Besides, he's out for Bard himself."

The deputy said with much meaning: "You can do a lot of queer things, Nash."

"Forget it, Glendin."

"I will for a while. D'you really think I can let you take out Butch and his gunmen ag'in' Bard? Why, they're ten times worse'n the tenderfoot."

"Maybe, but there's nothin' proved ag'in' 'em —nothin' but a bit of cattle-liftin', maybe, and things like that. The point is, they're all hard men, and with 'em along I can't help but get Bard."

"Murder ain't proved on Butch and his men, but it will be before long."

"Wait till it's proved. In the meantime use 'em all."

"You've a long head, Nash."

"Glendin, I'm makin' the biggest play of my life. I'm off to find Butch. You'll stand firm with Drew?"

"I won't hear a word he says."

"S'long! Be back in ten minutes. Wait for me."

He was as good as his word. Even before the ten minutes had elapsed he was back, and behind followed a crew of heavy thumping boots up the stairs of Glendin's house and into the room where he sat with Dr. Young and Shorty Kilrain. They rose, but not from respect, when Nash entered with Conklin and his four ill-famed followers behind.

The soiled bandage on the head of Butch was far too thick to allow his hat to sit in its normal position. It was perched high on top, and secured in place by a bit of string which passed from side to side under the chin. Behind him came Lovel, an almost albino type with straw-coloured hair and eyes bleached and passionless; the vacuous smile was never gone from his lips.

More feared and more hated than Conklin himself was Isaacs. The latter, always fastidious, wore a blue-striped vest, without a coat to obscure it, and about his throat was knotted a flaming vermilion necktie, fastened in place with a diamond stickpin—obviously the spoil of some recent robbery. Glendin, watching, ground his teeth.

McNamara followed. He had been a squatter, but his family had died of a fever, and McNamara's mind had been unsettled ever since; whisky had finished the work of sending him on the downward path with Conklin's little crew of desperadoes. Men shrank from facing those too-bright, wandering eyes, yet it was from pity almost as much as horror.

Finally came Ufert. He was merely a round-faced boy of nineteen, proud of the distinguished bad company he kept. He was that weak-minded type which is only strong when it becomes wholly evil. With a different leadership he would have become simply a tobacco-chewing hanger-on at cross-roads saloons and general merchandise stores. As it was, feeling dignified by the brotherhood of crime into which he had been admitted as a full member, and eager to prove his qualifications, he was as dangerous as any member of the crew.

The three men who were already in the room had been prepared by Glendin for this new arrival, but the fact was almost too much for their credence. Consequently they rose, and Dr. Young muttered at the ear of Glendin: "Is it possible, Deputy Glendin, that you're going to use these fellows?"

"A thief to catch a thief," whispered Glendin in reply.

He said aloud: "Butch, I've been looking for you for a long time, but I really never expected to see you quite as close as this."

"You've said it," grinned Butch, "I ain't been watchin' for you real close, but now that I see you, you look more or less like a man should look. H'ware ye, Glendin?"

He held out his hand, but the deputy, shifting his position, seemed to overlook the grimy proffered palm.

"You fellows know that you're wanted by the law," he said, frowning on them.

A grim meaning rose in the vacuous eye of Lovel; Isaacs caressed his diamond pin, smiling in a sickly fashion; McNamara's wandering stare fixed and grew unhumanly bright; Ufert openly dropped his hand on his gun-butt and stood sullenly defiant.

"You know that you're wanted, and you know why," went on Glendin, "but I've decided to give you a chance to prove that you're white men and useful citizens. Nash has already told you what we want. It's work for seven men against one, but that one man is apt to give you all plenty to do. If you are—successful"—he stammered a little over the right word—"what you have done in the past will be forgotten. Hold up your right hands and repeat after me."

And they repeated the oath after him in a broken, drawling chorus, stumbling over the formal, legal phraseology.

He ended, and then: "Nash, you're in charge of the gang. Do what you want to with them, and remember that you're to get Bard back in town unharmed—if possible."

Butch Conklin smiled, and the same smile spread grimly from face to face among the gang. Evidently this point had already been elucidated to them by Nash, who now mustered them out of the house and assembled them on their horses in the street below.

"Which way do we travel?" asked Shorty Kilrain, reining close beside the leader, as though he were anxious to disestablish any relationship with the rest of the party.

"Two ways," answered Nash. "Of course I don't know what way Bard headed, because he's got the girl with him, but I figure it this way: if a tenderfoot knows any part of the range at all, he'll go in that direction after he's in trouble. I've seen it work out before. So I think that Bard may have ridden straight for the old Drew place on the other side of the range. I know a short cut over the hills; we can reach there by morning. Kilrain, you'll go there with me.

"It may be that Bard will go near the old place, but not right to it. Chances may be good that he'll put up at some place near the old ranchhouse, but not right on the spot. Jerry Wood, he's got a house about four or five miles to the north of Drew's old ranch. Butch, you take your men and ride for Wood's place. Then switch south and ride for Partridge's store; if we miss him at Drew's old house we'll go on and join you at Partridge's store and then double back. He'll be somewhere inside that circle and Eldara, you can lay to that. Now, boys, are your hosses fresh?"

They were.

"Then ride, and don't spare the spurs. Hoss flesh is cheaper'n your own hides."

The cavalcade separated and galloped in two directions through the town of Eldara.

CHAPTER XXXIII

NOTHING NEW

GLENDIN and Dr. Young struck out for the ranch of William Drew, but they held a moderate pace, and it was already grey dawn before they arrived; yet even at that hour several windows of the house were lighted. They were led directly to Drew's room.

The big man welcomed them at the door with a hand raised for silence. He seemed to have aged greatly during the night, but between the black shadows beneath and the shaggy brows above, his eyes gleamed more brightly than ever. About his mouth the lines of resolution were worn deep by his vigil.

"He seems to be sleeping rather well—though you hear his breathing?"

It was a soft, but ominously rattling sound.

"Through the lungs," said the doctor instantly.

The cowpuncher was completely covered, except for his head and feet. On the latter, oddly enough, were still his grimy boots, blackening the white sheets on which they rested.

"I tried to work them off—you see the laces are untied," explained Drew, "but the poor fellow recovered consciousness at once, and struggled to get his feet free. He said that he wants to die with his boots on."

"You tried his pulse and his temperature?" whispered the doctor.

"Yes. The temperature is not much above normal, the pulse is extremely rapid and very faint. Is that a bad sign?"

"Very bad."

Drew winced and caught his breath so sharply that the others stared at him. It might have been thought that he had just heard his own death sentence pronounced.

He explained: "Ben has been with me a number of years. It breaks me up to think of losing him like this."

The doctor took the pulse of Calamity with lightly touching fingers that did not waken the sleeper; then he felt with equal caution the forehead of Ben.

"Well?" asked Drew eagerly.

"The chances are about one out of ten."

It drew a groan from the rancher.

"But there is still *some* hope."

The doctor shook his head and carefully un‧wound the bandages. He examined the wound with care, and then made a dressing, and recovered the little purple spot, so small that a five-cent piece would have covered it.

"Tell me!" demanded Drew, as Young turned at length.

"The bullet passed right through the body, eh?"

"Yes."

"He ought to have been dead hours ago. I can't understand it. But since he's still alive we'll go on hoping."

"Hope?" whispered Drew.

It was as if he had received the promise of heaven, such brightness fell across his haggard face.

"There's no use attempting to explain," answered Young. "An ordinary man would have died almost instantly, but the lungs of some of these rangers seem to be lined with leather. I suppose they are fairly embalmed with excessive cigarette smoking. The constant work in the open air toughens them wonderfully. As I said, the chances are about one out of ten, but I'm only astonished that there is any chance at all."

"Doctor, I'll make you rich for this!"

"My dear sir, I've done nothing; it has been

your instant care that saved him—as far as he is saved. I'll tell you what to continue doing for him; in half an hour I must leave."

Drew smiled faintly.

"Not till he's well or dead, doctor."

"I didn't quite catch that."

"You won't leave the room, Young, till this man is dead or on the way to recovery."

"Come, come, Mr. Drew, I have patients who——"

"I tell you, there is no one else. Until a decision comes in this case your world is bounded by the four walls of this room. That's final."

"Is it possible that you would attempt——"

"Anything is possible with me. Make up your mind. You shall not leave this man till you've done all that's humanly possible for him."

"Mr. Drew, I appreciate your anxiety, but this is stepping too far. I have an officer of the law with me——"

"Better do what he wants, Doc," said Glendin uneasily.

"Don't mouth words," ordered Drew sternly. "There lies your sick man. Get to work. In this I'm as unalterable as the rocks."

"The bill will be large," said Young sullenly, for he began to see that it was as futile to resist the grey giant as it would have been to attempt to stop the progress of a landslide.

"I'll pay you double what you wish to charge."

"Does this man's life mean so much to you?"

"A priceless thing. If you save him, you take the burden of murder off the soul of another."

"I'll do what I can."

"I know you will."

He laid the broad hand on Young's shoulder.

"Doctor, you must do more than you can; you must accomplish the impossible; I tell you, it is impossible for this man to die; he *must* live!"

He turned to Glendin.

"I suppose you want the details of what happened here?"

"Right."

"Follow me. Doctor, I'll be gone only a moment."

He led the way into an adjoining room, and lighted a lamp. The sudden flare cast deep shadows on the face leaning above, and Glendin started. For the moment it seemed to him that he was seeing a face which had looked on hell and lived to speak of it.

"Mr. Drew," he said, "you'd better hit the hay yourself; you look pretty badly done up."

The other looked up with a singular smile, clenching and unclenching his fingers as if he strove to relax muscles which had been tense for hours.

"Glendin, the surface of my strength has not been scratched; I could keep going every hour for ten days if it would save the life of the poor fellow who lies in there."

He took a long breath.

"Now, then, let's get after this business. I'll tell you the naked facts. Anthony Bard was approaching my house yesterday and word of his coming was brought to me. For reasons of my own it was necessary that I should detain him here for an uncertain length of time. For other reasons it was necessary that I go to any length to accomplish my ends.

"I had another man—Lawlor, who looks something like me—take my place in the eyes of Bard. But Bard grew suspicious of the deception. Finally a girl entered and called Lawlor by name, as they were sitting at the table with all the men around them. Bard rose at once with a gun in his hand.

"Put yourself in his place. He found that he had been deceived, he knew that he was surrounded by armed men, he must have felt like a cornered rat. He drew his gun and started for the door, warning the others that he meant to go the limit

19

in order to get free. Mind you, it was no sudden gun-play.

"Then I ordered the men to keep him at all costs within the room. He saw that they were prepared to obey me, and then he took a desperate chance and shot down the gasoline lamp which hung over the table. In the explosion and fire which resulted he made for the door. One man blocked the way, levelled a revolver at him, and then Bard shot in self-defence and downed Calamity Ben. I ask you, Glendin, is that self-defence?"

The other drummed his finger-tips nervously against his chin; he was thinking hard, and every thought was of Steve Nash.

"So far, all right. I ain't askin' your reasons for doin' some pretty queer things, Mr. Drew."

"I'll stand every penalty of the law, sir. I only ask that you see that punishment falls where it is deserved only. The case is clear. Bard acted in self-defence."

Glendin was desperate.

He said at length: "When a man's tried in court they bring up his past career. This feller Bard has gone along the range raisin' a different brand of hell everywhere he went. He had a run-in with two gunmen, Ferguson and Conklin. He had Eldara within an ace of a riot the first night he hit the town. Mr. Drew, that chap looks the part of a killer; he acts the part of a killer; and by God, he *is* a killer."

"You seem to have come with your mind already made up, Glendin," said the rancher coldly.

"Not a bit. But go through the whole town or Eldara and ask the boys what they think of this tenderfoot. They feel so strong that if he was jailed they'd lynch him."

Drew raised a clenched fist and then let his arm fall suddenly limp at his side.

"Then surely he must not be jailed."

"Want me to let him wander around loose and kill another man—in self-defence?"

"I want you to use reason—and mercy, Glendin!

"From what I've heard, you ain't the man to talk of mercy, Mr. Drew."

The other, as if he had received a stunning blow, slipped into a chair and buried his face in his hands. It was a long moment before he could speak, and when his hands were lowered, Glendin winced at what he saw in the other's face.

"God knows I'm not," said Drew.

"Suppose we let the shootin' of Calamity go. What of hoss-liftin', sir?"

"Horse stealing? Impossible! Anthony—he could not be guilty of it!"

"Ask your man Duffy. Bard's ridin' Duffy's grey right now."

"But Duffy will press no claim," said the rancher eagerly. "I'll see to that. I'll pay him ten times the value of his horse. Glendin, you can't punish a man for a theft of which Duffy will not complain."

"Drew, you know what the boys on the range think of a hoss thief. It ain't the price of what they steal; it's the low-down soul of the dog that would steal it. It ain't the money. But what's a man without a hoss on the range? Suppose his hoss is stole while he's hundred miles from nowhere? What does it mean? You know; it means dyin' of thirst and goin' through a hundred hells before the finish. I say shootin' a man is nothin' compared with stealin' a hoss. A man that'll steal a hoss will shoot his own brother; that's what he'll do. But I don't need to tell you. You know it better'n me. What was it you done with your own hands to Louis Borgen, the hoss-rustler, back ten years ago?"

A dead voice answered Glendin: "What has set you on the trail of Bard?"

"His own wrong doin'."

The rancher waved a hand of careless dismissal.
"I know you, Glendin," he said.

The deputy stirred in his chair, and then cleared
his throat.

He said in a rising tone: "What d'you know?"

"I don't think you really care to hear it. To
put it lightly, Glendin, you've done many things
for money. I don't accuse you of them. But if
you want to do one thing more, you can make more
money at a stroke than you've made in all the
rest."

With all his soul the deputy was cursing Nash,
but now the thing was done, and he must see it
through.

He rose glowering on Drew.

"I've stood a pile already from you; this is one
beyond the limit. Bribery ain't my way, Drew,
no matter what I've done before."

"Is it war, then?"

And Glendin answered, forcing his tone into
fierceness: "Anything you want—any way you
want it!"

"Glendin," said the other with a sudden lowering of his voice, "has some other man been talking
to you?"

"Who? Me? Certainly not."

"Don't lie."

"Drew, rein up. They's one thing no man can say to me and get away with it."

"I tell you, man, I'm holding myself in harder than I've ever done before. Answer me!"

He did not even rise, but Glendin, his hand twitching close to the butt of his gun, moved step by step away from those keen eyes.

"Answer me!"

"Nash; he's been to Eldara."

"I might have known. He told you about this?"

"Yes."

"And you're going the full limit of your power against Bard?"

"I'll do nothin' that ain't been done by others before me."

"Glendin, there have been cowardly legal murders before. Tell me at least that you will not send a posse to 'apprehend' Bard until it's learned whether or not Ben will die—and whether or not Duffy will press the charge of horse stealing."

Glendin was at the door. He fumbled behind him, found the knob, and swung it open.

"If you double-cross me," said Drew, "all that I've ever done to any man before will be nothing to what I'll do to you, Glendin."

And the deputy cried, his voice gone shrill and

high, "I ain't done nothin' that ain't been done before!"

And he vanished through the doorway. Drew followed and looked after the deputy, who galloped like a fugitive over the hills.

"Shall I follow him?" he muttered to himself, but a faint groan reached him from the bedroom.

He turned on his heel and went back to Calamity Ben and the doctor.

CHAPTER XXXIV

CRITICISM

AFTER the first burst of speed, Bard resigned himself to following Sally, knowing that he could never catch her, first because her horse carried a burden so much lighter than his own, but above all because the girl seemed to know every rock and twist in the trail, and rode as courageously through the night as if it had been broad day.

She was following a course as straight as a crow's flight between the ranch of Drew and his old place, a desperate trail that veered and twisted up the side of the mountain and then lurched headlong down on the farther side of the crest. Half a dozen times Anthony checked his horse and shook his head at the trail, but always the figure of the girl, glimmering through the dusk ahead, challenged and drove him on.

Out of the sharp descent of the downward trail they broke suddenly onto the comparatively smooth floor of the valley, and he followed her at a

gallop which ended in front of the old house of
Drew. They had been far less than five hours on
the way, yet his long detour to the south had given
him three days of hard riding to cover the same
points. His desire to meet Logan again became
almost a passion. He swung to the ground, and
advanced to Sally with his hands outstretched.

"You've shown me the short cut, all right," he
said, "and I thank you a thousand times, Sally.
So-long, and good luck to you."

She disregarded his extended hand.

"Want me to leave you here, Bard?"

"You certainly can't stay."

She slipped from her horse and jerked the reins
over its head. In another moment she had untied
the cinch and drawn off the saddle. She held its
weight easily on one forearm. Actions, after all,
are more eloquent than words.

"I suppose," he said gloomily, "that if I'd asked
you to stay you'd have ridden off at once?"

She did not answer for a moment, and he
strained his eyes to read her expression through
the dark. At length she laughed with a new note
in her voice that drew her strangely close to him.
During the long ride he had come to feel toward
her as toward another man, as strong as himself,
almost, as fine a horseman, and much surer of

herself on that wild trail; but now the laughter in an instant rubbed all this away. It was rather low, and with a throaty quality of richness. The pulse of the sound was like a light finger tapping some marvellously sensitive chord within him.

"D'you think that?" she said, and went directly through the door of the house.

He heard the crazy floor creak beneath her weight; the saddle dropped with a thump; a match scratched and a flight of shadows shook across the doorway. The light did not serve to make the room visible; it fell wholly upon his own mind and troubled him like the waves which spread from the dropping of the smallest pebble and lap against the last shores of a pool. Dumfounded by her casual surety, he remained another moment with the rein in the hollow of his arm.

Finally he decided to mount as silently as possible and ride off through the night away from her. The consequences to her reputation if they spent the night so closely together was one reason; a more selfish and more moving one was the trouble which she gave him. The finding and disposing of Drew should be the one thing to occupy his thoughts, but the laughter of the girl the moment before had suddenly obsessed him, wiped out the rest of the world, enmeshed them hopelessly to-

gether in the solemn net of the night, the silence.
He resented it; in a vague way he was angry with
Sally Fortune.

His foot was in the stirrup when it occurred to
him that no matter how softly he withdrew she
would know and follow him. It seemed to Anthony that for the first time in his life he was not
alone. In other days social bonds had fallen very
lightly on him; the men he knew were acquaint-
ances, not friends; the women had been merely
border decorations, variations of light and shadow
which never shone really deep into the stream of
his existence; even his father had not been near
him; but by the irresistible force of circumstances
which he could not control, this girl was forced
bodily upon his consciousness.

Now he heard a cheery, faint crackling from the
house and a rosy glow pervaded the gloom beyond
the doorway. It brought home to Anthony the
fact that he was tired; weariness went through all
his limbs like the sound of music. Music in fact,
for the girl was singing softly—to herself.

He took his foot from the stirrup, unsaddled,
and carried the saddle into the room. He found
Sally crouched at the fire and piling bits of wood
on the rising flame. Her face was squinted to
avoid the smoke, and she sheltered her eyes with

one hand. At his coming she smiled briefly up at him and turned immediately back to the fire. The silence of that smile brought their comradeship sharply home to him. It was as if she understood his weariness and knew that the fire was infinitely comforting. Anthony frowned; he did not wish to be understood. It was irritating—indelicate.

He sat on one of the bunks, and when she took her place on the other he studied her covertly, with side glances, for he was beginning to feel strangely self-conscious. It was the situation rather than the girl that gained upon him, but he felt shamed that he should be so uncertain of himself and so liable to expose some weakness before the girl.

That in turn raised a blindly selfish desire to make her feel and acknowledge his mastery. He did not define the emotion exactly, nor see clearly what he wished to do, but in a general way he wanted to be necessary to her, and to let her know at the same time that she was nothing to him. He was quite sure that the opposite was the truth just now.

At this point he shrugged his shoulders, angry that he should have slipped so easily into the character of a sullen boy, hating a benefactor for no reason other than his benefactions; but the same vicious impulse made him study the face of Sally

Fortune with an impersonal, coldly critical eye.
It was not easy to do, for she sat with her head
tilted back a little, as though to take the warmth
of the fire more fully. The faint smile on her lips
showed her comfort, mingled with retrospection.

Here he lost the trend of his thoughts by beginning to wonder of what she could be thinking,
but he called himself back sharply to the analysis
of her features. It was a game with which he had
often amused himself among the girls of his eastern
acquaintance. Their beauty, after all, was their
only weapon, and when he discovered that that
weapon was not of pure steel, they became nothing;
it was like pushing them away with an arm of
infinite length.

There was food for criticism in Sally's features.
The nose, of course, was tipped up a bit, and the
mouth too large, but Anthony discovered that it
was almost impossible to centre his criticism on
either feature. The tip-tilt of the nose suggested a
quaint and infinitely buoyant spirit; the mouth, if
generously wide, was exquisitely made. She was
certainly not pretty, but he began to feel with
equal certainty that she was beautiful.

A waiting mood came on him while he watched,
as one waits through a great symphony and en-
dures the monotonous passages for the sake of the

singing bursts of harmony to which the commoner parts are a necessary background. He began to wish that she would turn her head so that he could see her eyes. They were like the inspired part of that same symphony, a beauty which could not be remembered and was always new, satisfying. He could make her turn by speaking, and knowing that this was so, he postponed the pleasure like a miser who will only count his gold once a day.

From the side view he dwelt on the short, delicately carved upper lip and the astonishingly pleasant curve of the cheek.

"Look at me," he said abruptly.

She turned, observed him calmly, and then glanced back to the fire. She asked no question.

Her chin rested on her hands, now, so that when she spoke her head nodded a little and gave a significance to what she said.

"The grey doesn't belong to you?"

So she was thinking of horses!

"Well," she repeated.

"No."

"Hoss-lifting," she mused.

"Why shouldn't I take a horse when they had shot down mine?"

She turned to him again, and this time her gaze went over him slowly, curiously, but without speaking she looked back to the fire, as though explanation of what "hoss-lifting" meant were something far beyond the grasp of his mentality. His anger rose again, childishly, sullenly, and he had to arm himself with indifference.

"Who'd you drop, Bard?"

"The one they call Calamity Ben."

"Is he done for?"

"Yes."

The turmoil of the scene of his escape came back to him so vividly that he wondered why it had ever been blurred to obscurity.

She said: "In a couple of hours we'd better ride on."

CHAPTER XXXV

ABANDON

THAT was all; no comment, no exclamation—she continued to gaze with that faint, retrospective smile toward the fire. He knew now why she angered him; it was because she had held the upper hand from the minute that ride over the short pass began—he had never once been able to assert himself impressively. He decided to try now.

"I don't intend to ride on."

"Too tired?"

He felt the clash of her will on his, even like flint against steel, whenever they spoke, and he began to wonder what spark would start a fire. It made him think of a game of poker, in a way, for he never knew what the next instant would place in his hands while the cards of chance were shuffled and dealt. Tired? There was a subtle, scoffing challenge hidden somewhere in that word.

"No, but I don't intend to go any farther from Drew."

Her smile grew more pronounced; she even looked to him with a frank amusement, for apparently she would not take him seriously.

"If I were you, he'd be the last man I'd want to be near."

"I suppose you would."

As if she picked up the gauntlet, she turned squarely on the bunk and faced him.

"You're going to hit the trail in an hour, understand?"

It delighted him—set him thrilling with excitement to feel her open anger and the grip of her will against his; he had to force a frown in order to conceal a smile.

"If I do, it will be to ride back toward Drew."

Her lips parted to make an angry retort, and then he watched her steel herself with patience, like a mother teaching an old lesson to a child.

"D'you know what you'd be like, wanderin' around these mountains without a guide?"

"Well?"

"Like a kid in a dark, lonesome room. You'd travel in a circle and fall into their hands in a day."

"Possibly."

She was still patient.

"Follow me close, Bard. I mean that if you

don't do what I say I'll cut loose and leave you alone here."

He was silent, enjoying her sternness, glad to have roused her, no matter what the consequences; knowing that each second heightened the climax.

Apparently she interpreted his speechlessness in a different way. She said after a moment: "That sounds like quittin' cold on you. I won't do it unless you try some fool thing like riding back toward Drew."

He waited again as long as he dared, then: "Don't you see that the last thing I want is to keep you with me?"

There was no pleasure in that climax. She sat with parted lips, her hands clasped tightly in her lap, staring at him. He became as vividly conscious of her femininity as he had been when she laughed in the dark. There was the same sustained pulsing, vital emotion in this silence.

He explained hastily: "A girl's reputation is a fragile thing, Sally."

And she recovered herself with a start, but not before he saw and understood. It was as if, in the midst of an exciting hand, with the wagers running high, he had seen her cards and knew that his own hand was higher. The pleasant sense of mastery made a warmth through him.

"Meaning that they'd talk about me? Bard, they've already said enough things about me to fill a book—notes and all, with a bunch of pictures thrown in. What I can't live down I fight down, and no man never says the same thing twice about me. It ain't healthy. If that's all that bothers you, close your eyes and let me lead you out of this mess."

He hunted about for some other way to draw her out. After all, it was an old, old game. He had played it before many a time; though the setting and the lights had been different the play was always the same—a man, and a woman.

She was explaining: "And it *is* a mess. Maybe you could get out after droppin' Calamity, because it was partly self-defence, but there ain't nothin' between here and God that can get you off from liftin' a hoss. No, sir, not even returning the hoss won't do no good. I know! The only thing is speed—and a thousand miles east of here you can stop ridin'."

He found the thing to say, and he made his voice earnest and low to give the words wing and sharpness; it was like the bum of the bow string after the arrow is launched, so tense was the tremor of his tone.

"There are two reasons why I can't leave. The first is Drew. I must get back to him."

"Why d'you want Drew? Let me tell you, Bard, he's a bigger job than ten tenderfeet like you could handle. Why, mothers scare their babies asleep by tellin' of the things that William Drew has done."

"I can't tell you why. In fact, I don't altogether know the complete why and wherefore. It's enough that I have to meet him and finish him!"

Her fingers interlaced and gripped; he wondered at their slenderness; and leaning back so that his face fell under a slant, black shadow, he enjoyed the flame of the firelight, turning her brown hair to amber and gold. White and round and smooth and perfect was the column of her throat, and it trembled with the stir of her voice.

"The most fool idea I ever heard. Sounds like something in a dream—a nightmare. What d'you want to do, Anthony, make yourself famous? You will be, all right; they'll put up your tomb-stone by a public subscription."

He would not answer, sure of himself; waiting, tingling with enjoyment.

As he expected, she said: "Go on; is the other reason as good as that one?"

Making his expression grim, he leaned suddenly forward, and though the width of the room sepa-rated them, she drew back a little, as though the

shadow of his coming cast a forewarning shade
across her. He heard her breath catch, and as if
some impalpable and joyous spirit rushed to meet
and mingle with his, something from her, a spirit
as warm as the fire, as faintly, keenly sweet as an
air from a night-dark, unseen garden blowing in his
face.

"The other reason is you, Sally Fortune. You
can't go with me as far as I must go; and I can't
leave you behind."

Ah, there it was! He had fumbled at the keys
of the organ in the dark; he had spread his fingers
amply and pressed down; behold, back from the
cathedral lofts echoed a rising music of surpassing
beauty. Like the organist, he sank back again in
the shadow and wondered at the phrase of melody.
Surely he had not created it? Then what? God,
perhaps. For her lips parted to a smile that was
suggested rather than seen, a tender, womanly
sweetness that played about her mouth; and a light
came in her eyes that would never wholly die from
them. Afterward he would feel shame for what he
had done, but now he was wholly wrapped in the
new thing that had been born in her, like a bird
striving to fly in the teeth of a great storm, and
giving back with reeling, drumming wings, a beautiful and touching sight.

Her lips framed words that made no sound. Truly, she was making a gallant struggle. Then she said: "Anthony!" She was pale with the struggle, now, but she rose bravely to her part. She even laughed, though it fell short like an arrow dropping in front of the target.

"Listen, Bard, you make a pretty good imitation of Samson, but I ain't cut out for any Delilah. If I'm holding you here, why, cut and run and forget it."

She drew a long breath and went on more confidently: "It ain't any use; I'm not cut out for any man—I'd so much rather be—free. I've tried to get interested in others, but it never works."

She laughed again, more surely, and with a certain hardness like the ringing of metal against metal, or the after rhythm from the peal of a bell. With deft, flying fingers she rolled a cigarette, lighted it, and sat down cross-legged.

Through the first outward puff of smoke went these words: "The only thing that's a woman about me is skirts. That's straight."

Yet he knew that his power was besieging her on every side. Her power seemed gone, and she was like a rare flower in the hollow of his hand; all that he had to do was to close his fingers, and— He despised himself for it, but he could not resist

Moreover, he half counted on her pride to make her break away.

"Then if it's hopeless, Sally Fortune, go now."

She answered, with an upward tilt of her chin: "Don't be a fool, Anthony. If I can't be a woman to you, at least I can be a pal—the best you've had in these parts. Nope, I'll see you through. Better saddle now——"

"And start back for Drew?"

There was the thrust that made her start, as if the knife went through tender flesh.

"Are you such a plumb fool as that?"

"Go now, Sally. I tell you, it's no use. I won't leave the trail of Drew."

It was only the outward stretch of her arm, only the extension of her hand, palm up, but it was as if her whole nature expanded toward him in tenderness.

"Oh, Anthony, if you care for me, don't stay in reach of Drew! You're breaking——"

She stopped and closed her eyes.

"Breakin' all the rules, like any tenderfoot would be expected to do."

She glanced at him, wistful, to see whether or not she had smoothed it over; his face was a blank.

"You won't go?"

"Nope."

He insisted cruelly: "Why?"

"Because—because—well, can I leave a baby alone near a fire? Not me!"

Her voice changed. The light and the life was gone from it, but not all the music. It was low, a little hoarse.

"I guess we can stay here tonight without no danger. And in the morning—well, the morning can take care of itself. I'm going to turn in."

He rose obediently and stood at the door, facing the night. From behind came the rustle of clothes, and the sense of her followed and surrounded and stood at his shoulder calling to him to turn. He had won, but he began to wonder if it had not been a Pyrrhic victory.

At length: "All right, Anthony. It's your turn."

She was lying on her side, facing the wall, a little heap of clothes on the foot of her bunk, and the lithe lines of her body something to be guessed at—sensed beneath the heavy blanket. He slipped into his own bunk and lay a moment watching the heavy drift of shadows across the ceiling. He strove to think, but the waves of light and dark blotted from his mind all except the feeling of her nearness, that indefinable power keen as the fragrance of a garden, which had never quite become disentangled from his spirit. She was there, so close. If he called, she would answer; if she answered——

He turned to the wall, shut his eyes, and closed his mind with a Spartan effort. His breathing came heavily, regularly, like one who slept or one who is running. Over that sound he caught at length another light rustling, and then the faint creak as she crossed the crazy floor. He made his face calm—forced his breath to grow more soft and regular.

Then, as if a shadow in which there is warmth had crossed him, he knew that she was leaning above him, close, closer; he could hear her breath. In a rush of tenderness, he forgot her beauty of eyes and round, strong throat, and supple body— he forgot, and was immersed, like an eagle winging into a radiant sunset cloud, in a sense only of her being, quite divorced from the flesh, the mysterious rare power which made her Sally Fortune, and would not change no matter what body might contain it.

It was blindingly intense, and when his senses cleared he knew that she was gone. He felt as if he had awakened from a night full of dreams more vivid than life—dreams which left him too weak to cope with reality.

For a time he dared not move. He was feeling

for himself like a man who fumbles his way down a dark passage dangerous with obstructions. At last it was as if his hand touched the knob of a door; he swung it open, entered a room full of dazzling light—himself. He shrank back from it; closed his eyes against what he might see.

All he knew, then, was an overpowering will to see her. He turned, inch by inch, little degree by degree, knowing that if, when he turned, he looked into her eyes, the end would rush upon them, overwhelm them, carry them along like straws on the flooding river. At last his head was turned; he looked.

She lay on her back, smiling as she slept. One arm hung down from the bunk and the graceful fingers trailed, palm up, on the floor, curling a little, as if she had just relaxed her grasp on something. And down past her shoulder, half covering the whiteness of her arm, fled the torrent of brown hair, with the firelight playing through it like a sunlit mist.

He rose, and dressed with a deadly caution, for he knew that he must go at once, partly for her sake that he must be seen apart from her this night —partly because he knew that he must leave and never come back.

He had hit upon the distinctive feature of the

girl—a purity as thin and clear as the air of the uplands in which she drew breath. He stooped and smoothed down the blankets of his bunk, for no trace of him must be seen if any other man should come during this night. He would go far away—see and be seen—apart from Sally Fortune. He picked up his saddle.

Before he departed he leaned low above her as she must have done above him, until the dark shadow of lashes was tremulous against her cheek. Then he straightened and stole step by step across the floor, to the door, to the night; all the myriad small white eyes of the heavens looked down to him in hushed surprise.

CHAPTER XXXVI

JERRY WOOD

WHEN he was at the old Drew place before, Logan had told him of Jerry Wood's place, five miles to the north among the hills; and to this he now directed his horse, riding at a merciless speed, as if he strove to gain, from the swift succession of rocks and trees that whirled past him, new thoughts to supplant the ones which already occupied him.

He reached in a short time a little rise of ground below which stretched a darkly wooded hollow, and in the midst the trees gave back from a small house, a two-storied affair, with not a light showing. He wished to announce himself and his name at this place under the pretence of asking harbourage for the brief remainder of the night. The news of what he had done at Drew's place could not have travelled before him to Wood's house; but the next day it would be sure to come, and Wood could say that he had seen Bard—alone—the previous night.

It would be a sufficient shield for the name of Sally.
Fortune in that incurious region.

So he banged loudly at the door.

Eventually a light showed in an upper window,
and a voice cried: "Who's there?"

"Anthony Bard."

"Who the devil is Anthony Bard?"

"Lost in the hills. Can you give me a place to
sleep for the rest of the night? I'm about done
up."

"Wait a minute."

Voices stirred in the upper part of the house;
the lantern disappeared; steps sounded, descending the stairs, and then the door was unbarred and
held a cautious inch ajar. The ray of light jumped
out at Bard like an accusing arm.

Evidently a brief survey convinced Jerry Wood
that the stranger was no more than what he pretended. He opened the door wide and stepped
back.

"Come in."

Bard moved inside, taking off his hat.

"How d'you happen to be lost in the hills?"

"I'm a bit of a stranger around here, you see."

The other surveyed him with a growing grin.

"I guess maybe you are. Sure, we'll put you up
for the night. Where's your hoss?"

He went out and raised the lantern above his head to look. The light shone back from the lustrous, wide eyes of the grey.

Wood turned to Bard.

"Seems to me I've seen that hoss."

"Yes. I bought it from Duffy out at Drew's place."

"Oh! Friend of Mr. Drew?"

Half a life spent on the mountain-desert had not been enough to remove from Drew that distinguishing title of respect. The range has more great men than it has "misters."

"Not exactly a friend," answered Bard.

"'Sall right. Long's you know him, you're as good as gold with me. Come on along to the barn, and we'll knock down a feed for the hoss."

He chuckled as he led the way.

"For that matter, there ain't any I know that can say they're friends to William Drew, though there's plenty that would like to if they thought they could get away with it. How's he lookin'?"

"Why, big and grey."

"Sure. He never changes none. Time and years don't mean nothin' to Drew. He started bein' a man when most of us is in short pants; he'll keep on bein' a man till he goes out. He ain't got many friends—real ones—but I don't know of any enemies, neither. All the time he's been on the range Drew has never done a crooked piece of work. Every decent man on the range would take his word ag'in'—well, ag'in' the Bible, for that matter."

They reached the barn at the end of this encomium, and Bard unsaddled his horse. The other watched him critically.

"Know somethin' about hosses, eh?"

"A little."

"When I seen you, I put you down for a tenderfoot. Don't mind, do you? The way you talked put me out."

"For that matter, I suppose I am a tenderfoot."

"Speakin' of tenderfoots, I heard of one over to Eldara the other night that raised considerable hell. You ain't him, are you?"

He lifted the lantern again and fixed his keen eyes on Bard.

"However," he went on, lowering the lantern with an apologetic laugh, "I'm standin' here askin' questions and chatterin' like a woman, and what you're thinkin' of is bed, eh? Come on with me."

Upstairs in the house he found Bard a corner room with a pile of straw in the corner by way of a mattress. There he spread out some blankets, wished his guest a good sleep, and departed.

Left to himself, Anthony stretched out flat on his back. It had been a wild, hard day, but he felt not the slightest touch of weariness; all he wished was to relax his muscles for a few moments. Moreover, he must be away from the house with the dawn—first, because Sally Fortune might waken, guess where he had gone, and follow him; secondly because the news of what had happened at Drew's place might reach Wood at any hour.

So he lay trying to fight the thought of Sally from his mind and concentrate on some way of getting back to Drew without riding the gauntlet of the law.

The sleep which stole upon him came by slow degrees; or, rather, he was not fully asleep, when a sound outside the house roused him to sharp consciousness compared with which his drowsiness had been a sleep.

It was a knocking at the door, not loud, but repeated. At the same time he heard Jerry Wood cursing softly in a neighbouring room, and then the telltale creak of bedsprings.

The host was rousing himself a second time that night. Or, rather, it was morning now, for when Anthony sat up he saw that the hills were stepping out of the shadows of the night, black, ugly shapes revealed by a grey background of the sky. A window went up noisily.

"Am I runnin' a hotel?" roared Jerry Wood. "Ain't I to have no sleep no more? Who are ye?"

A lowered, muttering voice answered.

"All right," said Jerry, changing his tone at once. "I'll come down."

His steps descended the noisy stairs rapidly; the door creaked. Then voices began again outside the house, an indistinct mumble, rising to one sharp height in an exclamation.

Almost at once steps again sounded on the stairs, but softly now. Bard went quietly to the door, locked it, and stole back to the window. Below it extended the roof of a shed, joining the main body of the house only a few feet under his window and sloping to what could not have been a dangerous distance from the ground. He raised the window-sash.

Yet he waited, something as he had waited for Sally Fortune to speak earlier in the night, with a sense of danger, but a danger which thrilled and delighted him. No game of polo could match suspense like this. Besides, he would be foolish to go before he was sure.

The walls were gaping with cracks that carried the sounds, and now he heard a sibilant whisper with a perfect clearness.

"This is the room."

There was a click as the lock was tried.

"Locked, damn it!"

"Shut up, Butch. Jerry, have you got a bar, or anything? We'll pry it down and break in on him before he can get in action."

"You're a fool, McNamara. That feller don't take a wink to get into action. Sure he didn't hear you when you hollered out the window? That was a fool move, Wood."

"I don't think he heard. There wasn't any sound from his room when I passed it goin' downstairs. Think of the nerve of this bird comin' here to roost after what he done."

"He didn't think we'd follow him so fast."

But Anthony waited for no more. He slipped out on the roof of the shed, lowered himself hand below hand to the edge, and dropped lightly to the ground.

The grey, at his coming, flattened back its ears, as though it knew that more hard work was coming, but he saddled rapidly, led it outside, and rode a short distance into the forest. There he stopped.

His course lay due north, and then a swerve to the side and a straight course west for the ranch of William Drew. If the hounds of the law were so close on his trace, they certainly would never suspect him of doubling back in this manner, and he would have the rancher to himself when he arrived.

Yet still he did not start the grey forward to the north. For to the south lay Sally Fortune, and at the thought of her a singular hollowness came about his heart, a loneliness, not for himself, but for her. Yes, in a strange way all self was blotted from his emotion.

It would be a surrender to turn back—now.

And like a defeated man who rides in a lost cause, he swung the grey to the south and rode back over the trail, his head bowed.

CHAPTER XXXVII

"TODO ES PERDO"

IT was not long after the departure of Bard that Sally Fortune awoke. For a step had creaked on the floor, and she looked up to find Steve Nash standing in the centre of the room with the firelight gloomily about him; behind, blocking the door with his squat figure, stood Shorty Kilrain.

"Where's your side-kicker?" asked Nash. "Where's Bard?"

And looking across the room, she saw that the other bunk was empty. She raised her arms quickly, as if to stifle a yawn, and sat up in the bunk, holding the blanket close about her shoulders. The face she showed to Nash was calmly contemptuous.

"The bird seems to be flown, eh?" she queried.

"Where is he?" he repeated, and made a step nearer.

She knew at last that her power over him as a woman was gone; she caught the danger of his tone, saw it in the steadiness of the eyes he fixed upon her. Behind was a great, vague feeling of loss, the old hollowness about the heart. It made her reckless of consequences; and when Nash asked, "Is he hangin' around behind the corner, maybe?" she cried:

"If he was that close you'd have sense enough to run, Steve."

The snarl of Nash showed his teeth.

"Out with it. The tenderfoot ain't left his woman fur away. Where's he gone? Who's he gone to shoot in the back? Where's the hoss he started out to rustle?"

"Kind of peeved, Nash, eh?"

One step more he made, towering above her.

"I've done bein' polite, Sally. I've asked you a question."

"And I've answered you: I don't know."

"Sally, I'm patient; I don't mean no wrong to you. What you've been to me I'm goin' to bust myself tryin' to forget; but don't lie to me now."

Such a far greater woe kept up a throbbing ache in the hollow of her throat that now she laughed, laughed slowly, deliberately. He leaned, caught her wrist in a crushing pressure.

"You demon; you she-devil!"

She whirled out of the bunk, the blanket caught

about her like the toga of some ancient Roman girl; and as she moved she had swept up something heavy and bright from the floor.

All this, and still his grip was on her left arm.

"Drop your hand, Nash."

With a falling of the heart, she knew that he did not fear her gun; instead, a light of pleasure gleamed in his eyes and his lower jaw thrust out.

She would never forget his face as he looked that moment.

"Will you tell me?"

"I'll see you in hell first."

By that wrist he drew her resistlessly toward him, and his other arm went about her and crushed her close; hate, shame, rage, love were in the contorted face above her. She pressed the muzzle of her revolver against his side.

"You're in beckoning distance of that hell, Steve!"

"You she-wolf—shoot and be damned! I'd live long enough to strangle you."

"You know me, Steve; don't be a fool."

"Know you? Nobody knows you. And God Almighty, Sally, I love you worse'n ever; love the very way you hate me. Come here!"

He jerked her closer still, leaned; and she remembered then that Anthony had never kissed her. She said:

"You're safe; you know he can't see you."

He threw her from him and stood snarling like a dog growling for the bone it fears to touch because there may be poison in the taste—a starving dog, and a bone full of toothsome marrow which has only to be crushed in order that it may be enjoyed.

"I'm wishin' nothin' more than that he could see me."

"Then you're a worse fool than I took you for, Steve. You know he'd go through ten like you."

"There ain't no man has gone through me yet."

"But he would. You know it. He's not stronger, maybe not so strong. But he was born to win, Steve; he's like—he's like Drew, in a way. He can't fail."

"If I wrung that throat of yours," he said, "I know I couldn't get out of you where he's gone."

"Because I don't know, you see."

"Don't know?"

"He's given me the slip."

"You!"

"Funny, ain't it? But he has. Thought I couldn't ride fast enough to keep up with him, maybe. He's gone on east, of course."

"That's another lie."

"Well, you know."

"I do."

His voice changed.

"Has he really beat it away from you, Sally?"

She watched him with a strange, sneering smile. Then she stepped close.

"Lean your ear down to me, Steve."

He obeyed.

"I'll tell you what ought to make you happy. He don't care for me no more than I care for—you, Steve."

He straightened again, wondering.

"And you?"

"I threw myself at him. I dunno why I'm tellin' you, except it's right that you should know. But he don't want me; he's gone on without me."

"An' you like him still?"

She merely stared, with a sick smile.

"My God!" he murmured, shaken deep with wonder. "What's he made of?"

"Steel and fire—that's all."

"Listen, Sally, forget what I've done, and——"

"Would you drop his trail, Steve?"

He cursed through his set teeth.

"If that's it—no. It's him or me, and I'm sure to beat him out. Afterwards you'll forget him."

"Try me."

"Girls have said that before. I'll wait. There ain't no one but you for me—damn you—I know that. I'll get him first, and then I'll wait."

"Ten like you couldn't get him."

"I've six men behind me."

She was still defiant, but her colour changed.

"Six, Sally, and he's out here among the hills, not knowing his right from his left. I ask you: has he got a chance?"

She answered: "No; not one."

He turned on his heel, beckoned to Kilrain, who had stood moveless through the strange dialogue, and went out into the night.

As they mounted he said: "We're going straight for the place where I told Butch Conklin I'd meet him. Then the bunch of us will come back."

"Why waste time?"

"Because he's sure to come back. Shorty, after a feller has seen Sally smile—the way she can smile —he couldn't keep away. I *know!*"

They rode off at a slow trot, like men who have resigned themselves to a long journey, and Sally watched them from the door. She sat down, cross-legged, before the fire, and stirred the embers, and strove to think.

But she was not equipped for thinking, all her

life had been merely action, action, action, and now, as she strove to build out some logical sequence and find her destiny in it, she failed miserably, and fell back upon herself. She was one of those single-minded people who give themselves up to emotion rarely, but when they do their whole body, their whole soul burns in the flame.

Into her mind came a phrase she had heard in her childhood. On the outskirts of Eldara there was a little shack owned by a Mexican—José, he was called, and nothing else, "Greaser" José. One night an alarm of fire was given in Eldara, and the whole populace turned out to enjoy the sight; it was a festival occasion, in a way. It was the house of Greaser José.

The cowpunchers manned a bucket line, but the source of water was far away, the line too long, and the flames gained faster than they could be quenched. All through the work of fire-fighting Greaser José was everywhere about the house, flinging buckets of water through the windows into the red furnace within; his wife and the two children stood stupidly, staring, dumb. But in the end, when the fire was towering above the roof of the house, roaring and crackling, the Mexican suddenly raised a long arm and called to the bucket line, "It is done. *Señors*, I thank you."

Then he had folded his arms and repeated in a monotone, over and over again: "*Todo es perdo; todo es perdo!*"

His wife came to him, frantic, wailing, and threw her arms around his neck. He merely repeated with heavy monotony: "*Todo es perdo; todo es perdo!*"

The phrase clung in the mind of the girl; and she rose at last and went back to her bunk, repeating: "*Todo es perdo; todo es perdo!* All is lost; all is lost!"

No tears were in her eyes; they were wide and solemn, looking up to the shadows of the ceiling, and so she went to sleep with the solemn Spanish phrase echoing through her whole being: "*Todo es perdo!*"

She woke with the smell of frying bacon pungent in her nostrils.

CHAPTER XXXVIII

BACON

THE savour of roasting chicken, that first delicious burst of aroma when the oven door is opened, would tempt an angel from heaven down to the lowly earth. A Southerner declares that his nostrils can detect at a prodigious distance the cooking of "possum and taters." A Kanaka has a cosmopolitan appetite, but the fragrance which moves him most nearly is the scent of fish baking in Ti leaves. A Frenchman waits unmoved until the perfume of some rich lamb ragout, an air laden with spices, is wafted toward him.

Every man and every nation has a special dish, in general; there is only one whose appeal is universal. It is not for any class or nation; it is primarily for "the hungry man," no matter what has given him an appetite. It may be that he has pushed a pen all day, or reckoned up vast columns, or wielded a sledge-hammer, or ridden a wild horse from morning to night; but the savour of peculiar excellence to the nostrils of this universal hungry man is the smell of frying bacon.

A keen appetite is even stronger than sorrow, and when Sally Fortune awoke with that strong perfume in her nostrils, she sat straight up among the blankets, startled as the cavalry horse by the sound of the trumpet. What she saw was Anthony Bard kneeling by the coals of the fire over which steamed a coffee-pot on one side and a pan of crisping bacon on the other.

The vision shook her so that she rubbed her eyes and stared again to make sure. It did not seem possible that she had actually wakened during the night and found him gone, and with this reality before her she was strongly tempted to believe that the coming of Nash was only a vivid dream.

"Morning, Anthony."

He turned his head quickly and smiled to her.

"Hello, Sally."

He was back at once, turning the bacon, which was done on the first side. Seeing that his back was turned, she dressed quickly.

"How'd you sleep?"

"Well."

"Where?"

He turned more slowly this time.

"You woke up in the middle of the night?"

"Yes."

"What wakened you?"

"Nash and Kilrain."

He sighed: "I wish I'd been here."

She answered: "I'll wash up; we'll eat; and then off on the trail. I've an idea that the two will be back, and they'll have more men behind them."

After a little her voice called from the outside: "Anthony, have you had a look at the morning?"

He came obediently to the doorway. The sun had not yet risen, but the fresh, rose-coloured light already swept around the horizon throwing the hills in sharp relief and flushing, far away, the pure snows of the Little Brothers. And so blinding was the sheen of the lake that it seemed at first as though the sun were about to break from the waters, for there all the radiance of the sunrise was reflected, concentrated.

Looking in this manner from the doorway, with the water on either side and straight ahead, and the dark, narrow point of land cutting that colour like a prow, it seemed to Anthony almost as if he stood on the bridge of a ship which in another moment would gather head and sail out toward the sea of fresh beauty beyond the peaks, for the old house of William Drew stood on a small peninsula, thrusting out into the lake, a low, shelving shore, scattered with trees.

Where the little tongue of land joined the main shore the ground rose abruptly into a shoulder of rocks inaccessible to a horse; the entrance and exit to the house must be on either side of this shoulder hugging closely the edge of the water.

Feeling that halo of the morning about them, for a moment Anthony forgot all things in the lift and exhilaration of the keen air; and he accepted the girl as a full and equal partner in his happiness, looking to her for sympathy.

She knelt by the edge of the water, face and throat shining and wet, her head bending back, her lips parted and smiling. It thrilled him as if she were singing a silent song which made the brightness of the morning and the colour beyond the peaks. He almost waited to see her throat quiver—hear the high, sweet tone.

But a scent of telltale sharpness drew him a thousand leagues down and made him whirl with a cry of dismay: "The bacon, Sally!"

It was hopelessly burned; some of it was even charred on the bottom of the pan. Sally, returning on the run, took charge of the cookery and went about it with a speed and ability that kept him silent; which being the ideal mood for a spectator, he watched and found himself learning much.

Whatever that scene of the night before meant in the small and definite, in the large and vague it meant that he had a claim of some sort on Sally Fortune and it is only when a man feels that he has this claim, this proprietorship, as it were, that he begins to see a woman clearly.

Before this his observance has been half blind through prejudice either for or against; he either sees her magnified with adulation, or else the large end of the glass is placed against his eye and she is merely a speck in the distance. But let a woman step past that mysterious wall which separates the formal from the intimate—only one step—at once she is surrounded by the eyes of a man as if by a thousand spies. So it was with Anthony.

It moved him, for instance, to see the supple strength of her fingers when she was scraping the charred bacon from the bottom of the pan, and he was particularly fascinated by the undulations of the small, round wrist. He glanced down to his own hand, broad and bony in comparison.

It was his absorption in this criticism that served to keep him aloof from her while they ate, and the girl felt it like an arm pushing her away. She had been very close to him not many hours before; now she was far away. She could understand nothing but the pain of it.

As he finished his coffee he said, staring into a corner: "I don't know why I came back to you, Sally."

"You didn't mean to come back when you started?"

"Of course not.

She flushed, and her heart beat loudly to hear his weakness. He was keeping nothing from her; he was thinking aloud; she felt that the bars between them were down again.

"In the first place I went because I had to be seen and known by name in some place far away from you. That was for your sake. In the second place I had to be alone for the work that lay ahead."

"Drew?"

"Yes. It all worked like a charm. I went to the house of Jerry Wood, told him my name, stayed there until Conklin and several others arrived, hunting for me, and then gave them the slip."

She did not look up from her occupation, which was the skilful cleaning of her gun.

"It was perfect; the way clear before me; I had dodged through their lines, so to speak, when I gave

Conklin the slip, and I could ride straight for Drew and catch him unprepared. Isn't that clear?"

"But you didn't?"

She was so calm about it that he grew a little angry; she would not look up from the cleaning of the gun.

"That's the devil of it; I couldn't stay away. I had to come back to you."

She restored the gun to her holster and looked steadily at him; he felt a certain shock in countering her glance.

"Because I thought you might be lonely, Sally."

"I was."

It was strange to see how little fencing there was between them. They were like men, long tried in friendship and working together on a great problem full of significance to both.

"Do you know what I kept sayin' to myself when I found you was gone?"

"Well?"

"*Todo es perdo; todo es perdo!*"

She had said it so often to herself that now some of the original emotion crept into her voice. His arm went out; they shook hands across their breakfast pans.

She went on: "The next thing is Drew?"

"Yes."

"There's no changing you." She did not wait for his answer. "I know that. I won't ask questions. If it has to be done we'll do it quickly; and afterward I can find a way out for us both."

Something like a foreknowledge came to him, telling him that the thing would never be done—that he had surrendered his last chance of Drew when he turned back to go to Sally. It was as if he took a choice between the killing of the man and the love of the woman. But he said nothing of his forebodings and helped her quietly to rearrange the small pack. They saddled and took the trail which pointed up over the mountains—the same trail which they had ridden in an opposite direction the night before.

He rode with his head turned, taking his last look at the old house of Drew, with its blackened, crumbling sides, when the girl cried softly: "What's that? Look!"

He stared in the direction of her pointing arm. They were almost directly under the shoulder of rocks which loomed above the trail along the edge of the lake. Anthony saw nothing.

"What was it?"

He checked his horse beside hers.

"I thought I saw something move. I'm not sure. And there—back, Anthony!"

And she whirled her horse. He caught it this time clearly, the unmistakable glint of the morning light on steel, and he turned the grey sharply. At the same time a rattling blast of revolver shots crackled above them; the grey reared and pitched back.

By inches he escaped the fall of the horse, slipping from the saddle in the nick of time. A bullet whipped his hat from his head. Then the hand of the girl clutched his shoulder.

"Stirrup and saddle, Anthony!"

He seized the pommel of the saddle, hooked his foot into the stirrup which she abandoned to him, and she spurred back toward the old house.

A shout followed them, a roar that ended in a harsh rattle of curses; they heard the spat of bullets several times on the trees past which they whirled. But it was only a second before they were once more in the shelter of the house. He stood in the centre of the room, stunned, staring stupidly around him. It was not fear of death that benumbed him, but a rising horror that he should be so trapped—like a wild beast cornered and about to be worried to death by dogs.

As for escape, there was simply no chance—it was impossible. On three sides the lake, still beautiful, though the colour was fading from it, effectively blocked their way. On the fourth and narrowest side there was the shoulder of rocks, not only blocking them, but affording a perfect shelter for Nash and his men, for they did not doubt that it was he.

"They think they've got us," said a fiercely exultant voice beside him, "but we ain't started to make all the trouble we're goin' to make."

Life came back to him as he looked at her. She was trembling with excitement, but it was the tremor of eagerness, not the unmistakable sick palsy of fear. He drew out a large handkerchief of fine, white linen and tied it to a long splinter of wood which he tore away from one of the rotten boards.

"Go out with this," he said. "They aren't after you, Sally. This is west of the Rockies, thank God, and a woman is safe with the worst man that ever committed murder."

She said: "D'you mean this, Anthony?"

"I'm trying to mean it."

She snatched the stick and snapped it into small pieces.

"Does that look final, Anthony?"

He could not answer for a moment. At last he said: "What a woman you would have made for a wife, Sally Fortune; what a fine pal!"

But she laughed, a mirth not forced and harsh, but clear and ringing.

"Anthony, ain't this better'n marriage?"

"By God," he answered, "I almost think you're right."

For answer a bullet ripped through the right-hand wall and buried itself in a beam on the opposite side of the room.

"Listen!" she said.

There was a fresh crackle of guns, the reports louder and longer drawn.

"Rifles," said Sally Fortune. "I knew no bullet from a six-gun could carry like that one."

The little, sharp sounds of splintering and crunching began everywhere. A cloud of soot spilled down the chimney and across the hearth. A furrow ploughed across the floor, lifting a splinter as long and even as if it had been grooved out by a machine.

"Look!" said Sally, "they're firin' breast high to catch us standing, and on the level of the floor to get us if we lie down. That's Nash. I know his trademark."

"From the back of the house we can answer them," said Bard. "Let's try it."

"Pepper for their salt, eh?" answered Sally, and they ran back through the old shack to the last room.

CHAPTER XXXIX

LEGAL MURDER

As Drew entered his bedroom he found the doctor in the act of restoring the thermometer to its case. His coat was off and his sleeves rolled up to the elbow; he looked more like a man preparing to chop wood than a physician engaging in a struggle with death; but Dr. Young had the fighting strain. Otherwise he would never have persisted in Eldara.

Already the subtle atmosphere of sickness had come upon the room. The shades of the windows were drawn evenly, and low down, so that the increasing brightness of the morning could only temper, not wholly dismiss the shadows. Night is the only reality of the sick-bed; the day is only a long evening, a waiting for the utter dark. The doctor's little square satchel of instruments, vials, and bandages lay open on the table; he had changed the apartment as utterly as he had changed his face by putting on great, horn-rimmed

343

spectacles. They gave an owl-like look to him, an air of omniscience. It seemed as if no mortal ailment could persist in the face of such wisdom.

"Well?" whispered Drew.

"You can speak out, but not loudly," said the doctor calmly. "He's delirious; the fever is getting its hold."

"What do you think?"

"Nothing. The time hasn't come for thinking."

He bent his emotionless eye closer on the big rancher.

"You," he said, "ought to be in bed this moment."

Drew waved the suggestion aside.

"Let me give you a sedative," added Young.

"Nonsense. I'm going to stay here."

The doctor gave up the effort; dismissed Drew from his mind, and focused his glance on the patient once more. Calamity Ben was moving his head restlessly from side to side, keeping up a gibbering mutter. It rose now to words.

"Joe, a mule is to a hoss what a woman is to a man. Ever notice? The difference ain't so much in what they do as what they don't do. Me speakin' personal, I'll take a lot from any hoss and lay it to jest plain spirit; but a mule can make me mad by standin' still and doin' nothing but wabblin' them long ears as if it understood things it wasn't goin' to speak about. Y' always feel around a mule as if it knew somethin' about you— had somethin' on you—and was laughin' soft and deep inside. Damn a mule! I remember——"

But here he sank into the steady, voiceless whisper again, the shadow of a sound rather than the reality. It was ghostly to hear, even by daylight.

"Will it keep up long?" asked Drew.

"Maybe until he dies."

"I've told you before; it's impossible for him to die."

The doctor made a gesture of resignation.

He explained: "As long as this fever grows our man will steadily weaken; it shows that he's on the downward path. If it breaks—why, that means that he will have a chance—more than a chance—to get well. It will mean that he has enough reserve strength to fight off the shock of the wound and survive the loss of the blood."

"It will mean," said Drew, apparently thinking aloud, "that the guilt of murder does not fall on Anthony."

"Who is Anthony?"

The wounded man broke in; his voice rose high and sharp: "Halt!"

He went on, in a sighing mumble: "Shorty—help—I'm done for!"

"The shooting," said the doctor, who had kept his fingers on the wrist of his patient; "I could feel his pulse leap and stop when he said that."

"He said 'halt!' first; a very clear sign that he tried to stop Bard before Bard shot. Doctor, you're witness to that?"

He had grown deeply excited.

"I'm witness to nothing. I never dreamed that you could be so interested in any human being."

He nodded to himself.

"Do you know how I explained your greyness to myself? As that of a man ennuied with life—tired of living because he had nothing in the world to occupy his affections. And here I find you so far from being ennuied that you are using your whole strength to keep the guilt of murder away from another man. It's amazing. The boys will never believe it."

He continued: "A man who raised a riot in your own house, almost burned down your place, shot your man, stole a horse—gad, Drew, you are sublime!"

But if he expected an explanatory answer from the rancher he was disappointed. The latter pulled up a chair beside the bed and bent his stern eyes

on the patient as if he were concentrating all of
a great will on bringing] Calamity Ben back to
health.

He worked with the doctor. Every half hour a
temperature was taken, and it was going up steadily. Drew heard the report each time with a
tightening of the muscles about his jaws. He
helped pack the wounded man with wet cloths.
He ran out and stopped a wrangling noise of the
cowpunchers several times. But mostly he sat
without motion beside the bed, trying to will the
sufferer back to life.

And in the middle of the morning, after taking
a temperature, the doctor looked to the rancher
with a sort of dull wonder.

"It's dropping?" whispered Drew.

"It's lower. I don't think it's dropping. It
can't be going down so soon. Wait till the next
time I register it. If it's still lower then—he'll get
well."

The grey man sagged forward from his chair
to his knees and took the hands of Calamity, long-
fingered, bony, cold hands they were. There he
remained, moveless, his keen eyes close to the
wandering stare of the delirious man. Out of the
exhaustless reservoir of his will he seemed to be
injecting an electric strength into the other, a

steadying and even flow of power that passed from his hands and into the body of Calamity.

When the time came, and Young stood looking down at the thermometer, Drew lifted haggard eyes, waiting.

"It's lower!"

The great arms of the rancher were thrown above his head; he rose, changed, triumphant, as if he had torn his happiness from the heart of the heavens, and went hastily from the room, silent.

At the stable he took his great bay, saddled him, and swung out on the trail for Eldara, a short, rough trail which led across the Saverack—the same course which Nash and Bard had taken the day before.

But the river had greatly fallen—the water hardly washed above the knees of the horse except in the centre of the stream; by noon he reached the town and went straight for the office of Glendin. The deputy was not there, and the rancher was referred to Murphy's saloon.

There he found Glendin, seated at a corner table with a glass of beer in front of him, and considering the sun-whitened landscape lazily through the window. At the sound of the heavy footfall of Drew he turned, rose, his shoulders flattened

against the wall behind him like a cornered man
prepared for a desperate stand.

"It's all right," cried Drew. "It's all over,
Glendin. Duffy won't press any charges against
Bard; he says that he's given the horse away. And
Calamity Ben is going to live."

"Who says he will?"

"I've just ridden in from his bedside. Dr.
Young says the crisis is past. And so—thank
God—there's no danger to Bard; he's free from
the law!"

"Too late," said the deputy.

It did not seem that Drew heard him. He
stepped closer and turned his head.

"What's that?"

"Too late. I've sent out men to—to apprehend
Bard."

"'Apprehend' him?" repeated Drew. "Is it
possible? To murder him, you mean!"

He had not made a threatening move, but the
deputy had his grip on the butt of his gun.

"It was that devil Nash. He persuaded me to
send out a posse with him in charge."

"And you sent him?"

"What could I do? Ain't it legal?"

"Murder is legal—sometimes. It has been in
the past. I've an idea that it's going to be again."

"What d'you mean by that?"

"You'll learn later. Where did they go for Bard?"

He did not seem disappointed. He was rather like a man who had already heard bad news and now only finds it confirmed. He knew before. Now the fact was simply clinched.

"They went out to your old place on the other side of the range. Drew, listen to me——"

"How many went after him?"

"Nash, Butch Conklin, and five more. Butch's gang."

"Conklin!"

"I was in a hole; I needed men."

"How long have they been gone?"

"Since last night."

"Then," said Drew, "he's already dead. He doesn't know the mountains."

"I give Nash strict orders not to do nothin' but apprehend Bard."

"Don't talk, Glendin. It disgusts me—makes my flesh crawl. He's alone, with seven cutthroats against him."

"Not alone. Sally Fortune's better'n two common men."

"The girl? God bless her! She's with him; she knows the country. There may be a hope; Glen-

din, if you're wise, start praying now that I find
Bard alive. If I don't——"

The swinging doors closed behind him as he
rushed through toward his horse. Glendin stood
dazed, his face mottled with a sick pallor. Then
he moved automatically toward the bar. Murphy
hobbled down the length of the room on his
wooden leg and placed bottle and glass before the
deputy.

"Well?" he queried.

Glendin poured his drink with a shaking hand,
spilling much liquor across the varnished wood.
He drained his glass at a gulp.

"I dunno; what d'you think, Murphy?"

"You heard him talk, Glendin. You ought to
know what's best."

"Let's hear you say it."

"I'd climb the best hoss I owned and start west,
and when I come to the sea I'd take a ship and keep
right on goin' till I got halfway around the world.
And then I'd climb a mountain and hire a couple
of dead-shots for guards and have my first night's
sleep. After that I'd begin thinkin' of what I could
do to get away from Drew."

"Murphy," said the other, "maybe that line
of talk would sound sort of exaggerated to some,
but I ain't one of them. You've got a wooden leg,

but your brain's sound. But tell me, what in God's name makes him so thick with the tender-foot?"

He waited for no answer, but started for the door.

CHAPTER XL

PARTNERS

IF Drew had done hard things in his life, few were more remorseless than the ride on the great bay horse that day. Starting out, he reckoned coldly the total strength of the gallant animal, the distance to his old house, and figured that it was just within possibilities that he might reach the place before evening. From that moment it was certain that the horse would not survive the ride.

It was merely a question as to whether or not the master had so gaged his strength that the bay would not collapse before even the summit of the range had been reached. As the miles went by the horse loosened and extended finely to his work; sweat darkened and polished his flanks; flecks of foam whirled back and spattered his chest and the legs of his rider; he kept on; almost to the last the rein had to be drawn taut; to the very last his heart was even greater than his body.

Up the steep slopes Drew let the horse walk;

every other inch of the way it was either the fast trot or a swinging gallop, not the mechanical, easy pace of the cattle-pony, but a driving, lunging speed. The big hoofs literally smashed at the rocks, and the ringing of it echoed hollowly along the rock face of the ravine.

At the summit, for a single moment, like a bird of prey pausing in mid circle to note the position of the field mouse before it closes wings and bolts down out of the blue, Drew sat his horse motionless and stared down into the valleys below until he noted the exact location of his house—the lake glittered back and up to him in the slant light of the late afternoon. The bay, such was the violence of its panting, literally rocked beneath him.

Then he started the last downward course, sweeping along the treacherous trail with reckless speed, the rocks scattering before him. When they straightened out on the level going beneath, the bay was staggering; there was no longer any of the lilt and ease of the strong horse running; it was a succession of jerks and jars, and the panting was a sharper sound than the thunder of the hoofs. His shoulders, his flanks, his neck—all was foam now; and little by little the proud head fell, reached out; still he drove against the bit; still the rider had to keep up the restraining pressure.

Until at last he knew that the horse was dying
on his feet; dying with each heavy stride it made.
Then he let the reins hang limp. It was sad to
see the answer of the bay—a snort, as if of happiness; a pricking of the ears; a sudden lengthening
of stride and quickening; a nobler lift to the
head.

Past the margin of the lake they swept, crashed
through the woods to the right; and now, very distinctly, Drew heard the heavy drum of firing.
He groaned and drove home the spurs. And still,
by some miracle, there was something left in the
horse which responded; not strength, certainly
that was gone long ago, but there was an indomitable spirit bred into it with its fine blood by gentle
care for generations. The going was heavier among
the trees, and yet the bay increased its pace. The
crackle of the rifles grew more and more distinct.
A fallen trunk blocked the way.

With a snort the bay gathered speed, rose,
cleared the trunk with a last glorious effort, and
fell dead on the other side.

Drew disentangled his feet from the stirrup,
raised the head of the horse, stared an instant into the glazing eyes, and then turned and ran on
among the trees. Panting, dripping with sweat,
his face contorted terribly by his effort, he came

at last behind that rocky shoulder which commanded the approach to the old house.

He found seven men sheltered there, keeping up a steady, dropping fire on the house. McNamara sat propped against a rock, a clumsy, dirty bandage around his thigh; Isaacs lay prone, a stained rag twisted tightly around his shoulder; Lovel sat with his legs crossed, staring stupidly down to the steady drip of blood from his left forearm.

But Ufert, Kilrain, Conklin, and Nash maintained the fight; and Drew wondered what casualties lay on the other side.

At his rush, at the sound of his heavy footfall over the rocks, the four turned with a single movement; Ufert covered him with a rifle, but Nash knocked down the boy's arm.

"We've done talkin'; it's our time to listen; understand?"

Ufert, gone sullen, obeyed. He was at that age between youth and manhood when the blood, despite the songs of the poets, runs slow, cold; before the heart has been called out in love, or even in friendship; before fear or hate or anything saving a deep egoism has possessed the brain.

He looked about to the others for his cue. What he saw disturbed him. Shorty Kilrain, like a boy caught playing truant, edged little by little back against the rock; Butch Conklin, his eyes staring, had grown waxy pale; Steve Nash himself was sullen and gloomy rather than defiant.

And all this because of a grey man far past the prime of life who ran stumbling, panting, toward them. At his nearer approach a flash of understanding touched Ufert. Perhaps it was the sheer bulk of the newcomer; perhaps, more than this, it was something of stern dignity that oppressed the boy with awe. He fought against the feeling, but he was uneasy; he wanted to be far away from that place.

Straight upon them the big grey man strode and halted in front of Nash.

He said, his voice harsh and broken by his running: "I ordered you to bring him to me unharmed. What does this mean, Nash?"

The cowpuncher answered sulkily: "Glendin sent us out."

"Don't lie. You sent yourself and took these men. I've seen Glendin."

His wrath was tempered with a sneer.

"But here you are four against one. Go down and bring him out to me alive!" ·

There was no answer.

"You said you wanted no odds against any one man."

"When a man and a woman stand together," answered Nash, "they're worse than a hundred. That devil, Sally Fortune, is down there with him."

A gun cracked from the house; the bullet chipped the rock with an evil clang, and the flake of stone whirled through the air and landed at the feet of Drew.

"There's your answer," said Nash. "But we've got the rat cornered."

"Wrong again. Calamity Ben is going to live——"

A cry of joy came from Shorty Kilrain.

"Duffy says that he gave his horse away to Bard—Glendin has called back your posse. Ride, Nash! Or else go down there unarmed and bring Bard up to me."

The shadow of a smile crossed the lips of Nash.

"If the law's done with him, I'm not. I won't ride, and I won't go down to him. I've got the upper hand and I'm going to hold it."

"If you're afraid to go down, I will."

Drew unbuckled his cartridge belt and tossed it with his gun against the rocks. He drew out a white handkerchief, and holding it above him, at a full arm's length, he stepped out from the shelter. The others, gathering at their places of vantage, watched his progress toward the house. Steve Nash described it to the wounded men, who had dragged themselves half erect.

"He's walkin' right toward the house, wavin' the white rag. They ain't goin' to shoot. He's goin' around the side of the house. He's stopped there under the trees."

"Where?"

"At that grave of his wife under the two trees. He waits there like he expected Bard to come out to him. And, by God, there goes Bard to meet him—right out into the open."

"Steady, Steve! Drop that gun! If you shoot now you'll have Drew on your head afterward."

"Don't I know it? But God, wouldn't it be easy? I got him square inside the sights. Jest press the trigger and Anthony Bard is done for. He walks up to Drew. He's got no gun on. He's empty-handed jest like Drew. He's said something short and quick and starts to step across the grave.

"Drew points down to it and makes an answer. Bard steps back like he'd been hit across the face and stands there lookin' at the mound. What did Drew say? I'd give ten years of life to hear that talk!

"Bard looks sort of stunned; he stands there with a hand shadin' his eyes, but the sun ain't that bright. Well, I knew nobody could ever stand up to Drew.

"The chief is talkin' fast and hard. The young feller shakes his head. Drew begins talkin' again. You'd think he was pleadin' for his life in front of a jury that meant him wrong. His hands go out like he was makin' an election speech. He holds one hand down like he was measurin' the height of a kid. He throws up his arms again like he'd lost everything in the world.

"And now Bard has dropped the hand from his face. He looks sort of interested. He steps closer to the grave again. Drew holds out both his arms. By God, boys, he's pleadin' with Bard.

"And the head of Bard is dropped. How's it goin' to turn out? Drew wins, of course. There goes Bard's hand out as if it was pulled ag'in' his will. Drew catches it in both his own. Boys, here's where we grab our hosses and beat it."

He turned from the rocks in haste.

"What d'you mean?" cried Conklin. "Steve, are you goin' to leave us here to finish the job you started?"

"Finish it? You fools! Don't you see that Drew and Bard is pals now? If we couldn't finish Bard alone, how'd we make out ag'in' the two of them? The game's up, boys; the thing that's left is for us to save our hides—if we can—before them two start after us. If they *do* start, then God help us all!"

He was already in the saddle.

"Wait!" called Conklin. "One of 'em's a tenderfoot. The other has left his gun here. What we got to fear from 'em?"

And Nash snarled in return: "If there was a chance, don't you think I'd take it? Don't you see I'm givin' up everythin' that amounts to a damn with me? Tenderfoot? He may act Eastern and he may talk Eastern, but he's got Western blood. There ain't no other way of explainin' it. And Drew? He didn't have no gun when he busted the back of old Piotto. I say, there's two men, armed or not, and between 'em they can do more'n all of us could dream of. Boys, are you comin'?"

They went. The wounded were dragged to their feet and hoisted to their horses, groaning. At a slow walk they started down through the trees. Evening fell; the shadows slanted about them. They moved faster—at a trot—at a gallop. They were like men flying from a certain ruin. Beyond the margin of the bright lake they fled and lost themselves in the vast, secret heart of the mountain-desert.

CHAPTER XLI

ALL that day, in a silence broken only by murmurs and side glances, Anthony and Sally Fortune moved about the old house from window to window, and from crack to crack, keeping a steady eye on the commanding rocks above. In one of those murmurs they made their resolution. When night came they would rush the rocks, storm them from the front, and take their chance with what might follow. But the night promised to give but little shelter to their stalking.

For in the late afternoon a broad moon was already climbing up from the east; the sky was cloudless; there was a threat of keen, revealing moonshine for the night. Only desperation could make them attempt to storm the rock, but by the next morning, at the latest, reinforcements were sure to come, and then their fight would be utterly hopeless.

So when the light of the sun mellowed, grew

362

yellow and slant, and the shadows sloped from tree to tree, the two became more silent still, drawn and pale of face, waiting. Anthony at a window, Sally at a crack which made an excellent loophole, they remained moveless.

It was she who noted a niche which might serve as a loophole for one of the posse, and she fired at it, aiming low. The clang of the bullet against rock echoes clearly back to her, like the soft chime of a sheep bell from the peaceful distance. Then, as if in answer to her shot, around the edge of the rocks appeared a moving rag of white which grew into William Drew, bearing above his head the white sign of the truce.

In her astonishment she looked to Bard. He was quivering all over like a hound held on a tight leash, with the game in sight, hungry to be slipped upon it. The edge of his tongue passed across his colourless lips. He was like a man who long has ridden the white-hot desert and is now about to drink. There was the same wild gleam in his eyes; his hand shook with nervous eagerness as he shifted and balanced his revolver. Listening, in her awe, she heard the sound of his increasing panting; a sound like the breath of a running man approaching her swiftly.

She slipped to his side.

"Anthony!"

He did not answer; his gun steadied; the barrel began to incline down; his left eye was squinting. She dropped to her knees and seized his wrist.

"Anthony, what are you going to do?"

"It's Drew!" he whispered, and she did not recognize his voice. "It's the grey man I've waited for. It's he!"

In such a tone a dying man might speak of his hope of heaven—seeing it unroll before him in his delirium.

"But he's carrying the flag of truce, Anthony. You see that?"

"I see nothing except his face. It blots out the rest of the world. I'll plant my shot there—there in the middle of those lips."

"Anthony, that's William Drew, the squarest man on the range."

"Sally Fortune, that's William Drew, who murdered my father!"

"Ah!" she said, with sharply indrawn breath. "It isn't possible!"

"I saw the shot fired."

"But not this way, Anthony; not from behind a wall!"

His emotion changed him, made him almost a

stranger to her. He was shaking and palsied with eagerness.

"I could do nothing as bad as the crime he has done. For twenty years the dread of his coming haunted my father, broke him, aged him prematurely. Every day he went to a secret room and cared for his revolver—this gun here in my hand, you see? He and I—we were more than father and son—we were pals, Sally. And then this devil called my father out into the night and shot him. Damn him!"

"You've got to listen to me, Anthony——"

"I'll listen to nothing, for there he is and——"

She said with a sharp, rising ring in her voice: "If you shoot at him while he carries that white flag I'll—I'll send a bullet through your head—that's straight! We got only one law in the mountains, and that's the law of honour. If you bust that, I'm done with you, Anthony."

"Take my gun—take it quickly, Sally, I can't trust myself; looking at him, I can see the place where the bullet should strike home."

He forced the butt of his revolver into her hands, rose, and stepped to the door, his hands clasped behind his back.

"Tell me what he does."

"He's comin' straight toward us as if he didn't

fear nothin'—grey William Drew! He's not packin' a gun; he trusts us."

"The better way," answered Bard. "Bare hands—the better way!"

"He has killed men with those bare hands of his. I can see 'em clear—great, blunt-fingered hands, Anthony. He's coming around the side of the house. I'll go into the front room."

She ran past Anthony and paused in the habitable room, spying through a crack in the wall. And Anthony stood with his eyes tightly closed, his head bowed. The image of the leashed hound came more vividly to her when she glanced back at him.

"He's walkin' right up the path. There he stops."

"Where?"

"Right beside the old grave."

"Anthony!" called a deep voice. "Anthony, come out to me!"

He started, and then groaned and stopped himself.

"Is the sign of the truce still over his head, Sally?"

"Yes."

"I daren't go out to him—I'd jump at his throat."

She came beside him.

"It means something besides war. I can see it in his face. Pain—sorrow, Anthony, but not a wish for fightin'."

From the left side of his cartridge belt a stout-handled, long-bladed hunting-knife was suspended. He disengaged the belt and tossed it to the floor. Still he paused.

"If I go, I'll break the truce, Sally."

"You won't; you're a man, Anthony; and remember that you're on the range, and the law of the range holds you."

"Anthony!" called the deep voice without.

He shuddered violently.

"What is it?"

"It sounds—like the voice of my father calling me! I must go!"

She clung to him.

"Not till you're calmer."

"My father died in my arms," he answered; "let me go."

He thrust her aside and strode out through the door.

On the farther side of the grave stood Drew, his grey head bare, and looking past him Anthony saw the snow-clad tops of the Little Brother, grey also in the light of the evening. And the trees whose branches interwove above the grave—grey also with moss. The trees, the mountain, the old headstone, the man—they blended into a whole.

"Anthony!" said the man, "I have waited half my life for this!"

"And I," said Bard, "have waited a few weeks that seem longer than all my life, for this!"

His own eager panting stopped him, but he stumbled on: "I have you here in reach at last, Drew, and I'm going to tear your heart out, as you tore the heart out of John Bard."

"Ah, Anthony," said the other, "my heart was torn out when you were born; it was torn out and buried here."

And to the wild eyes of Anthony it seemed as if the great body of Drew, so feared through the mountain-desert, was now enveloped with weakness, humbled by some incredible burden.

After that a mist obscured his eyes; he could not see more than an outline of the great shape before him; his throat contracted as if a hand gripped him there, and an odd tingling came at the tips of his fingers. He moved forward.

"It is more than I dreamed," he said hoarsely, as his foot planted firmly on the top of the grave, and he poised himself an instant before flinging himself on the grey giant. "It is more than I dreamed for—to face you—alone!"

And a solemn, even voice answered him, "We are not alone."

"Not alone, but the others are too far off to stop me."

"Not alone, Anthony, for your mother is here between us."

Like a fog under a wind, the mist swept from the eyes of Anthony; he looked out and saw that the face of the grey man was infinitely sad, and there was a hungry tenderness that reached out, enveloped, weakened him. He glanced down, saw that his heel was on the mount of the grave; saw again the headstone and the time-blurred inscription: "Here sleeps Joan, the wife of William Drew. She chose this place for rest."

A mortal weakness and trembling seized him. The wind puffed against his face, and he went staggering back, his hand caught up to his eyes.

He closed his mind against the words which he had heard.

But the deep organ voice spoke again: "Oh, boy, your mother!"

In the stupor which came over him he saw two faces: the stern eyes of John Bard, and the dark, mocking beauty of the face which had looked down

24

to him in John Bard's secret room. He lowered his hand from his eyes; he stared at William Drew, and it seemed to him that it was John Bard he looked upon. Their names differed, but long pain had touched them with a common greyness. And it seemed to Anthony that it was only a moment ago that the key turned in the lock of John Bard's secret room, the hidden chamber which he kept like Bluebeard for himself, where he went like Bluebeard to see his past; only an instant before he had turned the key in that lock, the door opened, and this was the scene which met his eyes—the grave, the blurred tombstone, and the stern figure beyond.

"Joan," he repeated; "your wife—my mother?"

He heard a sob, not of pain, but of happiness, and knew that the blue eyes of Sally Fortune looked out to him from the doorway of the house.

The low voice, hurried now, broke in on him.

"When I married Joan, John Bard fled from the range; he could not bear to look on our happiness. You see, I had won her by chance, and he hated me for it. If you had ever seen her, Anthony, you would understand. I crossed the mountains and came here and built this house, for your mother was like a wild bird, Anthony, and I did not dare to let men near her; then a son was born, and she died giving him birth. Afterward I lived on here, close to the place which she had chosen herself for rest. And I was happy because the boy grew every day into a more perfect picture of his dead mother.

"One day when he was almost three I rode off through the hills, and when I came back the boy was gone. I rode with a posse everywhere, hunting him; aye, Anthony, the trail which I started then I have kept at ever since, year after year, and here it ends where it began—at the grave of Joan!

"Finally I came on news that a man much like John Bard in appearance had been seen near my house that day. Then I knew it was Bard in fact. He had seen the image of the woman we both loved in the boy. He was all that was left of her on earth. After these years I can read his heart clearly; I know why he took the boy.

"Then I left this place. I could not bear the sight of the grave; for she slept in peace, and I lived in hell waiting for the return of my son.

"At last I went East; I was at Madison Square Garden and saw you ride. It was the face of Joan that looked back at me; and I knew that I was close to the end of the trail.

"The next night I called out John Bard. He had been in hell all those years, like me, for he had waited for my coming. He begged me to let him have you; said you loved him as a father; I only laughed. So we fought, and he fell; and then I saw you running over the lawn toward us.

"I remembered Joan, her pride and her fierceness, and I knew that if I waited a son would kill his father that night. So I turned and fled through the trees. Anthony, do you believe me; do you forgive me?"

The memory of the clumsy, hungered tenderness of John Bard swept about Anthony.

He cried: "How can I believe? My father has killed my father; what is left?"

The solemn voice replied: "Anthony, my son!"

He saw the great, blunt-fingered hands which had killed men, which were feared through the length and breadth of the mountain-desert, stretched out to him.

"Anthony Drew!" said the voice.

His hand went out, feebly, by slow degrees, and was caught in a mighty double clasp. Warmth flowed through him from that grasp, and a great emotion troubled him, and a voice from deep to deep echoed within him—the call of blood to blood. He knew the truth, for the hate burned out in him and left only an infinite sadness.

He said: "What of the man who loved me? Whom I love?"

"I have done penance for that death," answered William Drew, "and I shall do more penance before I die. For I am only your father in name, but he is the father in your thoughts and in your love. Is it true?"

"It is true," said Anthony.

And the other, bitterly: "In his life he was as strong as I; in his death he is still stronger. It is his victory; his shadow falls between us."

But Anthony answered: "Let us go together and bring his body and bury it at the left side of—my mother."

"Lad, it is the one thing we can do together, and after that?"

A plaintive sound came to the ear of Anthony, and he looked down to see Sally Fortune weeping at the grave of Joan. Better than both the men she understood, perhaps. In the deep tenderness which swelled through him he caught a sense of the drift of life through many generations of the past and projecting into the future, men and women strong and fair and each with a high and passionate love.

The men died and the women changed, but the love persisted with the will to live. It came from a thousand springs, but it rolled in one river to one sea. The past stood there in the form of William

Drew; he and Sally made the present, and through his love of her sprang the hope of the future.

It was all very clear to him. The love of Bard and Drew for Joan Piotto had not died, but passed through the flame and the torment of the three ruined lives and returned again with gathering power as the force which swept him and Sally Fortune out into that river and toward that far-off sea. The last mist was brushed from his eyes. He saw with a piercing vision the world, himself, life. He looked to William Drew and saw that he was gazing on an old and broken man.

He said to the old man: "Father, she is wiser than us both."

And he pointed to Sally Fortune, still weeping softly on the grave of Joan.

But William Drew had no eye for her; he was fallen into a deep muse over the blurred inscription on the headstone. He did not even raise his head when Anthony touched Sally Fortune on the shoulder. She rose, and they stole back together toward the house. There, as they stood close together, Sally murmured: "It is cruel to leave him alone. He needs us now, close to him."

His hand wandered slowly across her hair, and he said: "Sally, how close can we *ever* be to him?"

"We can only watch and wait and try to understand," murmured Sally Fortune.

They were so close to the door of the ruined house, now, that a taint of burnt powder crept out to them, a small, keen odour, and with a sudden desire to protect her, he drew her close to him. There was no tensing of her body when his arm went around her and he knew with a rush of tenderness how completely, how perfectly she accepted him. Over the hand which held her he felt soft fingers settle to keep it in its place, and when he looked down he found that her face was raised, and the eyes which brooded on him were misty bright, like the eyes of a child when joy overflows in it, but awe keeps it quiet.

THE END